The War Before
The War

Based on True Events

David Lee Corley

DEDICATION

I dedicate this story to all of those who fought in the Indochina Wars. History will not forget your sacrifices.

TABLE OF CONTENTS

ACKNOWLEDGMENTS

I wish to acknowledge Robert McNamara for commissioning the Report of the Office of the Secretary of Defense Vietnam Task Force, also known as The Pentagon Papers. The study was a U.S. Department of Defense history of the political and military involvement in Indochina from 1945 to 1967. Reading the study gave me great insight into what the political and military leaders were thinking leading up to and during the First and Second Indochina Wars. While I do not agree with many of McNamara's decisions about the war, I appreciate the historical significance of the study that he secretly commissioned.

I also wish to acknowledge Daniel Ellsberg's role in revealing the study and ensuring that it was published. I, like many Americans during that time, had mixed feelings about what he did, but I don't doubt the act took great courage. It could very well be that his actions prevented future conflicts as we are now able to look back at the decision-making process that brought about the Indochina Wars.

Both McNamara and Ellsberg are now an essential part of history.

WAR GEOGRAPHY

French Indochina, commonly known as 'Indochina,' was a French colony divided into five territories - Laos, Cambodia, Tonkin, Amman, and Cochinchine. After a French declaration in 1949, Tonkin, Amman, and Cochinchine would be known as Vietnam while Cambodia and Laos retained their original names and became independent protectorates.

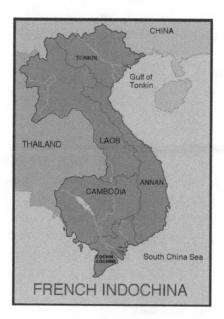

The major cities in Vietnam were Saigon, Hanoi, and Hue. The major waterways were the Mekong River, Saigon River, and Red River. The Mekong River ran through China, Burma, Laos, Cambodia, and Vietnam. Hanoi was the administrative center of French Indochina.

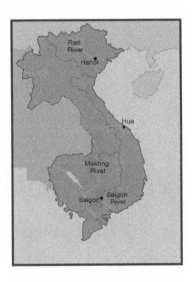

Most of the major battles in the First Indochina War were fought in the Tonkin Territory in the Northern part of the country.

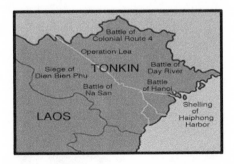

"War Is Too Important to Be Left to the Generals."

- Georges Clemenceau

PROLOGUE

World War II was over. The Japanese emperor had finally capitulated after the U.S. Air Force dropped two atomic bombs on Hiroshima and Nagasaki, destroying large parts of the cities and killing over two hundred thousand Japanese. Most were civilians. The Allies had avoided the invasion of Japan, and the lives of hundreds of thousands of soldiers and civilians were saved. It was a trade-off that would be argued by philosophers and historians for centuries. Regardless, the Allies won.

Peace had never been easy, especially in Indochina, whose fate was decided at the Potsdam Conference by Winston Churchill, Joseph Stalin, and Harry Truman. The Indochinese were not asked their opinion, and neither were the French. The world was divided by three great leaders, and a new post-war order was established.

Indochina was made up of Cambodia, Laos, and three Vietnamese territories - Tonkin, Amman, and Cochinchina. Per the new agreement, Indochina was divided at the 16th parallel. The Chinese were given control of North Indochina and the British control of the South. The question of whether Indochina was still a French colony was simply put off until later in hopes that the Viet Minh and the French could negotiate a settlement that both sides could accept. It was wishful thinking from Allied leaders that had bigger fish to fry, namely the division of Europe.

After trying unsuccessfully to engage the French in meaningful negotiations, the patience of Ho Chi Minh and his followers grew thin. Ho declared Vietnam independent from France and took control of much of the country using his Viet Minh rebels. They would not give up their country without a fight, no matter what the three world leaders had decided.

The British commander, Major-General Douglas Gracey, was backed by the 20th Indian Infantry Division, which landed in Saigon in September 1945. The reoccupation of the South was called "Operation Masterton" by the British. The only thing standing in Gracey's way was U.S. General MacArthur, who insisted that the British commander wait on taking control of the South until after the Japanese had formally surrendered the country to the Allies. The British forces formed a garrison outside the city. They watched helplessly as the Viet Minh took full advantage of the delay by consolidating their forces and shoring up their defensive positions.

Here our story begins...

CHAPTER ONE

Indochina was a country of floating mist. It clung to everything – the mountains, the rice paddies, the rivers, and the villages – until a gentle breeze pushed it onward. Mist created the mystery that filled Indochina, a country where foreigners went to escape the boredom of civilization. One rarely knew what to expect in Indochina, and that made it all the more enticing. It was the Wild West of Southeast Asia, a place of danger and boundless opportunity. A place where one could reinvent themselves. A place of second chances.

Indochina was a country of two cultures – French and Southeast Asian. Much of the country looked the same as it had for hundreds of years. Field after field, mostly of rice surrounded by mud-packed dikes and filled with knee-deep water, sprouting green. Rubber plantations with lines of trees, the bark cut with sharp knives to bleed a white gummy fluid that was

1

collected and processed by cheap labor. Primitive villages made of wood, of which there was an abundance. Flat-bottom sampans sailing their crops to market, floating down slow-moving rivers, passing under monkey bridges made of bamboo. It was a land of intense green, dark shadows, and a black mold that permeated everything. A sky more often grey than blue with clouds that trapped the heat. The sour smell of rotting vegetation and animal excrement combined with starch from the rice pots boiling in every home overpowered the senses. The countryside was more primeval than civilized, and that is why everyone loved it so.

The cities were a different story. They were a strange mixture of Southeast Asia and Europe. Brown faces mingling with white faces. The neighborhoods were divided – some Asian, some European. It was easy to tell the difference.

The buildings in the Asian communities were open, allowing the air to circulate. Bright colored banners hanging from the ceiling offered the occupants some privacy. The roof spans were curved and decorated with stone dragons to keep the demons away. The streets were clogged with trishaws, bicycles, and the occasional car or truck. The road edges were lined with food carts, each offering a specialty and cooked in an iron wok or over coals in a small barbeque. Customers squatted, sitting on their heels as they ate. Pho – a rich broth filled with fresh vegetables and a few slices of pork or fish – was the favorite. In Asian neighborhoods, humanity was on display for everyone to see.

The European communities were much more

reserved, and secrets were kept behind thick walls with doors and windows. Shutters provided privacy, and open slats let the air flow through the houses and buildings, but many times the shutters were flung open to allow more ventilation during the hot season. The streets and parks were kept immaculate and uncluttered. Lights on iron lamp posts cast a yellow hue throughout the night, making the neighborhoods safe. Young mistresses known as Congaie were an accepted vice as long as they were used with discretion, never in public or in front of a spouse. Opium was also legal and socially acceptable but confined to dark parlors where one could smoke and dream. Pleasures to while away the long hot nights and fight the longings for home. The men wore white suits with ties and the women long European-style dresses with brimmed hats to shield their faces from the sun when it appeared. White was sensible and clean.

Foreigners came to Southeast Asia looking for something different, and when they arrived, they changed everything to look just like home. Two different worlds living side by side – one incredibly poor and the other rich beyond the imagination of the average Indochinese. It was all so very civilized... until it was not.

Saigon - September 24, 1945

On the northern outskirts of Saigon sat Cité Héraud, a peaceful French-Eurasian quarter. The streets were lined with concrete sidewalks and lush dipterocarp trees that provided welcome shade. Children played on the manicured lawns of colonial villas with their steeply pitched roofs, deep overhangs, and yellow paint. Peugeot 202s with their headlights hidden behind a grill and Citroen sedans with their long noses drove down the paved streets that crisscrossed the neighborhood. A slow-moving river, Arroyo De Avalanche, flowed on the backside of the community offering the wealthy families additional protection against the masses and a cool breeze off its waters. For over a century, the French lived apart from the Indochinese slums and factories in the inner city. Their children were raised away from chaos and extreme poverty. The only Indochinese allowed in the neighborhood were the workers that tended gardens, picked up the trash, cooked the meals, and kept the houses clean. Cité Héraud was its own world. Idyllic. French.

At the end of World War II, the British had been placed in charge of Saigon. Although the Japanese army had surrendered, the British required their help to protect the French citizens until the rest of the British army had arrived by sea, and the question of potential French reoccupation of Indochina had been settled. Conquered and at the mercy of the Allies, the Japanese officers had no choice but to accept the British request. But that didn't mean they were happy about it. Japanese guards were placed around the French neighborhoods and businesses. Cité Héraud was no exception. The British commander expected the Japanese officers and soldiers to act professionally, no matter the circumstances. The Japanese troops were demoralized from the loss of the war, and discipline was sorely lacking. The Japanese officers, who just wanted to go home, did the absolute minimum to supervise their troops. Small bribes were all it took to circumvent Japanese guard posts or to commit crimes while the soldiers looked the other way.

Just beyond the Boulevard Paul Bert bordering the southern side of Cité Héraud, a group of Vietnamese men gathered. They were armed with metal pipes, machetes, and hammers. A few had pistols with two or three bullets in them; that was all they could afford. They were mostly factory workers and farmers. Peasants working for the French to feed their families.

Dang Phi Hung, a mid-level boss in the Binh Xuyen Crime Syndicate, was the self-proclaimed leader of the group. Hung didn't care about politics. He was a gangster. Only two things interested him - money and revenge. Today was about revenge.

Hung's brother had been buried alive by a French plantation owner for disrespecting the man's wife. Hung and his followers knew that it wouldn't be long before the British army took control of the city and re-established order. Once that happened, any thoughts of settling old scores would have to wait. It was during the chaos that a man could sow retribution upon his enemies and get away with it. The French were the enemy. In many cases, the Indochinese had been treated as slaves by their French masters. They were often beaten for not making their quota or trying to escape a plantation. Their pay was docked on a whim with not even a pretense of justice. They were forced to pay bribes to the foreman to keep their jobs. The lawless slums in which they lived were filled with vermin and disease. French law and magistrates protected the colonists but did little for the natives. Today, Hung and his men would seek the justice they had been denied. They were determined to teach the French the cost of tyranny.

As the dull sun fell in the cloud-covered sky, more angry Indochinese joined the ranks of the mob. Hung waited until the group numbered over two hundred. He divided his followers into raiding parties of nine with one member as the leader. Nine was a lucky number in Indochina. They needed luck not to get caught. None of the men knew if the Frenchmen that had actually caused them harm were in the Cité Héraud quarter. It wasn't important. The residents were French. That was all that mattered.

Hung was not educated. He could barely read and didn't know how to use an abacus. But as a gang leader, he had proven that he understood how to motivate men – a simple appeal to their basic instincts. "The French are thieves. They have taken your land on which you are now forced to work. Your sweat and blood make them rich while you stay poor. They have taken rice from your children's mouths. They stuff themselves in fancy restaurants while your families dine on the bones of pigs and fish heads without the eyes. I am tired of their promises that things will soon change for the better. They are liars and conmen. They have no interest in justice or equality. They only wish to fill their pockets with coins earned from your labor, not theirs. It is time to take back what is ours," he said to the cheers of his men. "They killed my brother. For what? For refusing to clean the vomit of a drunken French woman. I ask you, is this justice? If so, I want none of it. Like you, I want revenge for their sins. I want revenge for the scars on my back from their canes. I want revenge for the young women they raped and beat. We must do to them what they have done to us. It is the time of the ax and hammer. Show no mercy. They have shown none to you. You keep what you take. I want nothing but French blood."

A roar went up from the mob as their rage swelled. At Hung's command, the mob split up. Some went straight across the boulevard, stopping traffic, while others circled around the sides of the neighborhood to cut off any French that tried to escape. The river behind the neighborhood helped coral the French. Having been sufficiently bribed, the Japanese guards turned a blind eye to the mob as it passed. Each raiding party picked a house. They kicked in the front door and went room to room. They took captive men, women, and children. Anything of value was looted. Everything else was smashed or slashed. Men carried armfuls of jewelry, pocket watches, tea sets, and silverware. Two men tried to carry out an upright piano, but it slipped through their hands and crashed into pieces on the ground. Cars were filled with valuables and driven away by the very men that once chauffeured them, some dragging their owners behind, their feet tied to the bumpers. Furniture, wall clocks, leather-bound books, and stone sculptures were tossed through the windows, shattering the glass and landing on the manicured lawns.

There were no mock trials. There was no time for

civilized gestures. The French men were herded into the street. Their genitals were removed with butcher knives, followed by decapitation as their wives and children watched. The women were raped, mutilated, then left to bleed to death. The children's limbs were hacked off or crushed with hammers.

Upon first hearing of the massacre, General Gracey was outraged. He rebuked the Japanese commander in Saigon and demanded the Japanese army take action. The Japanese commander was already considering seppuku for dishonoring his emperor by losing the war. Gracey's scolding only fed his depression, and he became unresponsive. He did nothing, and the French continued to die as the minutes ticked by. Gracey had no choice but to take control of the situation.

The massacre had already lasted several hours when the British Army finally arrived in force. A battalion of Indian Gurkhas from the 20th Division with their famous boomerang-shaped kukri knives surrounded the neighborhood. The Indian Gurkha troops were actually Nepalese and considered by many to be the fiercest fighters in the world. They were shock colonial troops and extremely loyal to their British commanders.

Upon seeing the British troops, the mob took furniture from the houses and threw up barricades across the main entrances of the community. They were outnumbered three to one, and the British troops had much better weapons. And yet, they continued to torture, rape, and pillage. Their bloodlust was like a drug that only grew stronger as they practiced their vengeance. No matter what happened, the French in Saigon would not forget this day.

British mortar and machinegun teams took up positions. The troops could hear the hair-raising screams of men, women, and children coming from the neighborhood. The British major commanding the battalion did not make a move until he was sure he would win the fight that he knew was coming. His desire for victory no doubt cost the lives of a dozen or more French civilians. When three armored cars arrived, the major felt well-prepared and gave the order to start the attack.

The mortar teams shelled the enemy positions, and the machine-gunners raked the barricades while the armored cars advanced firing their 25 mm main guns. The troops, armed with Lee-Enfield rifles, followed on foot, shooting anybody that appeared above the barricade.

The enemy barricade was blown into kindling, and the defenders were quickly overrun. Once past the barrier, the Gurkhas spread throughout the community. While the Gurkhas were accustomed to violence, the young British officers were shocked by what they saw and found it difficult not to toss their lunch.

Most of the mob was killed on the spot. Any resistance whatsoever was met with a bullet to the forehead or a kukri knife across the throat. Those survivors that knew how to swim made it across the river to the safety of the opposite shore and escaped. Those that remained were taken captive and turned over to the French authorities for trial. Most would rot in jail for several months, then be guillotined – French justice for traitors and hardened criminals.

Over one hundred and fifty French civilians had been brutally murdered, while another one hundred and fifty survived with terrible disfigurements and nightmares for what remained of their lives.

The next day as the news of the massacre spread throughout the city, most of the French civilians fled Saigon for the countryside, where they hoped it would be safer. Others abandoned Indochina entirely and sailed home to France.

The Vietnamese living in Saigon threw up more barricades throughout the city and its suburbs. They used axes and saws to cut down trees blocking the streets. Cars and trucks were turned on their sides. Furniture was stacked to fill the holes of the blockades. Travel through the city was hindered, and many French abandoned the safety of their cars to escape on foot. Many were robbed or murdered. Chaos prevailed.

The Gurkhas continued to have running street battles with the gangsters from the Binh Xuyen and Cao Dai Syndicates. The Gurkhas won the battles when British artillery and armor were brought into play, but not without suffering some losses. It was the duty of the Gurkhas to fight and die for the British. As was their tradition, their sacrifices were made without complaint.

Viet Minh rebels and communist cadres captured the power plant, slaughterhouse, and central market. Knowing that they could not hold the facilities long once the British arrived, the Viet Minh troops and cadres set fire to the buildings. Plumes of black smoke rose above the city. Civilians covered their mouths with wet scarves to hold back the choking fumes. The flames spread, and Saigon burned.

General Vo Nguyen Giap, the Viet Minh commander, and Ho Chi Minh's longtime friend, used the confusion in the cities to consolidate Ho's position by attacking the leaders of the non-communist forces. He had his troops round up and kill hundreds of militia leaders, French sympathizers, government officials, and Catholics, at times burying them alive so as not to waste valuable bullets. This brutal demonstration of force, even against their fellow citizens, caused thousands of Vietnamese to flock to Ho Chi Minh's side so they could similarly fight the French. They wanted a strong and determined leader that, no matter the cost, would guide them to victory and freedom. There was a feeling throughout the country that now was the time to fight for independence and kick the French out of Indochina once and for all.

As the civilians left for the countryside and others joined Ho's army of rebels, the city of Saigon became a ghost town with major neighborhoods abandoned to the Indochina gangs who reveled in looting the French homes and businesses. They brutalized anybody crazy enough to remain.

This made General Gracey's job easier. Anyone left in Saigon was considered the enemy. Without civilians in the way, his troops were free to use their artillery, armored vehicles, and tanks to root out the gangs hidden in the downtown buildings and houses.

Block by block, the British forces took control of Saigon until the surviving gang members fled to the countryside.

The Viet Minh in Saigon broke off their attacks against the British and headed north, where they would link up with Ho Chi Minh's main force near Hanoi. They knew the French were coming, and when they arrived, the main struggle for Indochina would begin. It was time to consolidate, train, and plan. As they traveled north, the Viet Minh were joined by civilians that wanted to enlist in Ho's army. The Viet Minh raided Japanese supply depots to equip the recruits with weapons and ammunition. When the two armies combined in Hanoi, the fighting force numbered more than one hundred thousand soldiers. The Viet Minh leaders were ill-prepared for their success and unable to feed their troops. Looting was the solution and encouraged, especially against European businesses and shipping warehouses in Haiphong Harbor. Ho and his followers redistributed rice earmarked for export to those that needed it. It made Ho more popular than ever.

The Viet Minh set up camps in the mountains where the veterans taught the recruits. Their numbers grew as the legend of Ho Chi Minh spread throughout Indochina, and civilians left their homes to join the cause of independence. He was Indochina's messiah. Finding enough food and supplies was a constant problem. Some of the older volunteers were told to go back to their homes and await word of the final uprising. They would have to wait to do their duty. At that moment in the war, Ho needed a young army that could travel hundreds of miles on foot and still have enough energy to fight the French when they finally arrived at their destination.

Thousands of communist cadres were ordered to stay in the south and wait for orders. When the orders came, they were instructed not to attack the British or the French troops in and around Saigon. Instead, they were to perform non-violent political resistance. Ho Chi Minh did not want to appear as if he and his followers were invading the south. Not yet anyway. He still had hopes that the Americans would eventually side with the Viet Minh and help free Indochina. This was highly frustrating to the cadres who had joined the party to fight the French and drive them out of Indochina. Morale and discipline became a problem in the south for Ho and the communist party leaders. They needed the cadres to pave the way for an eventual military campaign, but not before the Viet Minh were ready. They were still very short on supplies, weapons, and food.

After witnessing the chaos in Saigon, General Gracey decided to hand over Southern Indochina to the French. He wanted to wash his hands of the entire affair. World War II had been won, and Indochina had served its purpose. He didn't see the need to sacrifice more British troops during peacetime simply to meddle in another nation's affairs. Since the French were determined to keep Indochina in French hands, the growing resistance within

13

Indochina was a problem of their making. It was up to them to find a solution. As a courtesy, Gracey created a beachhead out of Saigon that would allow the French forces traveling by ship to land without resistance. From a secured position, the French could organize, resupply, and launch an offensive to retake the rest of Indochina. After that, Gracey and his troops would simply leave the French and the people of Indochina to "sort it out." Besides, he was getting old and longed for a good cup of tea that could only be found in British India, his home.

CHAPTER TWO

Arlington, Virginia - October 23, 1945

Arlington National Cemetery was a sea of Kentucky bluegrass and white marble headstones. The trees covering the rolling hills and sprinkled throughout the gravesites were showing their autumn colors with generous bursts of yellow and orange. Even in peacetime, gunshots from honor guard salutes and bugles playing taps were heard twenty to thirty times a day, breaking the stillness that loomed over the cemetery. Veterans never stopped dying. It was a sad and thoughtful place where warriors were brought home to rest.

Lieutenant Colonel Peter Dewey, the first American soldier killed in Indochina, was buried in section three of the Arlington Cemetery. He was an officer in the OSS and the commander of the Deer Team in their mission to assist Ho Chi Minh and his Viet Minh in their struggle against the Japanese during the Second World War. At the end of the war, he and his team were preparing to leave Indochina and return to their base in southern China. Dewey was shot and killed by a Viet Minh soldier that mistook him for a French officer.

Ho Chi Minh considered Dewey a trusted friend and was deeply saddened by his death. They had fought side by side against the Japanese. At Ho's request, it was Dewey that had edited his speech to declare the independence of Vietnam. Ho sent a letter to President Truman offering his condolences and apologizing for Dewey's accidental death. Ho had no quarrel with the Americans. He hoped they would support the Viet Minh or at least stay neutral in the upcoming war with the French. The events surrounding Dewey's untimely death did not help Ho's cause.

Dewey was the son of U.S. Senator Charles Dewey, and that meant that all the stops were pulled out to honor the fallen hero. Although few knew the young commander that had died in a place that nobody could pronounce, hundreds came and paid their respects. President Truman sent a personal note and a beautiful wreath to the family. Photo-journalists came in droves in hopes of snapping a photo of a socialite or politician crying. It was a good bet. There were plenty. The chaplain waxed poetic, quoting Abraham Lincoln, Socrates, and reading from the Psalms.

Rene Granier and the other members of the Deer team were granted leave to attend Dewey's funeral. They wore their dress uniforms of the military branch they served under before they joined the OSS. Granier wore his Marine dress blues with a gold eagle, globe, and anchor emblems on the standing collar and red piping on his jacket, known as the blood stripe. Granier did not consider Dewey a friend. By choice, Granier had no friends and considered relationships in general as useless baggage. But he had grown to respect his commanding officer and felt his death a loss. He did not flinch when the honor volley was fired. He was well adjusted to gunfire, much of it his own. As always, Granier was sullen but did not shed a tear. What was the point? The man was dead and at peace. Not such a bad thing.

Granier suffered from a twinge of guilt. He had the Viet Minh soldier in his gunsight moments before Dewey was killed. Dewey was trying to reason with the young man, speaking to him in French. Granier had hesitated, giving heed to morality, hoping he would not need to take the young Vietnamese soldier's life. His hope was misplaced, and now Dewey was dead. He swore to himself he would never hesitate again. He would do what needed to be done.

After the funeral, a reception was held at the Fort Meyer's Officer Club. The buffet was befitting the son of a senator, and an open bar helped the guests console with the Dewey family.

Granier sat with the other Deer Team members. They were unaccustomed to mingling with politicians and socialites. There was an overabundance of generals from the Pentagon wearing their 'fruit salad' of medals on freshly pressed uniforms. The team didn't like them either. It wasn't wise to get too close to a general. Nothing good could come of it.

Colonel Archimedes Patti, Dewey's superior officer and commander of OSS operations in Indochina, walked over to the Deer Team table and said, "Are you men getting enough to eat?"

"Yes, sir," said Paul Hoagland, the team medic and the team member closest to Dewey.

"It's a nice spread," said Weapon Specialist Herbert Green. "Commander Dewey would have liked it."

"That and the whiskey," said Victor Santana, the team's communication specialist. "Never knew him to pass up a drink when offered."

"How are you holding up, Sergeant?" Patti said to Granier.

"Okay, sir," said Granier.

"When you have a moment, I'd like a private conversation on the patio."

"Now is as good a time as any."

The two soldiers excused themselves and walked out onto the patio. They moved to a corner where they could speak privately. "Sergeant, I know you went through a lot during your capture and internment with the Japanese," said Patti. "I trust your wounds are healing?"

"I'm fit for duty if that's what you are asking."

"That's good. We need you."

"We? I thought the OSS had been dismantled."

"It has. But something new has risen in its place - the Central Intelligence Group. Its primary mission is to collect and disseminate overseas intelligence to keep America safe from those that would do us harm.

A select group of soldiers from the OSS have been asked to join. I was one. I would like you to be another."

"Me? Why? I'm a soldier, not a spy."

"Actually, you would be an intelligence officer. Spies are developed by the officers and gather intelligence."

"Officer," said Granier with a grunt. "That's even worse."

"Look, you are the only American that has fought alongside both the Viet Minh and the French. That makes you unique. So unique that the new director of the CIG would like you to write a report on the current status and abilities of both armies."

"A report?"

"Sergeant, this is important. The president will probably be given your report."

"All the more reason, you got the wrong guy."

"I don't think so. I think you are exactly what our country needs. With the removal of the Deer Team and the other covert operatives in Indochina, we are blind. Indochina is the linchpin to communist expansion into Southeast Asia. The Russians know it. The Chinese know it. And we know it. A war between the French and the Viet Minh has already begun. The outcome of that war may very well decide the fate of Southeast Asia. It is imperative that America chooses who it supports wisely."

"I thought we already decided to side with the French."

"No. We haven't. While we do send the French a small amount of aid, we've agreed to remain neutral for the moment. But that won't last long. There is no way America can stay out of this thing, especially if China and Russia side with the Viet Minh. We would have no choice but to support the French. What we really need to know, is can the French win?"

"I see."

"Good. Because right now, you are one of the few people that can answer that question."

"That's a big ask for a sniper-scout."

"Maybe, but you're all we have."

Granier considered for a long moment. He wasn't sure what he was going to do now that the OSS had been disbanded, and all the military branches were trimming down. He would have a hell of a time getting back into the Marines even with his record and experience. His skill set was not an advantage in corporate America. With his luck, he would end up as a security guard working the graveyard shift and chasing shadows. What he really needed was time to figure out what he was going to do with his life. Working for Patti would give him that time. "Alright. I'll write your report," said Granier. "But you may not like what I have to say."

"I'm willing to take that risk."

When Patti finally left, Granier had another drink with the Deer Team. He doubted he would see any of them again. He was not one to stand on ceremony, but a final drink seemed like the right thing to do. They toasted their dead commander and shook hands. Granier grabbed his overcoat and headed for the door. He was almost clear of the room when he heard a woman's voice ask, "How did you know Peter?"

Granier stopped and turned to see a young woman sitting by herself at a table, nursing a daiquiri. He thought she might be drunk because she was dropping her r's, but then he realized it was just her Bostonian accent. "Excuse me?" said Granier.

"How did you know Colonel Dewey?"

"We fought together."

"In Indochina?"

"I'm not at liberty to say."

"Oh. You're a spook."

"Hardly. He was my commander."

"Peter was good at that... giving orders. Always so damned organized."

"How did you know him?"

"Our families ran in the same circles."

"Military?"

"Politics."

"Ah."

"You don't approve of politics?"

"Don't know much about 'em."

"Well, they are very easy to understand."

She kicked out the chair beside her as an invitation for him to sit. Granier stared at the chair for a moment, wondering if he should just make an excuse like he needed to meet someone. She was attractive, well dressed, and slurring slightly. He didn't see the harm and sat. "The first thing to know about politics is that you must be willing to sacrifice your soul if you are going to be any good at them," she said, taking the last sip of her cocktail. "And the second is... never run out of liquor. It soothes the conscience and stills the mind."

Granier smiled a little. He liked her rebellious

attitude. "So, what office are you running for?" said Granier.

"Me? Oh, hell, no. The men in the family are the politicians. We girls are just expected to show up and say witty things. How am I doing?"

"Pretty good."

She nodded her thanks and asked. "What's your name, Sergeant?"

"Rene Granier."

"Are you French? That's a French name if I've ever heard one."

"I was when I was growing up. I'm an American now."

"Any regrets?"

"A few. But I'm pretty sure I'll survive."

"I bet you will," she said, giving him the once over with her eyes. "So, what's it like… Indochina? I adore travel."

"I never said I was in—"

"Save it. I know where Peter died. He was a senator's son."

"It's beautiful. And ancient. And rough like an unpolished diamond."

"Oh, Sergeant. You're a poet. Be still my heart."

Granier chuckled. "And you're drunk."

"Drunk? This is not drunk. I can show you drunk," she said, waving to a waiter. She motioned for two more daiquiris.

"I can't," said Granier.

"Who said one was for you?"

"Good, because I don't drink rum."

"Of course not. You're a marine. Whiskey?"

"Sure."

"Let's get you a double, so you can catch up."

"That's probably not a good idea."

"I think it's a perfect idea. Life is too short. Peter would agree if he hadn't gotten himself killed for no reason."

"No reason?"

"Oh, a faux pas. I apologize. It happens when I drink. I speak my mind."

"So, it's not really an apology if it's the way you feel."

"I suppose not. But I don't want to offend you. Men in uniform can be so sensitive."

"I think you'll find me far from sensitive."

"Really? The thought intrigues me. I am curious as to your opinion. Does war solve anything?"

"You know… I should really get going," he said, rising.

"Oh, come on, Sergeant. I was just trying to ruffle your feathers. Besides, I hate the thought I will never see Peter again. I don't want to be alone tonight."

"I'm sure you won't be. It's just not going to be me. Have a good night," he said, walking away.

"Shit," said the woman as the waiter sat two daiquiris in front of her.

Saigon, Indochina - December 23, 1945

As the sun rose in the early morning sky, the French troopship MS Maréchal Joffre sailed up the Sông Sài Gòn, also known as the Saigon River. Sampans bobbed in the wake as it passed. Its mighty horn announced the ship's arrival and broke the stillness of the morning. The vessel was an American hand-me-down from World War II. Most of France's navy, including its troopships, had been sunk by the Allies to keep it out of the hands of the Nazis. France could not afford a new troopship, and while the Maréchal Joffre was well-used, it still served its purpose.

On the bow of the ship, the 6th company of the 23rd Colonial Infantry Regiment was performing calisthenics. Leading them was Captain Marcel Bigeard. Those that knew him called him Little Bruno - his call sign when he was with the underground in Paris. He didn't object. Bruno was not one for formality. He measured his men by ability and bravery. Everyone under his command knew where they stood and what was expected of them. Today, and every morning before breakfast, was one hour of calisthenics. They were also expected to do a five-mile run, but Bruno had forgone the run while they were aboard ship because there were too many things to trip over and break an ankle. He needed his men fit when they landed. He planned on using them a great deal.

The other company commanders onboard believed it was better to forgo the exercise altogether until their troops had adjusted to the hot and muggy Southeast Asian weather. They let their men rest up for the fight ahead.

Bruno didn't understand this logic since the men would need to fight no matter the weather. He thought it stupid and told his fellow officers such whenever asked, which wasn't often. In their eyes, Bruno was a fanatic and an upstart captain looking to jump rank. The one thing nobody could argue was that Bruno was one of the fittest men in the French army. His men both loved him and hated him because he tended to volunteer for the most dangerous assignments.

"Good workout, gentlemen," Bruno said as he finished the final set of squats.

Bruno never asked his men to do anything he would not do himself, and that included the morning exercise routine. He always led from the front. Bruno also had one other peculiar habit that most thought foolish and drove his fellow commanders nuts. Bruno never carried a weapon into battle, not even an officer's sidearm. He felt as commander of his unit, his duty was to make sure that all of his men were positioned correctly and fighting efficiently. He couldn't do that if he were fighting himself. And Bruno loved to fight. It was instinctual. Hence, his self-imposed 'no weapon' rule. "The ship will be docking at the Port of Saigon at noon. We will be disembarking shortly after that. I have been assured that the British have secured the area around the port. However, since I do not trust the British as far as I can throw them, we will be landing with our weapons at the ready."

His men laughed. Classic Bruno. "I do have some good news. Once off the ship, I am sure we can find a safe place for our morning run," he said, and the men groaned. "I will make sure everyone is given a chance to stretch their legs at the earliest convenience. Speaking of which, after breakfast, we will have a full equipment check and inspection. Those caught lacking will give me ten miles before sundown. Welcome to Indochina, Gentlemen. It's a beautiful place to die."

CHAPTER THREE

Haiphong, Indochina - November 23, 1946

Ho Chi Minh did not want a war. He hoped to negotiate a peaceful withdrawal of the French from Indochina. He and his followers were not afraid of the French. They had been fighting the French since before World War II. They knew that the French were in a weakened state because of the toll from the Nazi occupation of France. With their economy in ruins, the French lacked money, supplies, and weapons. Ho and his advisors doubted that the French public would have much stomach for yet another prolonged conflict. The Viet Minh simply needed to outlast the French, racking up casualties whenever possible. The French media would do the rest, and their army would be called home.

It wasn't the French that worried Ho. It was the Americans. The French had been an ally of the Americans just as the Viet Minh had been an

American ally. But France was in Europe, and the Americans wanted to prevent Soviet expansion. The Americans were also concerned about Chinese expansion into Indochina. But Ho suspected that the two countries were not equal in the minds of the Americans. Ho knew his history. France had helped America achieve its independence from Britain. France was in the heart of Europe. The Americans believed that Europe falling to the communists was just as bad as Europe falling to the fascists. It was nonsense, of course.

While it was true that Ho was a communist, he was a nationalist first and foremost. He believed that Communism was the best political and economic system to lift the Vietnamese people out of poverty. He would do whatever was necessary to save his country and feed his people.

Still, if the Americans were forced to choose between Indochina and France, Ho was sure they would choose France. Southeast Asia was not a threat to America, but a communist Europe could be. In Ho's mind, war must be avoided at all costs. He had watched how the American military buildup had destroyed both the Nazis and the Japanese. He did not want the same fate to fall on Vietnam. He did not want to fight the Americans. He saw them as a natural ally to the Indochinese. The Americans had fought for their freedom just as the Indochinese were fighting for theirs. Ho had lived and worked in America. He supported many of the ideas of liberty and unalienable equal rights that the Americans accepted as core beliefs.

Besides, Ho didn't trust the Chinese. China had

invaded and occupied Vietnam many times over the centuries. Mao was an ardent communist and was willing to make great sacrifices to further global expansion of his beloved philosophy. He resented Ho's nationalistic tendencies and thought them counter-productive to the true communist agenda. China needed Vietnamese rice to feed its growing population and Vietnamese soldiers to support communist expansion into Southeast Asia. If Vietnam accepted Chinese military aid, it would be hard to stop the tiger once it had his foot in the door. Ho was stuck between a rock and a hard place. He needed the French to grant Vietnam independence and leave his country once and for all, but he needed the Chinese to force them to do it.

Things had settled down to a slow boil between the Viet Minh and the French since the first skirmishes after the end of World War II. France simply did not have enough military resources at its disposal to fight a protracted war with the Viet Minh, which were quickly growing in number and strength. Instead, France's commissioner for Northern Indochina, Jean Sainteny, negotiated a treaty with Ho Chi Minh that gave Vietnam independence as a free state within the French Union. Vietnam was allowed to have its own government, parliament, army, and finances. France was entitled to a military presence in Vietnam for five years to protect French citizens and France's financial interests.

Before long, and much to the dismay of Ho and his followers, France began to exert the same colonial authority it had previously renounced in the treaty.

French warships stationed in the Gulf of Tonkin virtually blockaded Haiphong Harbor. When a French patrol boat seized a Chinese junk running contraband, Vietnamese soldiers on shore opened fire on the French ship. Armed clashes between French and Vietnamese civilians broke out in the city of Haiphong. To stop the violence from escalating, the French agreed to respect Vietnamese sovereignty in Haiphong.

Once the news of the incident reached Paris, Admiral d'Argenlieu, High Commissioner of Indochina, was incensed. He fired off a cable to Jean Étienne Valluy, the commander of French forces in Indochina, demanding that he take control of Haiphong by force of arms.

An ultimatum was given to Ho Chi Minh and the Vietnamese demanding that they immediately withdraw from the French and Chinese sections of the city, including the port. When the Vietnamese refused, the French Cruiser Suffren and three Bougainville-class aviso ships were ordered to take up positions within the harbor.

Seeing the warships approach, the people of Haiphong ran for shelter. Two platoons of French marines went ashore and escorted the French and Chinese citizens for whom they were responsible back to the ships. The French knew the location of the French and Chinese neighborhoods and would avoid shelling them during the battle, but they weren't taking any chances. Any Vietnamese that stood in the way of the marines were quickly mowed down by a volley of gunfire. The marines were vastly outnumbered, and aggression was their only defense. After their violent display, any mob would think twice about attacking the marines as they twisted their way through the city. That brief respite was all they needed to reach the safety of the shoreline, where the ships' guns could protect them with direct fire.

With the French and Chinese civilians safely on board, the small flotilla opened fire. The ground shook as shells whistled in and exploded within the city. The aviso patrol boats with their five and a half inch guns raked the shoreline and destroyed many of the Vietnamese homes and businesses. The eight-inch guns on the Suffren were able to reach any structure within the entire city. One shell filled with high explosives would demolish a house, killing its occupants. A large stone or masonry building might take two or three rounds before the roof caved in and the walls collapsed. The ships' gunners were careful in their selection of targets, pounding one Vietnamese neighborhood or business district before moving on to the next.

Helldivers and Corsairs from the French aircraft carrier Arromanches carried out bombing raids over the city. Once their bombs were released, the pilots were free to strafe any enemy positions that fired at them. Any vehicle or pedestrian within the city limits was considered a target of opportunity. The French were ordered to make an example of the Vietnamese in Haiphong, and they carried out their mission with relish.

Fire was the most significant hazard to the people of Haiphong. Much of the city was old and was constructed with wood that had dried out over decades, even centuries, of use. Hot shrapnel from the shells tore deep into the wood structures and set them ablaze. Paper lanterns hung from the outside beams caught fire easily and acted as kindling. Any fire spread quickly, without warning. Wind from the sea was drawn in by the heat and created a firestorm consuming entire neighborhoods.

The shelling only lasted a few hours, but that was all that was necessary. The fire did the rest. Before daybreak of the following morning, over six thousand Vietnamese civilians had died in what history would call The Haiphong Massacre. The Indochina War had begun.

Hanoi, Indochina

Ho and General Giap were in conference in their new party headquarters in Hanoi when word came of the massacre. Both were crestfallen at the loss and the brutality of the French on their civilian population. "They won't have a full accounting of the losses and damage for a few days, but they believe dead are in the thousands, and over half the city has been destroyed by fire," said Giap reading the cable. "At least the harbor facilities were only lightly damaged."

"Of course. The French need the harbor to unload more troops and supplies," said Ho, disgusted.

"We cannot let this stand."

"And we won't. But a large portion of our troops are still untrained, and many are unarmed," said Ho.

"We should only fight the French if we cannot lose."

"We won't lose. Morale is high. Our soldiers are itching for a fight to prove themselves worthy. The French are weak, poorly supplied, and their numbers are still few. We should strike them now before they gain strength. A powerful blow could force them to rethink their reoccupation."

"And where would you make this blow?"

"Hanoi. It's only a matter of time before the French attempt to take control of Hanoi. They know it is our strongest bastion and our base of support."

"Are we ready to go on the offensive?"

"No. But if we wait until we are ready, we may lose the only opportunity to show the French the true opposition they face. Once they are entrenched, the cost will rise significantly to root them out. I know it is risky, but we must strike now."

"What about the French artillery and air force?"

"Both are surmountable problems. Our troops must keep moving during the battle and not let the French pin them down. To do so will be met with disaster."

"And French armor?"

"Their tanks are the biggest threat. We acquired a stockpile of lunge mines from the Japanese weapon depots that we raided before they left."

"Lunge mine?"

"It's a shaped charge using high explosives. Specially trained volunteers carry the conical charge on the end of a wooden pole. When a tank or armored car passes, the soldier springs from his hidden position, charges the side of the vehicle, and strikes the armored plates at a 90-degree angle. The mine detonates on impact, killing the crew, and disabling the vehicle."

"And the soldier?"

"It's a manual anti-tank weapon. It does not require much skill, so we can use some of our younger recruits rather than the veterans."

"You mean it's a suicide weapon?"

"Unfortunately, yes. The operator of the mine is killed by the explosion. But we have no lack of volunteers. The lunge mines are very effective against all types of armor. It's considered an honor to be selected for such a mission."

"Just because our people are brave does not mean we should take their lives lightly."

"I assure you I don't."

"I don't like it. How will our people feel if they know we are using their children for suicide attacks?"

"Proud, I would imagine. Their children will be dying for their country and saving the lives of their fellow soldiers. The French tanks will be devastating against our infantry if we do not stop them. We will lose by far more men than the few suicide operators we use to stop the French armor."

"I see."

"Good. We both know that independence will cost many lives. Maybe even our own. I take the sacrifice of our men seriously, but it is necessary."

"Of course. I don't doubt your prudence, General. I just want to make sure we have an army to win our people's freedom. What if we waited until our men are better prepared?"

"The French will see us as weak. We will be inviting additional attacks."

"I see. What about using the crime syndicates to attack the French? At least they are already armed and know how to fire a weapon."

"They are undisciplined thugs that damage our cause and turn the people against us."

"I suppose you are right. How long would you need before we could strike?"

"Two, maybe three weeks to reposition our troops and evacuate those civilians that can be convinced to leave the city before the shooting starts. We should consolidate our forces and send anyone unready to our mountain bases to continue training. Only our veterans and the lunge mine volunteers should fight the French. The recruits would just be cannon fodder. While there is some value in mass, we cannot waste them. We will need them as replacements after they are trained."

"I agree. We need to preserve every soldier that we can. The French will hit back hard. We must be prepared for a protracted engagement."

"Then we are in agreement?"

"We are. Keep me advised as you make preparations to carry out your plan."

"Of course, Uncle."

CHAPTER FOUR

York County, Virginia - December 10, 1946

Camp Perry was made up of 9,000 acres of hearty Virginia forest and bordered by the York River. It was an ideal location to train the Navy's elite combat engineers - The Seabees. It even had its own destroyer escort ship - Miss Never Sail - a wooden mock-up used for demolition training. The U.S. Navy abandoned the camp after World War II and turned it over to the U.S. Forestry Department for recreational use.

As the CIA was being formed, the director identified the need for a secret training facility for overseas field officers. His idea was to hide in plain sight. A small section of Camp Perry was cordoned off with signs that identified the area as impassable with dangerous swamps. An electrified fence surrounded the area, which seemed strange to visitors of the national park who were too busy enjoying the natural beauty of the area to pay much attention. In later years, the entire camp would be reclaimed by the U.S. Navy, and the secret CIA training facility would expand to include all the acreage. The electrified fences were extended, and the signs keeping visitors out took on a much more ominous tone with threats of imprisonment for trespassers. Guard dogs and M.P.s patrolled the perimeter 24 hours a day, 365 days a year. The CIA training facility would be nicknamed "The Farm."

Granier felt like he had unintentionally made a deal with the devil. When he turned in his report on the Viet Minh and the French, it created quite a stir. Patti was right. Even the president read it. This made Granier an expert on Indochina, and the new CIA director, Lieutenant General Hoyt Vandenberg, was not about to let him return to active duty. He would be given a desk and asked to analyze all intel from Southeast Asia. Granier refused and threatened to resign. He was technically a civilian working for the U.S. Government. Instead of accepting his resignation, Patti made a deal with Granier. Granier would spend half his time training field officers in sniper and reconnaissance techniques at The Farm and the other half reviewing and writing intelligence reports. Granier was not happy about this compromise. But he also knew he wasn't trained for a job in the real world, except maybe in law enforcement, which didn't suit his reclusive nature. Working for the CIA was the best he could do at the moment.

Three days a week, Granier would take ten

recruits into the woods of Camp Perry and instruct them on how to spy on and kill the enemy without being detected. His students were required to wade through swamps filled with snakes and other deadly critters; climb tall trees and create a sniper's perch; crawl a half-mile on their bellies through the dirt and mud. And anything else that he could think of that would make the recruits miserable, instill confidence, and teach them the true meaning of silence and stealth. His job lacked the thrill of being shot at but was entertaining at times; like the first time a recruit finds a leech sucking on his ball sack. He was a hard teacher and not afraid to put his boot up anyone's ass that wasn't giving 100%. He wasn't there to win popularity contests. His students didn't like him and often complained to their superiors. He was okay with that as long as they learned what was required to be a good scout and sniper. In his mind, he was saving the lives of the future CIA officers, whether they liked it or not.

The other two to three days a week, Granier sat at a desk in Washington, D.C., which he truly hated. He felt like his legs were continually cramping from lack of exercise. He would spend his lunch break hiking around the National Mall and the Memorial Parks while munching on a hot dog or roast beef sandwich and sipping a coke. Pickles were the only vegetable he liked, but sliced tomatoes were at times tolerated as long as they were firm and ripe.

It was during one of these walks that Granier saw a man sitting on a bench reading a newspaper – The Boston Globe. Wearing a long overcoat with a suit underneath and his hair combed with precision, the man was young, no more than thirty, and handsome. The man glanced above his newspaper and saw Granier passing. He folded and tucked his paper under his arm as he rose and walked toward Granier. Granier didn't like company, especially during his walks. It was an intrusion. The man seemed to grin as he spoke. His big white teeth were disarming. "Excuse me. Are you Rene Granier?" said the man.

Granier's defensive radar immediately went up. He didn't know this man, nor his intentions. "Who's asking?" he said.

"Jack," said the man offering his hand.

"I'm Granier," he said, shaking the man's hand. "How did you find me?"

"Your boss told me you like to take walks at lunch. And this is the best place to walk."

"My boss?"

"Lieutenant General Hoyt Vandenberg."

Granier chuckled. "He's a bit more than my boss."

The man smiled, "Yeah. I suppose you're right. But he's the only one I knew at the agency."

"How do you know the director?"

"My family's involvement in politics. Generals like politics. They all think they're going to be like Eisenhower or Grant – President of the United States – someday."

"Ain't that the truth. How can I help you, Jack?"

"I read your report."

"My report?"

"…on Indochina and the Viet Minh."

"How did you get your hands on a top-secret report?"

"President Truman suggested I read it."

"President Truman?"

"Yeah, just after I got elected to Congress."

"You're a Congressman?"

"Congressman-elect… for another month."

"Okay. So, you read my report."

"Actually, it's a little more than that. My sister Patricia said Paul Dewey was your commander. You two met at his funeral."

"That woman was your sister? I'm surprised she could remember anything."

"Yeah. She drinks a bit when she gets depressed. She's a creative type like Hemingway and Picasso. Anyway, you impressed her as a straightforward man. I need to have a straightforward conversation about Indochina."

"You read my report. What else do you need to know?"

"Most of our senators and congressmen believe Indochina is just a sideshow to the growing communist threat in Europe. I don't see it that way. Asia holds 60% of the world population. We can't just concede over half the world to live under Communism. Not without a fight. I agree with you that Indochina is the key to Southeast Asia. We must deny the Russians and the Chinese a foothold."

"Easier said than done."

"Obviously, yes. It will take a huge commitment to stop them. But after reading your report, I wonder if there is another way. You said that Ho Chi Minh is more a nationalist than a communist."

"I believe he is, yes. He sees Communism as a path to freedom for his country. He uses

Communism to offer his people something new, while the French only offer the status quo. It's a big reason why so many follow him. He gives them hope."

"I can see that. Would you say he sees Communism as a means to an end, but not necessarily the end itself?"

"I think he would agree that the struggle is all about freeing his people and making Vietnam a great nation. He sees Communism as the best way to achieve that goal."

"If he was shown a better way, would he recognize it? Would he be willing to abandon Communism?"

"If you mean Capitalism, I doubt it. The French were capitalists, and he saw what they did to his people."

"I see. So, there's no way to reason with him?"

"I wouldn't say that. But it's going to be an uphill battle. He's had a long time to think about it. He lived and worked in America for a few years and got to see our political and economic system first hand. It made quite an impression on him. I know he believes in liberty and equality. I heard him speak many times while we were with him in the mountains. Hearing him talk, it felt like he was cherry-picking from what he had seen and put together his own philosophical approach. He may be a communist, but I don't think his Communism is anything like Mao's and Stalin's Communism, and I don't think he is as dedicated to spreading his beliefs beyond the borders of Vietnam. Everyone thinks they understand what he truly believes. But I wonder."

"How is that?"

"He's a politician, and he has great instincts. He always says and does the right things to win over his audience. His followers are extremely loyal to him. They would die for him. But I can't help but feel he knows something that nobody else knows, and he keeps it hidden. And the only time we are going to find out what Ho believes is when the fighting is finally finished."

"So, you don't believe he can be trusted?"

"You're asking the wrong guy. While we were fighting the Japanese, he tried to have me killed. I'm a bit biased."

"Fair enough. But I still want to know what you think."

Granier considers before responding. He still wasn't sure about this young man, Jack, but he figured his opinion couldn't hurt. "People do things for a reason. Ho had his reasons."

"What would those be?"

"He thought I was a spy for the French. He hates the French and what they have done to his people."

"So, his reasons for betraying you were justified?"

"No. I wasn't a spy."

"Okay, but from his point of view?"

"I suppose I would have done the same thing if I were in his shoes. You protect your pack, whatever it takes."

"Your pack?"

"The men you fight alongside. They defend you, and you defend them."

"I know what you mean."

"You fought in the war?"

"I did. In the Pacific."

"You were a marine?"

"No. Navy. P.T. Boats."

"Dangerous duty."

"Says the man who parachuted behind enemy lines."

Granier grunted.

"Can he be reasoned with... Ho Chi Minh?" said Jack.

"Yeah, I suppose. He's smart and listens more than he talks. But he's also calculating. He only does what he thinks will help his cause."

"What about his ties with Russia?"

"I don't think he cares much for the Russians. He certainly doesn't trust them."

"And the Chinese?"

"The same. He doesn't trust them, and they don't trust him. They don't like his nationalistic viewpoint. But Ho won't refuse help from anyone that will help him win freedom for his people."

"How does he feel about the United States?"

"A couple of years ago, he loved it. He thought we would be a natural ally for his independence movement. Now, I don't know. A lot of water under the bridge."

"How could I find out?"

"I suppose you'd have to go there."

"To Indochina?"

"Sure. America is not at war with the Viet Minh or the French. You're about to become a U.S. congressman. I'm sure both sides would roll out the red carpet to impress you. Why not see for yourself?"

"Something to think about. Do you think the French will give the Indochinese their independence?"

Granier considered for a long moment, then said, "Cambodia and Laos, yes. Vietnam, I'm not so sure."

"Why is that?"

"Too valuable. The French need money to rebuild their country after World War II. Vietnam is a profitable colony. Lots of rice, rubber, iron, and wood, plus labor is damn near free. The French have built a great deal of infrastructure in Vietnam. They will want to see a return on their investment, especially now that they are strapped for cash."

"So, it's about money?"

"That and pride. France was once a great empire. The Nazis overrunning Paris with such ease gave France a black eye. The French need to prove to the world that they are still a great power and deserve a seat at the table. Giving up Vietnam would be seen as a weakness. If France is going to hang onto their empire, they must project strength. If Vietnam falls, France's colonies in North Africa will be next, especially Algeria."

"Can France win against the Viet Minh?"

"Honestly, I don't know. The French certainly know how to fight despite what the world thinks, and they seem determined to hang on to Vietnam. But the Viet Minh are getting stronger by the day. They flock to Ho Chi Minh like he is a god. I've never seen such dedication. The Vietnamese have nothing to lose and everything to gain. I think they will fight to the death to win their freedom."

"What do you think are the biggest misconceptions about the war?"

"I think there are two that are dangerous. The first is that all Communism is being directed by Moscow. It's not. The whole idea of Indochina being a launching platform into the rest of Southeast Asia may or may not be true, but I don't think the Indochinese are going to be too excited about sending their troops into Thailand or Malaysia. They've got enough problems in their own countries."

"Interesting. And the second?"

"I think the French underestimate the Viet Minh because they are not as educated or trained by professional soldiers. I've seen them fight. The Viet Minh are natural soldiers and brave. They've learned from experience. The longer they fight, the better they will become. It's their enemies that are teaching them."

"You've been a great help. You've given me a lot to think about, Rene."

"Call me, Granier."

"Okay, Granier. I'll let you get back to your walk. Can I call you if I have more questions?"

"I wouldn't object. Do you have my office number?"

"I'm pretty sure I can find it."

"Right. You know people."

"I suppose I do," said Congressman-elect John F. Kennedy as he grinned like the Cheshire Cat, shook Granier's hand, and walked away.

CHAPTER FIVE

Hanoi, Indochina – December 19, 1946

It was early morning. A thin layer of fog mixed with smoke from the wooden stoves hung over the rivers and neighborhoods of Hanoi. It was quiet. The windows of the houses and buildings stayed shut, and the doors remained locked tight. Unlike most days, nobody was going to work, and no children played in the streets. There was an uneasy feeling throughout the city, and nobody wanted to talk about it. Talking was dangerous and could get you killed.

Three men carrying a shovel and two sledgehammers walked along a vacant street of a Saigon business district. All the shops were closed with their window shades down. They would not open that day. The Vietnamese business owners had been warned of what was about to happen, and it would be far too risky to open for whatever money might be earned.

Another Vietnamese man standing in a doorway signaled the three men as they approached. He took a quick survey of the area to ensure that no French eyes were watching, then disappeared through an open door.

The three men followed him inside a furniture store and moved through a showroom into the warehouse area in the back of the building. The men moved to a masonry wall that had an outline in chalk of a crude doorway. Two of the men went to work hammering the wall with the sledgehammers while the third man shoveled away the debris. It didn't take long before they broke through the wall into the warehouse area of a clothing store on the opposite side. A Vietnamese woman was waiting. As soon as the hole was large enough and the debris was cleared away, they stepped through the hole with their sledgehammers and shovels. The men followed the woman to the wall on the opposite side of her store, where they saw another chalk outline of a rough doorway. They went to work, pounding away at the wall. Within a few hours, they had created a long tunnel through seven buildings.

A delivery truck pulled into the alley behind the furniture store. The driver parked next to the loading doorway and got out. He knocked on the loading door, and the door opened. The driver and the business owner nodded politely to each other. The driver looked for prying French eyes as he walked to the back of the truck. It was clear. He opened the tailgate. Seven Viet Minh disguised as delivery men jumped out of the back of the truck. They carried three large carpets and four large boxes inside the store, and the back door of the warehouse was closed.

Inside the furniture store warehouse, the Viet Minh unrolled the carpets revealing weapons hidden inside. The boxes were opened to reveal ammunition and grenades. The Viet Minh went to work distributing the firearms and ammunition to the front areas and upper levels of each of the seven buildings. They set up recently-filled sandbags to create reinforced defensive positions behind the display windows with their shades drawn. They were careful to set up the positions far enough from the windows so the soldiers manning them would not be hurt by the falling glass when the first shots were fired. More Viet Minh arrived as the day wore on until there was an entire company of soldiers in the seven buildings, hidden and waiting.

A Vietnamese woman walked out of an alley and into the street. She looked both ways down the road. It was vacant, as she hoped. She motioned toward the alley.
A dozen Vietnamese men and women carrying picks, hoes, and shovels exited the alley. They moved into the street. Six men went to work, tearing up the asphalt with their picks and hoes. Six men and women placed the blades of their shovels beneath the broken pavement and used the shovel handles to pry up the remaining asphalt. They rolled up the asphalt like a carpet creating a thick roadblock across the entire street.

More men and women brought furniture,

trashcans, logs, and empty crates to pile on top of the rolled-up asphalt. Dirt, rocks, and sand transported in wheelbarrows and carts were used to fill in the gaps of the defensive wall. A deep and wide trench was dug in front of the roadblock making the wall seem even more impenetrable and preventing French vehicles from ramming the barricade. Similar roadblocks were created throughout the business districts, industrial areas, and neighborhoods of Hanoi.

Bridges were blocked at both ends. The wooden planks that formed the bridges' deck were torn up with picks and crowbars, making them impassable. The roadblocks would force the French vehicles to stop. Hamstrung, the vehicles and their occupants would become easy targets for the Viet Minh and militias.

Vietnamese women collected hundreds of glass bottles, candles, and cloth rags from their neighbors, restaurants, and markets around Hanoi. The bottles, candles, and rags were brought to a central location in the back of a food market in a Vietnamese neighborhood.

A truck pulled up and parked behind the market. The driver retrieved two large metal cans, one filled with gasoline and the other with motor oil, from the back of the truck. He carried the metal containers through the backdoor into the warehouse of the market. A pharmacist arrived with several liters of naphthenic acid and palmitic acid. The market owner contributed a few liters of kerosene to the project.

An assembly line was created. Six women cut up the rags into strips. Another six tied the strips around the necks of the bottles, leaving an extra length of cloth to hang from each knot. Next, the pharmacist stirred the two acids in with a half and half mixture of gasoline and motor oil. The combined ingredients created a crude form of napalm that would burn long and stick to whatever came in contact with it. The napalm was poured through a funnel into the individual bottles. Broken pieces of candle were pressed into the top of the container, sealing the napalm inside. Finally, the rag around the neck was dosed with kerosene so it would ignite quickly and hopefully light the napalm once the bottle was broken and the liquid ran out. When a box of the firebombs was filled, it was taken by bicycle or motor scooter to one of the dozen chokepoints around Hanoi, where the Viet Minh and militia hoped to ambush the French soldiers and vehicles.

A Vietnamese blacksmith waited patiently while stoking his fire. Three men dropped off burlap bags filled with 60D common nails. The blacksmith removed a handful of the 6-inch nails and used his tongs to place them deep in the orange coals of his fire. He pumped the bellows to increase the heat even further.

Once the nails were reddish-orange, he removed them with the tongs, used a chisel to cut off the nails' heads, then placed them on his anvil and used his hammer to pound them into ninety degrees angles.

When all the nails were finished and cooled with a dousing of water, the blacksmith's assistant linked the center of two nails and welded them together. The nails had become caltrops - four-sided spikes arranged in such a manner that one spike always pointed upward from a stable base. The caltrops were placed back in the burlap bags for transportation.

French roadblocks at the entrances to industrial areas prevented any non-authorized Vietnamese from getting near key installations. There was an armored car with a machinegun in the turret manned by two men. Another four soldiers would check documents and search visitors and vehicles waiting to pass. For the French troops, it was mind-numbing work. Most of the Vietnamese that approached the roadblock were women who wanted to sell the soldiers sodas or cigarettes. Some were prostitutes willing to sell themselves to feed their families.

Twice in the morning and twice in the afternoon, a French soldier from the mess hall would ride a bicycle to bring coffee to the soldiers at the roadblock. It was always a welcome break from the boredom. He would pour the hot liquid into the soldiers' cups from a large metal container strapped to the back of the bicycle. He joked with the soldiers and gave them updates on troop movements, plus any messages from company headquarters. Once everyone had their fill, he rode off for the next roadblock making the rounds, stop after stop, day after day.

As expected, the coffee delivery soldier had come twice in the morning and once in the early afternoon. But he was late for the late afternoon coffee break, and the soldiers at the roadblock were grumpy and complaining. "It's a soft duty if there ever was one. He has one job to do, and he can't even do it right," said the sergeant in charge of the roadblock.

"Maybe something happened," said another soldier.

"What? He burned his fingers and had to go to the hospital?"

"It could happen."

"You're an idiot."

"Maybe he had a flat tire," said a different soldier.

"You're even more of an idiot than him," said the sergeant motioning to the first soldier. "It doesn't take an hour to fix a flat."

"He would need to take the coffee container off the back of his bike. That takes time."

"You're just making excuses for him. He's just a lazy bastard."

"Wait, there he is," said the first soldier pointing.

Everyone turned to see a soldier stopping at the top of a hill and getting off his bicycle. He moved to the back of his bike, where the coffee container was strapped, and seemed to be checking the coffee inside using his cigarette lighter for illumination. "What the hell is he doing?" said the sergeant. "It's coffee. It's not like it's going to run off by itself."

The sergeant waved for the delivery soldier to come on down. The soldier closed the lid to the container, waved back at the sergeant, remounted his bicycle, and rode down the hill. "It's about fucking time," said the sergeant as the bike approached.

The soldier riding the bicycle had his helmet low over his eyes, casting a shadow over his face. He rode past the sergeant and over to the armored car as if to serve the crew first. The soldier stopped his bicycle and leaned it up against the side of the armored vehicle. "What the hell are you doing?" said the angry sergeant. "Get back over here!"

The soldier ran into the field next to the road. One of the soldiers in the armored car climbed out and opened the lid to the coffee container. It was smoky inside. He blew the smoke away and saw a fuse burning. "Oh, shit," he said. "Bomb!"

The soldiers dove for cover, but it was too late. The explosion was massive. The armored vehicle was rocked violently and tipped over on its side. The soldiers closest to the container were shredded by red-hot shrapnel flying in all directions and died within moments. The survivors had blood pouring from their eyes, noses, and ears. The sergeant regained his wits, picked up a rifle, and opened fire at the delivery soldier running across the field.

The delivery soldier was hit in the back and fell to the ground. The helmet came off, revealing a Vietnamese woman wearing an ill-fitting French uniform. She died.

The sergeant turned to see a platoon of Viet Minh soldiers appear at the top of the hill. He looked around at the surviving men in his unit badly mauled and disoriented. He knew there was little hope they would be able to fend off the Viet Minh now running down the hillside toward the shattered roadblock. He saw the radio lying on the ground near the overturned armored car. He had to warn his headquarters of the attack. He found it hard even to stand and imagined it was his shattered eardrums, causing his dizziness. Slow and steady, he thought. As he moved toward the radio, the Viet Minh closed their distance on the roadblock and opened fire.

Bullets zinged through the air, some hitting his men. The sergeant found it hard to walk straight, but he wobbled toward the radio as best he could. A bullet hit him in the hip and spun him around. He toppled to the ground. He looked back at the Viet Minh less than thirty yards away and closing on his position. There wasn't much time. Another rifle shot sliced across his back and stopped in his shoulder. He dragged himself to the radio and flipped on the power switch. He picked up the handset and called his commander on the radio. It took a moment before he realized that the cord between the handset and the radio had been severed by a piece of shrapnel from the explosion. The radio was useless. He chuckled at the irony. A Viet Minh soldier ran up behind him, aimed his rifle, and put the sergeant out of his misery. The Viet Minh fired on the remaining survivors and killed them all. They wasted no time and ran past the roadblock toward their intended target - Hanoi's power plant.

The Viet Minh feared the French armored units. They had little armor themselves. They had developed techniques to deal with the steel beasts, but most required the sacrifice of one or more Vietnamese soldiers, and those sacrifices were no guarantee that they could stop the vehicles permanently.

The French had an uncanny ability to recycle weapons that many thought wholly destroyed. They had learned to make do with what they had on hand, and if that meant refurbishing a demolished tank in which the original crew had died, then so be it. The blood was washed out, and steel plates were welded over the shell holes. Nothing was wasted, especially in the early part of the war.

Lieutenant Yves Hervouet commanded the 3rd Squadron, 1st Light Horse Regiment, the only armored unit in Hanoi. His round spectacles gave his youthful face a wise owl appearance that matched his superior intellect. He was brave and tenacious. Tank crews in World War II had very short life expectancies. To be effective, a tank commander had to accept that he and his team probably wouldn't survive the war. It made them ornery and mean. Hervouet had fought on the Maginot Line before it was overrun and again in North Africa against Rommel. He was an experienced veteran before his twenty-sixth birthday. A promotion to first lieutenant brought him his current command.

The squadron was made up of 9 Hotchkiss H-39 light tanks, 12 Panhard 178B armored cars, and 14 troop trucks that carried his infantry, mechanics, supplies, and spare parts. It was far less than what would be required to defend a city the size of Hanoi from the Viet Minh. What made matters worse was that his commander had piecemealed out most of his vehicles to other infantry units protecting critical installations and roadways in and around the city. It was only his insistence on maintaining an armored reactionary force that kept one platoon of three tanks, two armored cars, and three troop trucks under his command. That was it – one platoon. Hardly the honor he thought he was being given when he was assigned command of the 3rd squadron. Still, he was determined to make its presence known.

His plan was simple - be in all places at once, so the Viet Minh thought the squadron bigger than it was. To do this, he needed to crisscross Hanoi with all the speed his tanks and armored cars could muster. He would run his vehicles, and troops ragged to fool the enemy. He would even have his men switch out the platoon identification flags on the vehicle antennas to extend the illusion of more vehicles. He knew the Viet Minh had spies throughout the city that would report their sightings of the unit flags to their Viet Minh commanders. Typically, the flags were only used for military parades and training, but Hervouet reckoned that the Viet Minh didn't know that.

As the sun set, the city became more dangerous. The Viet Minh were masters at hiding, and darkness was their ally. They only needed to blow off one of the vehicles' tracks or wheels to cripple the platoon. The French soldiers would not leave a damaged vehicle for the Viet Minh to capture and potentially use against them in the future. When a vehicle was disabled, Hervouet and his men would take up defensive positions and fight to protect the crew of the mangled vehicle while they repaired the damage, and it became mobile once again. If the vehicle could not be repaired, it had to be towed away or destroyed beyond all usefulness before it could be abandoned. This procedure usually involved a satchel charge or multiple incendiary grenades to burn out the wiring inside the vehicle and bake off the ammunition. When incendiary grenades were not available, or they were under heavy fire, the survivors would make a run for it, then the other French tanks and armored cars would shell the damaged vehicle with their cannons until it blew up. The idea that nobody would be left behind by his comrades emboldened the French soldiers. It was a promise to each other they all took seriously.

On that night, Hervouet felt particularly uneasy. He had studied the intelligence reports and knew that the Viet Minh were repositioning their units. That meant they were up to something. It wasn't that Hervouet or his men were afraid. They weren't. They knew they were better trained than the Viet Minh, and they knew the territory just as well as the enemy. The French had lived and fought in Indochina for almost a century. The French soldiers thought themselves superior in intelligence to their Indochinese subjects. They certainly were larger in size and strength. And that mattered in battle, especially if the fight was reduced to hand-to-hand combat. The French could shoot better, and they fought well as a unit, which gave them the upper hand. All of those advantages gave them confidence that they could defeat their enemy… if they could only find him.

On the other hand, the Viet Minh followed the military strategies of Mao Zedung. Mao dictated that guerrilla fighters should ambush the enemy when they least expected it and have no concept of defense or battle lines. They should attack the enemy from all sides. The guerrilla leaders should always dictate the timing of conflicts and never fight unless they were sure they would win. If things did not go as expected, as often happens in war, the guerrilla fighters should be prepared to flee so they could fight another day. To the French and other western armies, this method of fighting and retreating seemed dishonorable and cowardly. To the Viet Minh, it seemed smart.

Like the other tank and armored vehicle commanders, Hervouet rode through the city with his legs inside the tank turret and the rest of his body sticking out the back hatch. It was dangerous. A sniper could easily pick him off, or an armed civilian could take a quick potshot as he passed. But it did give him a clear view of the surrounding area and the road ahead. Besides, it was cooler than inside the tank. Even in the cool, dry season, it was muggy in Hanoi, and a breeze was always welcome.

Hervouet's eight-vehicle column had been running for almost fourteen hours, and the drivers were fatigued. He knew he would need to call it a night after a few more hours, but he hated surrendering the night to the Viet Minh. The more time the Viet Minh had to move unimpeded within the city, the worse the expected assault would be for the French. Still, his men needed rest if they were to fight effectively. It was almost 2200 hours as he glanced at his watch. He decided midnight would be the cutoff time. He thought about telling his men his decision to cheer them up and give them something to look forward to but then reconsidered when the image of his men fixated on their wristwatches instead of the road and surrounding area popped into his head. They're tough. They can take it, he thought. I don't need to coddle them. Keep 'em focused on the mission at hand. Keep 'em alive.

The Hotchkiss light tank that Hervouet rode in was noisy as hell. The steel plates creaked. The hatch door bounced, clanging loudly each time it hit the turret. The heavy treads ground against the asphalt. It was a two-person vehicle that had been modified by the Germans during the occupation. The commander of the vehicle fought from the turret and was the gunner and loader of the 37mm main gun. The driver sat inside the chassis toward the front. There was also a 7.5 mm Reibel machinegun that could be mounted beside the main gun or on top of the turret to be used by the commander as an anti-aircraft gun. The turret was spun by a hand crank and could rotate 360 degrees. The tank carried 100 shells for the main gun and 3,500 rounds for the machinegun.

"How far to the Citadel?" Hervouet yelled down into the turret.

"Another five minutes," said Sgt. Lucas Malet, his driver. "You want me to pick up speed?"

"Do you think you can do it without blowing the engine?"

"No."

"Then no, you moron. Maintain current speed."

Hervouet didn't like the neighborhood they were entering, especially since his tank was in the lead. A fire had gutted many of the buildings, and some had collapsed. The blackened debris made perfect hiding places for the Viet Minh. If I was going to make an ambush, this is where I would do it, he thought. He reached down inside the turret and removed the machinegun from its mount next to the cannon. He pulled the weapon through the hatchway and attached it to its turret mount where he could reach it within a moment's notice. He checked the 150-round ammunition drum to ensure the bullets inside were properly aligned before replacing it on the gun. He wasn't taking any chances. He considered radioing the other commanders in his column but thought he might be micromanaging. His vehicle commanders were smart and knew the dangers. They would figure out their own strategies for defending their vehicles.

A bright flash lit up the horizon. It was an explosion of some sort — a big one. The lights in the surrounding buildings and the streetlights flickered and then went dark. "Shit," said Hervouet. "They hit the power plant."

"That can't be good," said Malet.

"You are a master of understatement, Sergeant."

"What do we do?"

"Keep driving and watch for the enemy."

"I can't see the road. Can I turn on the headlights?"

"Do you want to be the only moving target lit up like a Christmas tree?"

"No."

"Then I suggest you keep them off."

Hanoi was plunged into darkness except for the occasion cooking fire outside a few homes. The moonlight cast a soft outline on the tallest buildings leaving the others hidden in the blackness of their shadows. With the odds tilted in their favor, the Viet Minh were now free to roam the city and hunt the

French as they pleased. They would not waste the opportunity.

As his armored column drove past the buildings, Hervouet kept an eye on any position that might be used by a Viet Minh. It was unsettling. There were so many. He made a mental note to avoid the route on future patrols. He heard the whine of a siren and jerked around to the street in front. There were several burnt-out cars abandoned near the corner. The siren grew closer. Malet slowed the tank. "Don't slow down, Sergeant," snapped Hervouet.

Malet sped back up.

A fire truck appeared from the cross street at the end of the corner and turned toward the convoy. Its headlights were blinding. The truck swerved from side to side like the driver was drunk and finally crashed into a parked car. It was blocking the road. The siren faded to a warble.

Malet slammed on the brakes and slowed the tank to a stop. Hervouet knew instinctively what was happening; the fire truck was a blocking vehicle, and the column was about to be ambushed. He jumped up on the engine compartment and chambered a round into the machinegun.

The fire truck was still. The driver and crew nowhere in sight. "Fuck a duck," said Hervouet to himself.

"You think it's an ambush?" said Malet sheepishly.

"Of course it's an ambush. When's the last time you saw a fire truck crash right in front of you?"

"What do we do?"

"Fight."

Hervouet trained his machinegun sights on the fire truck cab. The driver was still inside. Hervouet was sure of it. Like a farmer waiting for a gopher, Hervouet held his fire. The driver's side door swung open, and the Viet Minh inside opened fire with a pistol. Hervouet gave him a short burst from his machinegun. The pistol went silent and dropped to the ground. The driver was dead.

From the corner of his eye, Hervouet saw something approach the side of his tank. It was a Viet Minh sapper charging from behind a debris pile and carrying a long pole with something bulky on the end. The lieutenant swung his machinegun around and opened fire. The sapper was hit several times and fell to the ground, dropping the pole.

More sappers sprung from their hiding places among the rubble and charged the armored vehicles in the column with their long poles. Other Viet Minh opened fire from their covered positions in and around the buildings. The French commanders focused on the sappers with poles, shooting them down as fast as they could, but there were too many.

One of the sappers reached a tank and struck his lunge mine against the thick steel panel on the side of the vehicle. The shaped-charge exploded with a blinding flash, killing the sapper instantly and dissolving a hole in the steel armor. The driver inside the tank was showered with molten metal and screamed until he died. The tank commander's legs, still inside the tank, were also splattered with the hot metal. He pulled his legs out. His pants were on fire. He tried to put the fire out with his hand, but some of the hot metal stuck to his palms and fingers, burning them badly. He finally rolled off the back of the tank onto the ground.

As bullets ricocheted off his tank, Hervouet turned to see several flaming Molotov cocktails launched from the rooftops of surrounding buildings arc across the night sky and land on the French troop trucks. The bottles holding the petrol mixture shattered on contact. The truck roofs and the canvass tarps over the trucks' passenger beds burst into flames. The French infantry soldiers poured out of the back of the trucks only to be met with a hail of gunfire from Viet Minh in the building windows. Six members of Hervouet's platoon were dead in the first minute of the battle. He was losing his command. His men were dying.

He turned back to his driver and said, "We gotta get out of here. Can we go around?"

"Not enough room. We'll just get wedged in," said Malet.

Hervouet's mind was racing. He had to do something... anything. He slid back inside the turret and spun the turret's hand crank until the main gun was aligned with the cab of the fire truck. He squeezed the trigger. There was a loud crack as the shell left the barrel. The round sailed through the open cab door and punched through the opposite side of the truck without exploding. "Fuck," said Hervouet as he reloaded the main gun, the empty casing clanking on the floor, the breach slamming shut.

He cranked the turret until the gun was aligned with the water tank on the back of the truck. He fired again.

The shell easily pierced the thin steel wall and exploded inside the tank. Water burst out, showering the French tank. But the fire truck still blocked the street. "Ram the bastard," said Hervouet.

Malet released his foot off the brake and gunned the engine. The tank lunged forward and picked up speed. "Aim for the back of the truck. We'll spin it out of the way," said Hervouet.

The tank had a top speed of only 22 mph. Malet quickly shifted through the gears. When he hit third gear, the tank smacked the back of the truck. The truck moved a few feet on initial impact, but it wasn't enough for the French vehicles to get by. Malet backed the tank up and made another run. The second impact helped a little more. On the third try, Malet repositioned the tank, so he struck the truck right over the back wheels. The fire truck's tires skidded across the asphalt. Debris was scattered all over the street but clear enough for the convoy to get past. "This is Rouge Leader Six. We are getting the hell out of here. Everyone load up and follow me," said Hervouet on the radio.

The infantry soldiers retrieved their dead and wounded comrades. The damaged tank was in flames and beyond repair. There was no way to retrieve the deceased driver. They would return and retrieve his body in daylight if it was still there. Everyone continued fighting as they made their way back to the trucks. One of the trucks was too severely damaged by the fire. A sergeant pulled the pin on a grenade and pitched it into the cab. It exploded, destroying the steering gear and instruments. He opened the front hood and tossed another grenade on top of the engine manifold. It exploded, tearing off the carburetor and shredding the hoses and belts. The truck was beyond repair and of no use to the Viet Minh. The infantrymen from the demolished truck climbed on the backs and sides of the armored cars. They continued to fire, keeping the Viet Minh pinned down.

With everyone loaded, Hervouet ordered Malet to leave the area. The battered convoy followed, leaving two of the vehicles burning in the street and one of their own behind. Even with their armor, the French had been forced to retreat. The Viet Minh had won the battle.

Foggy Bottom, Washington D.C., USA

Grumpier than usual, Granier sat at his desk, sipping his morning coffee. He was supposed to be in the woods with a new batch of students, but events in Hanoi had forced him to call off the class for today and go into the office. The thought that his recruits would be happy at the news bothered him. He liked to see them suffer. It meant he was doing his job as their instructor. Cables had been coming in all morning and were stacked on his desk. As the resident expert on Indochina, he was often asked to interpret the events unfolding in Hanoi. What's to interpret? he thought. The French and Viet Minh are trying to kill each other again. Big whoop.

Colonel Patti appeared in the doorway and said, "So, what do you think?"

"I think I need a bear claw to go with my coffee,"

said Granier.

"No, I meant Hanoi."

"I know what you meant. I just like busting your chops... Sir."

"The president is wondering if he should try to pass a supplementary aid bill for the French. He's asked the director for a recommendation, and the director asked me."

"Shit rolls downhill, don't it?"

"Damn right. Now it's in your lap. What do you think about the aid?"

"I'm sure the French would like more money."

"Yeah, but will it do any good? Will it keep Hanoi from falling to the communists?"

"How the hell am I supposed to know that?"

"It's your job to know."

"Yeah. Well, I'm really lousy at it. You should fire me."

"Granier, for god's sake, I gotta give the director a recommendation."

"Look, even if the president gets an aid package through Congress, it's gonna take weeks. The battle for Hanoi will be over before it ever arrives."

"So, that's a no."

"I didn't say that. If the French knew the aid was coming, they might commit more assets to the fight because they know they will be able to replace them."

"So, that's a yes."

"I didn't say that, either."

"What are you saying?"

"That I really want a bear claw."

"I'll buy you a fucking bear claw. Just give me a goddamn recommendation."

"Send 'em the money. Ten million ought to do it."

"See, now was that so hard?" said Patti looking at his watch, then disappearing from the doorway. "I've got to go see the director."

"What about my bear claw?" said Granier calling after him.

"I'm a spy. We lie sometimes. Shoot me," said Patti from down the hall.

Hanoi, Vietnam

It was early morning in Hanoi. The ever-moving mist hung over the city and mixed with the smoke from cooking fires to create a brownish smog. Everything seemed grey and hazy, a shadow of itself. The markets, usually busy with early morning buyers for restaurants and food carts were empty. The vendors anxious to sell their fruit, vegetables, fish, and pork before the heat of the day when they would spoil were nowhere in sight. The people of Hanoi had been warned, and experience taught them to listen. It would be another day of street battles.

After the Japanese surrendered, the Viet Minh immediately took up defensive positions on both sides of the Long Bien Bridge, formerly called the Paul Doumer Bridge by the French. A historic cantilever bridge 1.5 miles in length, it was considered the most strategic roadway in all of Northern Vietnam. It was the only bridge capable of supporting armored vehicles and trucks across the Red River. It connected Haiphong Harbor with Hanoi. For all practical purposes, whoever controlled the Long Bien Bridge also controlled Hanoi. On one side was Hoan Kiem district, and on the other the Long Bien district with its Gia Lam Airfield.

The French made the bridge their highest priority when they launched their attack to retake Hanoi. Every available French unit was part of the assault to retake the bridge. Bombarded by French artillery and harassed by aircraft, the Viet Minh fought bravely for one day and then retreated. Their commanders knew it was hopeless to hold such a fixed asset where the French could consolidate their firepower and air power. Before fleeing, the Viet Minh tried to blow up the bridge hoping to slow the French advance into downtown Hanoi. While they were able to tear up the roadway, their explosives did nothing to damage the superstructure of the bridge, which was made of high-grade steel. The French engineers repaired the damage within two days, and the bridge was once again operational. Tanks, armored cars, and troops trucks rolled across the Red River like it was a Sunday drive in the park. It was an unfortunate but necessary loss to the Viet Minh.

Knowing that they could not hold the bridge for an extended period of time, it was curious when the Viet Minh commanders sent a group of thirty militiamen to retake the bridge. Such a force was highly inadequate to take such a well-protected asset. It seemed like a complete waste of military resources and personnel. The French were happy to capitalize on such a mistake, especially when the attacking militia failed to close in and chose instead to fire at the French from afar. The French called in artillery and airstrikes to deal with the pesky militia.

Captain Cedric Marchand and his wingman, Lieutenant Noe Cheron, boarded their British-made Supermarine Spitfires on the French aircraft carrier Arromanches. Although the French had already captured several airfields in and around Hanoi and Haiphong, they were not considered secure. The Viet Minh could quickly move a mortar on to the rooftop of a surrounding building and bombard the airfields during landings and takeoffs. It was much safer to keep their aircraft on the Arromanches floating in the middle of Ha Long Bay. The Viet Minh didn't have much of a navy, and the French warships that protected the Arromanches could easily deal with any attack at sea.

With their aircraft industry decimated by the Nazis during the occupation, the French found it necessary to purchase aircraft from the British and Americans who had an abundance of warplanes after WW II. The two Spitfires were each armed with four 50-cal Browning machineguns and two Hispano auto-cannons. The 20mm Hispanos were overkill for any weapon the Viet Minh had in their arsenal, but they were well-adapted at punching large holes in masonry buildings and walls. The aircraft was maneuverable and considered fast, with a top speed of 370 mph.

As always, Marchand took off first, and Cheron followed. They formed up and headed inland. Hanoi was close in, and their mission was relatively simple, so they were not concerned about burning too much fuel. They throttled up to just under three-quarter speed so as not to overheat their supercharged engines.

As the two aircraft approached the bridge, the French commander on the ground had his mortar men mark the Indochinese positions with colored smoke rounds. It was hardly a challenge. Even with the low hanging fog, Marchand and Cheron could see the enemy as they discharged their weapons. Marchand led the attack and fired a brief burst from his four machineguns at the center of the enemy front line, dispersing them. He radioed Cheron not to attack but instead line up with him on the far side of the enemy so they could strafe the militia line. When the aircraft circled, the militia broke as militiamen often do when faced with a superior force. They jumped back in the three trucks that had carried them to the battlefield. The vehicles sped toward the safety of the city center, where the buildings were tall and made it difficult for the French aircraft.

Marchand and Cheron were determined to head them off before they drove too deep into the buildings. They increased their speed to full throttle and flew low to achieve a deep field of fire. Marchand again took the lead and flipped his weapon switch from machinegun to cannon. The aircraft's Hispano cannons were loaded with high explosive shells and fired at a rate of 200 rounds per minute.

The first five shells exploded behind the last truck. Marchand tipped the nose of his aircraft up slightly, and the next burst of rounds landed in the truck. Two rounds exploded in the back, killing several passengers and setting the vehicle on fire. Several more rounds found their way into the engine compartment via the truck cab and damaged the engine beyond repair. One round hit next to the gas tank sending hot shrapnel into the fuel. The explosion ripped the truck to pieces killing everyone inside. The remains of the burning vehicle crashed into a car parked along the curb.

Marchand lined up the next truck in his sights and pulled the trigger on his yolk. Nothing happened. Neither cannon fired, which meant the problem was most probably electrical, not mechanical. He flipped his weapon selection switch back to machinegun, realigned his sights on the truck, and pulled the trigger. Again, nothing happened. He cursed, then informed Cheron that it was his turn. Marchand pulled up and circled to watch Cheron's results.

Cheron had watched his commander using his cannons to great effect and decided on the same course of action. He selected his aircraft's cannons, lined up his sights on the second truck, and opened fire. His focus was on the truck, and he did not notice what was happening on the rooftop of a building a quarter of a mile from his position.

On the distant rooftop, eight Viet Minh sprung from their hiding places and pulled a canvas tarp off a Japanese Type 96 twin-barreled anti-aircraft gun. The Japanese gunner and his Indochinese assistant were already seated in the gun's cradle mount, and the first 25 mm shells rounds had been racked into the guns' chambers.

Upon occupying Hanoi, the Viet Minh had discovered the abandoned weapon. The Japanese had initially disassembled the gun, carried it up to the roof, and reassembled it to protect downtown Hanoi from Allied aircraft. When they left at the end of the war, there was no point in taking the gun with them since they were ordered to disarm anyway. It was abandoned and left to rust in place. When the Viet Minh found it, they had no idea how to operate the sophisticated aiming device that allowed the gunner to lead an aircraft the correct distance.

Six hundred Japanese soldiers had deserted their army and joined the Viet Minh during the war. A search was conducted, and the Viet Minh found one Japanese soldier that had operated a similar gun and knew the aiming system. He was recruited to be the weapon's operator and was sitting in the gunner's seat. The assistant gunner adjusted the weapon's height using a hand-wheel. Together they aimed the gun at the approaching aircraft. Eight Viet Minh loaders fed the ammunition into the twin guns using top-loaded 15-round magazines. The gunner opened fire.

The first rounds were short and exploded into a taller building across the street. Cheron saw the explosions and immediately recognized it as anti-aircraft fire. He pulled up his strafing run and banked his plane, exposing its belly. Two shells found their mark - one ripped through the left-wing, and the other entered the bottom of the fuselage. Cheron disappeared in a mist of red when the shell exploded inside the cockpit. The Spitfire continued to bank and flew into a tall building exploding in a ball of flame.

Marchand was horrified to see his young friend die in such a spectacular manner. He increased his altitude and maneuvered his aircraft so it was directly above the anti-aircraft gun. Unable to use his

71

weapons, he tipped his Spitfire into a steep dive and pushed his engine to maximum speed.

The anti-aircraft gun crew was frantic as they watched the aircraft approach. The Type 96 was difficult to adjust when firing directly overhead, and the violent vibration from each shot made aiming the weapon problematic. The gunner and his assistant did their best to shoot down the French warplane. It wasn't enough. Marchand's spitfire plowed into the rooftop gun at almost 400 mph. Both weapons were disintegrated in a massive ball of flame along with their crews. The thunderous secondary explosions from the ammunition baking off woke anyone still sleeping in the city and lit up the morning sky.

It was night, and downtown Hanoi was pitch dark. It would be weeks until the French engineers could repair the damage the saboteurs had done to the power plant. Four Panard armored cars drove down a dark street in a business district. Their turrets, armed with 47mm cannons and 7.5mm machineguns, swung slowly from side to side as they advanced, searching for targets. There were none. The street was void of human life. It made the French crews uneasy. This was a business district, and even at this time of night, there should be some pedestrians.

These four vehicles were the reconnaissance element of a mobile infantry battalion that was following their path a half-mile back in trucks and half-tracks protected by armored cars. If there was trouble, it was the recon element's job to find it before the battalion arrived. They were aggressive and audacious. Unlike the other units in the battalion, their mission was not to defeat the enemy. If an ambush was discovered or a firefight broke out, the French recon would engage the enemy long enough to determine its strength and position, then hold their position until the battalion arrived. If the fighting became too intense, they would break off contact and wait for the battalion in a safe location. The recon elements of a battalion were some of the bravest and most-valued soldiers – experienced fighters with a strong esprit de corps. They knew how to attract trouble and how to get out of it when needed.

Lieutenant Godefroy Boudet, the commander of the recon unit, rode in the first armored vehicle. He was an example to his men and always led from the front. But he wasn't stupid. He stayed buttoned up inside the vehicle, away from enemy sniper's sights. He didn't like what he was seeing through the commander's forward viewport in the turret. It was too quiet and still. Two bad signs in a battle zone. Two reasons to be very cautious. Because of his high viewpoint, he was the first to see the roadblock at the end of the street. "Halt," he said to the driver who stopped the vehicle.

The other commanders followed suit and brought their vehicles to a stop and swung their turrets to predetermined fields of fire on opposite sides of the street with the guns of the last vehicle covering the rear.

Boudet considered sending two of his four-person crew out to examine the roadblock, but he knew there was probably an ambush waiting for them. And if there was no ambush, then the roadblock was surely boobytrapped with a mine or grenades connected to tripwires. His mission was to find the enemy's main force, and he knew instinctively this was not it. The roadblock was a distraction meant to pin them down while a much larger force closed in to surround them. He and his men were anxious to fight the Viet Minh, but he wasn't going to bite. Not yet. He would find another way around and report back to the battalion. "Tin-tin Six, to all units. We are reversing direction. Proceed to the previous intersection. Acknowledge in sequence. Over," radioed Boudet.

The commanders in each vehicle acknowledged the order in a predetermined sequence, so Boudet was sure that all understood his orders. Reversing the direction of a column, even a small one, was dangerous work and, if not executed correctly, could leave the vehicles open to attack. Boudet had spent a significant amount of time training his men the correct procedure of reversing direction one vehicle at a time so the other vehicles could maintain covering fields of fire. It was like a mechanized ballet that seemed chaotic when one vehicle would move then stop in what seemed like an awkward position while another vehicle realigned itself. In only a minute, the entire column had reversed its position and was on its way back to the previous intersection.

Boudet's vehicle turned on the intersecting street, and the other vehicles followed. He radioed his battalion commander and informed him of the necessary detour. The recon column entered another sector of the business district. There was a line of buildings on the Northern side of the street and a park on the opposite side.

Inside the buildings, a Viet Minh commander peered out the edge of a drawn blind careful not to disturb it. Even the slightest movement could give away their position to the recon patrol. The Viet Minh held their fire. They were looking to bag a bigger trophy.

Boudet's column rolled out of the business district without incident. He still didn't feel right but searching the buildings door-to-door would take too much time and expose his men to ambush without the protection of his armored vehicles. The column drove through a residential neighborhood. The only light came from the explosions of distant battles around the city and flares dropped by French aircraft. There were no cooking fires in the neighborhood. That was never a good sign. Even the Vietnamese had to eat. They needed the fires to cook their rice and smoke their fish if they were lucky enough to have one.

The armored vehicles pulled into the center of the neighborhood and took up defensive positions. Boudet didn't like stopping for anything, but his recon units had outpaced the battalion and needed to wait until it caught up. At least in the residential neighborhood, he and his men didn't need to worry too much about snipers firing from high building windows and rooftops. Most of the homes were one to two stories tall.

The mobile battalion entered the business district and took the detour that Boudet had recommended. As the lead armored cars passed the seven buildings occupied by the Viet Minh, the troop transport trucks came into alignment with the building windows. Six Viet Minh sappers carrying lunge mines attacked the armored cars from both sides of the street. Two made it far enough to detonate their mines against the French armor. Both armored cars were destroyed, and the crews inside were killed. The street was blocked by the burning wreckage, and the battalion came to an abrupt halt. Moments later, the armored cars protecting the rear of the convoy were attacked by sappers and destroyed. In all, twelve Viet Minh sappers gave up their lives to stop the convoy and destroy the armored cars protecting it. The French were thrown into disarray, unable to advance or retreat.

The window shutters in the seven buildings rolled up, and the Viet Minh opened fire with their machineguns and rifles. A barrage of bullets pierced the sides of the trucks, shredding the troops that rode in back. It happened so fast there was no way to find cover before it was too late. Firebombs were thrown down from the building rooftops and burst into flames on top of the French vehicles. Grenades were rolled under the trucks by Viet Minh emerging from hidden positions. The explosions set the vehicles ablaze and ignited their gas tanks. Seventeen French troops died in the first two minutes of the ambush. Many more would follow.

Boudet watched the explosions from a distance. It was a recon commander's worst nightmare. He and his men had missed the danger, and now the battalion they were ordered to protect was under attack. Boudet radioed his battalion commander requesting instructions but received only static in return. The French were dying. Boudet radioed his vehicle commanders and ordered that they reverse direction and return to the battalion. The vehicles started their mechanized maneuver to turn around.

Viet Minh, waiting in the homes around the neighborhood, sprang into action. They carried burlap bags, ripped open the tops, and flung the contents on the asphalt around the French vehicles. Caltrops tumbled across the pavement covering the street with their metal spikes.

As the armored vehicles backed up to turn around, their tires were pierced with the four-sided metal spikes. The drivers refused to give up even with flat tires and continued to drive until their deflated tires collected enough spikes to prevent them from moving. The turrets swung around to face the threat and opened fire. The Viet Minh that had thrown the caltrops were already gone. The street was empty except for the French crews now beginning to panic. They were trapped in an ambush, and it wasn't over. Dozens of firebombs arced over the Vietnamese homes and smashed on the street around the French vehicles. As the flames engulfed the vehicles, the French continued to fire their weapons, but there were no targets.

A second wave of firebombs flew over the rooftops and crashed on top of the armored vehicles. After a few minutes, the armor turned red hot, and the men roasted inside. Some tried to escape the steel ovens only to step on the caltrops in the street, which pierced their boots. Writhing in pain and unable to run, they were engulfed in flames. One vehicle's gas tank ignited, blowing the hatches off and setting off the ammunition. The exploding shells rocked the other vehicles. Those inside and still alive screamed. Feeling his skin blistering, Boudet pulled out his sidearm and fired a bullet through his right temple. It seemed the only rational thing to do. The French crews still alive followed their commander's lead as always. There were no survivors.

CHAPTER SIX

Hanoi, Indochina - December 23, 1946

A flight of five tri-motor Amiot AAC Toucans flew over the Red River and landed at Gia Lam Airfield in the Eastern section of Hanoi. The French Toucans were based on the German Junker JU-52 with its unique three-engine design and carried eighteen troops plus their gear. The French Air Force was desperately short of aircraft. It would take two trips from Saigon to transport Captain 'Bruno' Bigeard's entire company.

As the first plane landed, a mortar shell exploded near the edge of the runway, causing the pilot to swerve. The plane fishtailed, throwing the men in back to the deck and piercing the aircraft's metal skin with shrapnel in several places. None of the troops or crew were seriously hurt as the plane rolled to a stop.

Bruno was the first out of the aircraft and immediately began organizing his men. The base commander approached in a jeep and pulled up next to Bruno, who snapped to attention and saluted. The Colonel saluted back and said, "Captain, you should get your men away from the aircraft as soon as possible. The Viet Minh have taken control of a nearby neighborhood and frequently shell the airfield. They target the aircraft."

"Why do you allow this, Colonel?" said Bruno as another shell exploded nearby.

"I don't allow anything, Captain. We're shorthanded. I barely have enough troops to patrol the airfield for saboteurs."

"Then allow me and my men to correct the situation on your behalf, Colonel. We shall instruct the Viet Minh that this is a French territory."

"Be my guest, Captain."

"Where is this area the Viet Minh have occupied?"

"To the Northeast," said the Colonel pointing. "Where those industrial buildings are clustered."

Bruno motioned to Lieutenant Nathanael De Villiers, who trotted over to Bruno and the Colonel. "Lieutenant De Villiers, take 2nd Platoon, find that mortar and destroy it."

"Yes, Bruno," said De Villiers, saluting and rushing off to gather his men.

"You let your men use your first name? It's insubordinate," said the Colonel.

"Colonel, it is not my first name. It is my call sign from the French underground. And I don't care what they call me as long as they obey my orders and kill the enemy. Now, if you will excuse me, Colonel. I have a war to fight."

The two officers saluted begrudgingly, and Bruno moved off.

The Viet Minh mortar crew was on top of an abandoned industrial building. The rooftop overlooked the entire airfield, giving them a perfect spotting and firing position. As the last plane landed, they launched another round, attempting to time the explosion with the path of the aircraft. It missed by only a few yards. Had it hit the plane, many of the troops inside would have been killed or wounded. The Viet Minh realigned their mortar to fire on the French aircraft clustered at the end of the runway.

Below, De Villiers and his men prepared to assault the building. Most of the platoon took up defensive positions inside and around the base of the building. Once the firefight began, more Viet Minh would come to reinforce the mortar crew. 2nd Platoon would be ready to greet them with an ambush. In the meantime, two fireteams went up opposite stairwells to reach the roof.

The two fireteams waited until both were in position. One fireteam opened fire, pinning the mortar crew down while the second team stayed hidden. The mortar crew fought back with their rifles. They hated the idea of abandoning their mortar, but they were outgunned by the better-trained French troops. They ran across the rooftop in the opposite direction toward the second staircase, where the other fireteam was hidden. As they approached, they were met with a hail of French gunfire. The entire Viet Minh mortar team was killed. The French gathered the Viet Minh mortar and the remaining ammunition to carry back to the airfield. De Villiers knew that Bruno would be displeased that they had not captured any prisoners to be interrogated, but his men needed a good bloodletting to boost their confidence. He saw it as a fair tradeoff and was prepared to justify his actions to his commander. He had, after all, obeyed orders and destroyed the mortar position.

The firefight between the French and the Viet Minh reinforcements was short and hardly worth mentioning, with only two Viet Minh killed before retreating. De Villiers and his men had won their first enemy encounter in the Battle of Hanoi.

In addition to losing their entire reconnaissance platoon, the French Mobile Infantry Battalion continued to take heavy losses. The majority of the surviving soldiers, including Major Delacroix, the officer in command, had taken up defensive positions in the park across from the seven buildings where the majority of the Viet Minh were positioned. The Viet Minh had moved troops to the upper floors and rooftops of the buildings where they could fire down on the French forces. The French were pinned down and unable to retreat.

The troop trucks carrying Bruno's rifle company pulled to a stop a half a mile from where the battle was raging. The troops dismounted and formed up in their platoons. Bruno suspected a Viet Minh ambush of any reinforcements, namely his company. Approaching in trucks would be suicide for his men.

They would march into battle. Bruno pulled a runner aside and said, "Private Haillet, find Major Delacroix and inform him that we are coming on foot. Tell him I would be much obliged if his men did not shoot us as we approach."

Haillet nodded and ran toward the battle in the distance. Bruno turned to address his men, "We will approach on foot. Two staggered columns. Make sure you keep your intervals. 1st Platoon will take the lead, followed by the weapons platoon, then 2nd Platoon. 3rd Platoon will guard the rear. The Viet Minh will be expecting us, so keep your eyes open and watch out for boobytraps and mines. Any questions?"

There were none. "Follow me," said Bruno taking the lead with no weapon in hand. His men took up their positions behind him.

Five minutes later, Bruno and his men arrived on the street behind the park, where the French were pinned down. The battle continued to rage with tracer rounds flying in all directions, bullets ricocheting of debris, and mortar rounds exploding.

Unknowingly, Bruno had been correct. A squad of Viet Minh had been hiding in a building positioned for an ambush, but their leader had decided against the attack when he saw the French on foot with their weapons at the ready. The Viet Minh were outnumbered and would not fight a battle they knew they could not win.

Bruno signaled his men to take up defensive positions and wait while he reported to Major Delacroix. Bruno and Lieutenant Maxime Chapelle, his executive officer, kept low as they approached and found the Major. "Captain Bigeard, 6th company, 23rd Colonial Infantry Regiment. This is my XO, Lieutenant Chapelle. We have been ordered to reinforce your battalion, Major Delacroix."

"It's about time, Captain. Where is your weapon?" said Delacroix.

"I am a commander. I do not use one."

"That's the stupidest thing I have ever heard. How many men do you have?"

"One hundred and forty-six."

"Alright. The enemy has taken up positions in those seven buildings across the street. They also have snipers in the surrounding buildings. Once we take out one position, another pops up. I don't know how they're doing it."

"I see."

"I want you and your men to take the left flank. Once you are in position, my men will withdraw back to the street behind the park. They will take up defensive positions and cover your withdrawal."

"We are to withdraw?"

"Yes. We have taken heavy losses. Half my men are dead or wounded. We are no longer operationally effective."

"I understand. We will protect your withdrawal to the best of our abilities."

"Dismissed, Captain," said the major saluting.

Bruno and Chapelle saluted and returned to their company, keeping low and using the terrain to protect against snipers.

As they rejoined their company, Bruno signaled his

commanders to gather. He drew a simple map on the ground and said, "Weapons and 1st Platoon will take up a position on the left flank and cover the withdrawal of the infantry battalion. 2nd and 3rd Platoons will leave their packs with 1st Platoon and follow me. Bring plenty of grenades and ammunition. We will need them. We move out in three minutes. Any questions?"

There were none. Bruno dismissed the commanders. Chapelle moved up beside him and spoke in a low voice, "Bruno, what are you doing?"

"Protecting the Major's withdrawal as ordered."

"With only Weapons and 1st Platoons?"

"Of course not. 2nd and 3rd will create a diversion by killing the enemy."

"A diversion?"

"Yes. Yes. The Major's battalion will be able to withdraw more effectively if the enemy is dead, will they not?"

"These are riflemen, not paratroopers like you and I, Bruno. They have not been trained to fight a battle such as this."

"As my father always said, 'They will never learn any younger.' Besides, you've seen them. They have the heart to fight and the will to win."

"Because you told them they can."

"Exactly. Now let's show them how."

"Some will die."

"I am well aware of the risks. Now, let's go, Lieutenant," said Bruno curtly.

Chapelle had spoken his peace. He nodded and followed Bruno as he led his men back across the park.

The Weapons platoon, commanded by Lieutenant Zacharie Dubost, set up their two 30-cal machineguns on opposite sides of 1st Platoon to give themselves an overlapping field of fire while still being able to cover each other's positions in the event of an enemy assault. Three Brandt Mle 1935 60-mm mortars were set up twenty yards back of the front line, which still gave them an effective range of up to one mile. The problem was finding enemy targets in an urban environment. Unless the enemy was on a rooftop or out in the open, the mortar teams could do little beyond illuminating the battlefield with parachute flares. The two bazooka teams in the Weapons platoon were far more effective at destroying fortified positions in buildings and far more mobile. The two-man bazooka teams could easily traverse behind the front line, searching for targets. They only took a few moments to load and fire. The problem they encountered was shooting around the wreckage from the burning troop trucks and armored cars in the street in front of the enemy-occupied buildings.

Commanded by Lieutenant Olivier Gueguen, 1st Platoon had 34 soldiers divided into two squads of sixteen men with a sergeant as commander. They were armed with MAS36 rifles with a smattering of MAS-38 submachineguns usually carried by the sergeants. Each squad also had a British-made BREN machinegun for extra firepower. Even before the soldiers of 1st Platoon settled into their firing positions, they came under fire by Viet Minh snipers on the rooftops and upper story windows. The Viet

Minh snipers were smart. They would fire one or two shots, then move to another position preventing the French from concentrating their rifle fire or the mortar crews from lobbing rounds onto the roof.

The Viet Minh tactics frustrated the young French troops, who saw them as cowards. The French veterans suggested the recruits stop complaining and learn from the enemy's strategy. Once situated along the front line, the French troops were able to lay down effective covering fire that allowed Bruno and the other two platoons to maneuver around the back of the first building.

Bruno signaled his men to stop their advance and take up hidden defensive positions one block from the mouth of the alley that ran behind the seven buildings where the Viet Minh were positioned. He left his XO in charge and moved up by himself to find the scouts he had sent to recon the alley. The scouts were well hidden and explained the layout of the Viet Minh to Bruno. The French troops stayed out of sight. "The enemy has set up a machinegun surrounded by sandbags at each end of the alley in back of the buildings," said the scout. "They also have a sniper on each end of the rooftops overlooking the alley and all approaches.

"A tough nut to crack," whispered Bruno. "I am less worried about the machineguns than I am the snipers. Do you think you can get two men up there without being spotted?"

"Yes."

"They'll need to use their knives so as not to tip off the other Viet Minh on the roof."

"Of course. No problem."

"Once you take out the snipers, we'll deal with the machinegun crews."

"You already have a plan?"

"Always."

"We'll get going then," said the scout moving off without a salute – a useless formality that often got the commanding officer killed on a battlefield.

The two scouts, armed only with knives, maneuvered silently into position, then scaled the opposite sides of the buildings using their bare hands and boots rather than using the fire escape ladders, which would make too much noise. It became even more dangerous as they reached the fourth floor more than fifty feet above the street. A fall would be fatal.

Once on top of the roof, they used the air vents and chimney stacks as cover as they maneuvered into position. Each approached his target cautiously and waited until the right moment when the snipers had their fingers off their weapons' triggers. Surprisingly, the two assaults were less than a minute apart from each other. Both scouts used their knives to kill their enemy sniper with little more than a grunt and a whimper. They signaled their success to the scout leader below. Using the Viet Minh sniper rifles, the two scouts would remain hidden on the rooftop and wait until the attack began when they would attempt to pick off the snipers on the front of the rooftop overlooking the French positions.

Bruno decided to attack the enemy machinegun positions at both ends of the alley simultaneously to prevent them from supporting each other's position. Even with the rooftop snipers out of action, Bruno knew there was little hope that the attack on the machineguns would go unnoticed by the enemy soldiers inside the building. Speed would be crucial. He sent a messenger back to Dubost and ordered the two bazooka teams to join the two assaulting platoons.

When the bazooka teams arrived, Bruno assigned one to each platoon. Bruno stayed with the 3rd Platoon and sent De Villiers with 2nd Platoon around the block to approach the opposite end of the alley. He expected a lot from his platoon commanders and didn't give them much time to get into position before the assault began. He figured the longer they waited, the higher the probability that his men would be discovered by the enemy.

The two assaults started with a hail of covering fire as the bazooka gunner moved around the corner of the ally, took aim, and fired. One of the explosions was a direct hit and killed the Viet Minh gunner and loader. The third member of the machinegun crew took over the machinegun and opened fire. De Villiers knew that the new gunner would quickly jam his machinegun without a loader to feed the ammunition. He had his men throw two smoke grenades into the alley and retreat around the corner. He waited until the machinegun went silent, then ordered his men to charge. They overran the position and killed the new gunner before he could unjam his gun.

Lieutenant Théodore Darche's 3rd Platoon didn't do as well. The bazooka rocket sailed over the machinegun position and exploded against a wall thirty feet deeper into the alley. He, too, had his troops follow the bazooka shot with two smoke grenades. They filled the alley with smoke, but that only made the machinegun crew invisible. Machinegun bullets continued to zip through the smoke forming tiny vortices and creating a deadly fog. Hand grenades were tossed blindly into the alley by the French. None of the explosions silenced the machinegun. It was the French sniper watching from the rooftop that came up with the solution. He could have used a grenade if he had one or shot them with his rifle, but he didn't want to expose his presence to the other Viet Minh on the rooftop. He could barely see the machinegun crew, but that was all he needed. He crawled over to a chimney stack and gave it a little shove to see which brick might be loose. As it turned out, the mortar holding the bricks together was well aged and cracked. He wrapped his arms around the chimney stack and lifted with his legs. The top of the chimney broke free. He slowly carried it to the edge of the roof and set it down on the ledge overlooking the machinegun position below. He estimated the distance of the machinegun from the back of the building, then gave the top of the chimney a shove. It worked far better than he had imagined. The chimney fell apart midair, and the bricks scattered. The masonry hit the gunner and loader on their heads, killing them instantly, and broke the third team member's shoulder. He went down, shrieking in pain.

Bruno looked confused when he heard the crash of the bricks and the machinegun go silent. He thought it might be some sort of diversion. The French scout on the roof signaled his comrades and gave them a thumbs up. Bruno ordered Darche to attack. Darche and his men charged only to find the machinegun crew out of action.

Bruno didn't hesitate. He knew the Viet Minh inside already knew of the French assault and would be preparing to meet them as they entered the buildings. He grabbed two grenades off a rifleman, kicked in the back door, pulled the safety rings, and threw both grenades inside at different angles. He pressed himself against the masonry wall by the door. There were two explosions, and smoke billowed out the open door. Darche ordered a squad of riflemen through the doorway. They fired their weapons blindly into the smoke as they entered and fanned out, careful not to hit each other.

The Viet Minh inside returned fire, unable to see who was firing but saw the muzzle blasts in the smoke cloud at the back of the building. One of them threw a grenade into the smoke cloud. There was a bright flash from the explosion.

One of the French riflemen yelped from a piece of hot shrapnel entering his thigh. Bruno waited as long as he thought prudent, which wasn't more than a few seconds and entered the doorway. He motioned for two riflemen to follow him on each side. As he spotted the enemy through the smoke, he pointed, and the riflemen fired in that direction. More French soldiers entered the building. It was chaos. Neither side knew where the enemy was located. Bruno ordered his men forward. They obeyed and soon secured the warehouse in the back of the first building. Bruno saw the crude doorway hammered through the wall. It appeared as a long tunnel of doorways. He could see the French soldiers attacking the Viet Minh seven buildings down. He moved to the doorway into the front of the furniture store, where a dozen Viet Minh were firing through the windows at the French positions outside. He motioned for four riflemen to ready their weapons. Darche handed Bruno two grenades and kept two for himself. He ordered his riflemen to stay behind the wall until he gave the signal. Bruno and Darche pulled the safety pins at the same time and tossed all four grenades through the doorway into the front of the store. The four grenades exploded. Several Viet Minh screamed and fell dead or wounded. Darche ordered his men to advance. They charged through the doorway and opened fire at anything moving. In less than a minute, the fight for the furniture storeroom was over, and all the Viet Minh were dead. Bruno ordered his men away from the front windows as the French units outside did not know of their success and might accidentally fire on them. He sent a rifleman back to 1st Platoon with orders to ceasefire on building one. Friendly fire was now just as deadly as the Viet Minh.

Bruno knew there would be more Viet Minh on the floors above. Clearing out the seven buildings would be a difficult task. He ordered Darche to take one of his squads up the stairs with grenades and clear out the building. In the meantime, Bruno took the second squad with him and prepared to breach the passageway into the second building. It was the same routine - grenades followed by a brief blind charge into the smoke with weapons fired from the hip. It was a deadly game of leapfrog that the Viet Minh did not understand how to play. The Viet Minh were much better at jungle warfare than urban house-to-house fighting.

He knew that De Villiers, a veteran fighter from WW II, would be performing the same operation of clearing each building. Bruno's biggest concern was no longer the Viet Minh, who seemed to be in a state of confusion as the French closed in and overran the Viet Minh positions. Bruno was worried about what would happen when the two French platoons met in the middle shrouded by smoke. He sent a messenger to De Villiers ordering not to proceed beyond the third building on his end. He knew De Villiers would understand the danger and hold his position.

It took two hours to clear all seven buildings. Many Viet Minh tried to escape out the back alley but were met with a barrage of French bullets from the four guards Bruno had stationed there. As the final building was cleared and the two platoons met up in the middle, Bruno sent a messenger to Major Delacroix informing him that he and his men were free to retreat anytime they wished. The battle was over, and the French had won.

Delacroix was furious that Bruno had disobeyed his orders and attacked the Viet Minh but decided not to make an issue of it since he, as commander, would be given credit for the victory once his battalion had been reinforced. In war, the truth always mattered less than rank.

Hanoi, Indochina - December 24, 1946

At the Viet Minh's headquarters in Hanoi, Ho and General Giap stood over a conference table examining maps and reading reports of military action. "The French forces are receiving reinforcements and resupply by the hour. While we had initially succeeded in capturing most of the city's key infrastructure facilities, the French are now retaking those facilities. The cost of our dead and captured is higher than expected. We are losing control of Hanoi," said Giap. "We could bring in more units from the surrounding area, but I fear without artillery they will only fall victim to the French air and ground assaults."

"We cannot lose Hanoi. It is the political center of Vietnam," said Ho.

"We may not have a choice."

"How long can we hold out?"

"If we can stop the French advance, a few more days, I think. But it will be costly. Perhaps the Chinese…"

"The Chinese cannot be trusted. We invite the tiger to eat the lion. Besides, if we accept help from the Chinese, America might enter the war on the side of the French."

"They will anyway. They only see the communist threat. An alliance with America is a pipe dream. It is a lost cause."

"No. It's not too late. The Americans can be convinced as long as we are not rash in our alliances."

"In the meantime, our troops die at the French

hand from American weapons and ammunition."

"We knew the cost of independence would be high. Our people are prepared to shoulder the burden."

"I know they will do what you ask. They are loyal and committed. But I believe we need to look at the larger picture. Even if we lose Hanoi and the other major cities, it does not mean the war is over. In fact, our troops are much more adept at fighting a guerrilla war against the French. In the cities and flatlands, it is much easier for the French to pin down our troops so they can use their artillery and air force. In the mountains and forests, we decide when to fight, not them."

"I understand. But most of our people are in the cities. They expect us to fight for their freedom."

"And we will. But let us do it on our terms, not the terms of the French."

They heard gunfire and explosions outside the headquarters building. Both Ho and Giap seemed concerned. "Uncle, please stay here. I will see what is happening," said the general, disappearing through the doorway.

Outside the building, bullets zinged through the air and ricocheted off the walls. A Viet Minh officer ran up to Giap and said, "General, the French have broken through our lines."

"How is that possible? They were nowhere near this position this morning," said Giap.

"I don't know. But they are attacking in force. There are reports of tanks and armored cars less than a mile away. I don't know how long my men can hold them off without reinforcements. Uncle Ho must leave now if we are to keep him safe."

"Yes. Yes. Of course."

"I will send as many troops with you as I can. Please hurry, General."

A mortar round exploded just ten yards from the building entrance wiping out a Viet Minh machinegun crew. Three British-made Supermarine Spitfires strafed the troops in front of the headquarters with their M2 Browning machineguns. A half dozen Viet Minh were killed and severely wounded by the large caliber bullets. With that kind of firepower, Giap knew it wouldn't take long for the French to overrun their position. He ran back inside.

Ho was gathering the maps and reports in preparation for leaving. "Leave them. You must leave now," said Giap.

"You will come with me," said Ho.

"No. Our men need me."

"Your country needs you more. I will not leave without you, General."

"Alright. Let's go."

Ho and Giap gathered essential maps and left the building out the back exit, where a squad of twelve Viet Minh was waiting for them to provide protection. They would not last long if cornered by the French. "Where to, General?" said the lieutenant in charge of the squad.

"The mountains," said Giap as they climbed into a medley of cars and jeeps and drove away.

Ten minutes later, after a fierce artillery bombardment, Bruno and his infantry company overran the Viet Minh headquarters killing over fifty enemy soldiers and taking dozens of prisoners. The building was scoured for enemy intelligence, then set fire and burned to the ground. The prisoners were interrogated as to Ho and Giap's destination. Many died, keeping that secret safe.

It took the French almost two months to secure Hanoi from the remaining Viet Minh units. The fighting settled down to the occasional terrorist attacks that would continue to plague the French during their entire occupation. The French fortified their positions in and around the city, hoping the Viet Minh would attack. But their hope was in vain. The Viet Minh stayed away and preserved their strength. They would fight another day when the odds were in their favor. Patience was the greatest ally of the Ho Chi Minh and his followers.

CHAPTER SEVEN

Tuyen Quang Province, Vietnam - January 14, 1947

Over the weeks following their retreat from the capital, Ho Chi Minh and General Giap gathered their forces in Tan Trao deep in the hills of Tuyen Quang Province, eighty miles west of Hanoi. The roads were in bad condition and were often washed out by the rains. This made travel for the Viet Minh difficult, but it made it even more arduous for the French with their heavy armored vehicles. The French troops were often forced to travel on just one road in an area, which made them an easy target for ambush. As was often the case, the geography of Indochina helped protect the Viet Minh, who were quite adept at traveling by foot and bicycle through the mountains and forests of the Northern Highlands. Unburdened by technology, the Viet Minh could often travel faster than the French and slowed their advance with harassing attacks.

The Vietnamese in the area surrounding Tan Trao were sympathetic to the Viet Minh. The Viet Minh needed help from the people of the highlands and often recruited new soldiers from the villages and farms. They were reluctant to harm anyone, but there were times when it could not be helped. Anyone that disagreed or seemed a potential threat to reveal the Viet Minh's location in the mountains was subject to reprisals or kidnapping. Secrecy was essential to their survival.

The journey had been trying for Ho, who was now fifty-eight years old with failing health. He had contracted pneumonia while traveling and was confined to bed rest by the camp doctor while he recovered. General Giap visited with him daily to report on the army's progress, review intelligence reports, and to plan. "Our remaining forces have left Hanoi and are on their way to our camps in the hills," said Giap drinking hot tea as he sat beside Ho's bed.

"And what was the final tally of our losses?" said Ho, knowing that Giap was avoiding the statistics.

"A little over twelve thousand killed or captured."

"An entire division?"

"I am afraid so. The French aircraft were quite effective until our men reached the forests."

"How can we possibly sustain such losses?"

"Surprisingly well. Even with the French assaults, we are recruiting faster than we are losing men. The big problem is training and weapons. Food is also an issue. We now have over 140,000 mouths to feed. Perhaps the Chinese could help?"

"No. They have already done enough. The

Soviets too. The Americans must not see us align ourselves with either. So far, the Americans have remained neutral and refrained from sending ground troops. We need to keep it that way."

"You worry about what the American will or won't do. In the meantime, we are starved for supplies."

"If the Americans support the French any more than they already have, we will be in real trouble. You have not seen America's capacity to produce weapons and supplies. They crushed both the Nazis and Japanese with their factories. We must do whatever is necessary to keep them out of the war, even if it means that our men go hungry."

"Uncle, with all due respect, not even you can convince them. The Americans need the French to help fend off the Soviets in Europe. The French will use that leverage to secure their support in Indochina. It's just a matter of time."

"You may be correct. But it is time that we need. We must build up our army before we face the French again."

"And where will we find the arms required?"

"We will raid the French supply convoys and armories as we did the Japanese."

"That will only supply a fraction of what we need, and it will cost us dearly when the French realize our desperation."

"So be it. We will just have to make do with what we have and what we can scavenge. We will not accept any more help from the Chinese or the Soviets. Not yet. I still believe there is hope the Americans will change their minds and see us once again as reliable allies. With America on our side, we could easily destroy the French."

"It is a dream, Uncle. But I will obey your will as always."

"I thank you for your honesty, General. The truth is rarely easy to hear but must always be welcomed. Now, tell me about the current distribution of our forces?"

"To avoid aerial assaults by the French aircraft, I have broken our army up into units no larger than a company, as you suggested. I am concerned with what would happen if the French are able to assemble enough units for a ground attack. The French could pin us down and use their aircraft and artillery to ravage our forces."

"We must act like a willow tree and bend with the wind. If the French attack on the ground, we should refuse combat and retreat further into the mountains."

"Such a strategy will be seen as weakness and embolden the French."

"Yes. But I have no interest in impressing the French. We follow Mao's advice - we do not fight until we are sure we can win."

"I understand. It will be done."

It was difficult for Giap to accept such a strategy. He was a warrior, and it seemed cowardly to retreat whenever combat was offered by the enemy. He knew that his Viet Minh army was capable of defeating the French, given the right circumstances. But Ho was right. Now was the time to build and train their army. His forces should harass and raid the French, but not fight them toe-to-toe, where the

French artillery and aircraft could be used to good effect, and the cost in Viet Minh lives would be great. The time for the Viet Minh to fight would come soon enough. His job was to keep his soldiers alive until that moment arrived.

Washington D.C., USA – March 1, 1947

President Harry S. Truman sat in the oval office with Secretary of State George Marshal and Under Secretary of State Dean Acheson, going over a list of foreign affairs. "And that brings us to Indochina," said Marshal. "The French now have complete control over Hanoi along with seventy percent of Vietnam, Cambodia, and Laos. The Viet Minh have retreated to their bases in the mountains."

"And are the Chinese staying out of it?" said Truman.

"So far, yes, except for some supplies and weapons they smuggle over the border to the Viet Minh," said Acheson.

"Well, that's good news," said Truman.

"How's that, Mr. President?" said Acheson.

"It puts to rest this whole discussion about the French being able to whip the communists."

"I'm not sure I would come to that conclusion, Mr. President," said Acheson. "The communists are still a very real threat."

"Are you suggesting we abandon our aid to the French?"

"Not at all. I think we need to increase it if we want to stop the communists from expanding in Southeast Asia."

"I think what Dean is saying is that we need to keep up the pressure until the French have a workable negotiated settlement with Ho Chi Minh and his followers," said Marshal.

"I don't trust the French. I need 'em to contain the Soviets, but I don't trust 'em. As far as we know, they could turn Indochina over to the communists and hightail it out of there. Then where would we be?" said Truman.

"Exactly, Mr. President. That's why we need to keep our foot in the door. See what is going on. Make sure this thing goes the way we want," said Acheson.

"And if it doesn't go our way?"

"We cannot leave Indochina to the communists. It would be a disaster," said Acheson. "If the French leave, we have to be prepared to take their place."

"You mean American troops?"

"If needed, yes."

"I don't like it. We cannot be all places at once. Our focus needs to be on Europe. That's where the real game is being played. I don't mind throwing war surplus to the French, but I sure as hell don't want our boys going to Indochina to fight while we got our hands full in Europe. Americans spent a fortune in blood and treasure bailing the French out after the Nazis took over. If the French are hell-bent on keeping their empire, then let them solve their own problems. No American troops in Indochina. That's final."

Granier sat at his desk at CIA headquarters located in Washington's Foggy Bottom in the E Street complex. The complex had been used by the OSS during World War II. He was having a shitty day. In their infinite wisdom, the Washington bureaucrats had just changed the name of the Central Intelligence Group to the Central Intelligence Agency. He supposed their reasoning was that an agency sounded bigger and more important than a group. For Granier, it meant he needed to order new stationery and business cards. That meant paperwork and using a typewriter. He loathed both, especially when the typewriter required a new ribbon as it did on that day. His fingertips were already blue from the carbon paper he used to make his requests in triplicate. The ribbon was making things worse. He could strip down an M1 carbine in less than thirty seconds but changing a typewriter ribbon was clearly beyond him. There was a knock at his door. He looked up to find a man wearing a white shirt and tie standing in his doorway, holding a briefcase. "Are you Rene Granier?" said the man.

"Yeah," Granier grunted.

The man stepped into the office, offering a handshake, "I'm Noah Bradley."

Granier looked down at his fingertips, covered in blue ink. "Oh, right," said Bradley looking at the ribbon in Granier's hands. "Do you mind?"

"Be my guest."

Bradley set down his briefcase, rolled up his sleeves, and went to work replacing the ribbon. "I'm with the CIA's new computer programming group. Officer Patti suggested we talk."

"I didn't even know we had one of those... a computer."

"Technically, we don't. Not yet. But the Navy does, and we are allowed to use it when we need to process."

"Process?"

"Ah, use the computer to calculate a solution."

"Like what?"

"Oh, well… ah… Suppose we want to figure out the trajectory of a political movement in a third world country or the number of Russian tanks being produced by a factory based on its purchases of raw materials."

"A computer can do that?"

"Given the correct data, yes."

Granier grunted. Bradley finished replacing the ribbon. His hands were clean. Granier grunted again.

"That's why I came to talk with you," said Bradley.

"How's that?"

"I was told you worked in Marine reconnaissance during the war."

"Yeah, so?"

"I was hoping you could help us figure out the correct data points to use as input."

"I don't know anything about computers."

"You don't need to know anything. You have military experience that we don't."

"Like what?"

"Um… like how fast can a supply convoy travel?"

"Depends."

"On what?"

"How many trucks in the convoy and what type? What are the road and weather conditions? What are the security requirements to protect the convoy?"

Bradley opened his briefcase and took out a notepad and pen. "Now see, that's great. That's exactly what we need to ask. Those are data points."

"What are you gonna do with all the information you collect?"

"Hopefully, predict when a war might start. Maybe even prevent it."

"Prevent a war? That'd be a neat trick."

"It would, wouldn't it?"

"Let me save you some time. A war will start when the diplomats stop talking, and the generals take over."

"That's a bit simplistic, don't you think?"

"Maybe, but it's the truth."

"Good. We can enter diplomacy as a data point."

Granier rolled his eyes as Bradley scribbled diplomacy on his pad. "I didn't sign up to be a computer programmer," said Granier, perturbed.

"Why did you sign up?"

"Damn good question. I've been asking myself that a lot lately."

"Look, this is the atomic age. Your input could save thousands if not millions of American lives."

"That's bullshit."

"No. It's not. There may not be any warning for an atomic bomb attack. Someone could just say the wrong thing in a moment of anger or press the wrong button and puff... an entire city gets wiped off the face of the earth."

"Hell, we're the only ones that have atomic bombs. It's the other guys that need to worry."

"And how long do you think that is going to last?

If America is going to survive, we need to get ahead of the ball. Computers can help us do that."

"Well, I don't see how, but I'll help you if I can. Ask your questions."

Bradley grinned like a pig in slop.

Bac Kan, Vietnam - October 7, 1947

Every available French transport plane flew over the forested hills of Northern Vietnam. The sky was overcast and threatened rain. It was the end of the wet season. The paratroopers inside the aircraft were hoping to catch the Viet Minh before they started their winter raids. An intelligence asset from one of the hill tribes had reported a sighting of Ho Chi Minh when the Viet Minh headquarters had been relocated to the town of Bac Kan in the province of the same name. The French gave the mission a code name - Operation Lea.

Because of his success in the Battle of Hanoi, Bruno was reassigned to lead a paratrooper company with just over 170 men. He had gained a reputation for aggressiveness and volunteered his new company to be the first to drop behind enemy lines. His new men were not thrilled. They had not yet learned to respect their new commander. Because of the shortage of planes, his company would be facing 40,000 Viet Minh troops stationed in the surrounding area until the limited number of aircraft could make the additional flights required to drop an additional 1,000 paratroopers. Even then, the French paratroopers would be vastly outnumbered until ground forces that included tanks and armored cars could reach the rendezvous point by roads that were sure to be washed out by the summer rains and heavily mined by the Viet Minh. An additional battalion of Foreign Legionaries was to travel upriver by boat. The river known for being clogged with downed trees and broken branches would make the going slow. Viet Minh ambushes would do their best to slow down the French on both the roads and rivers.

In addition to securing the landing zone, Bruno and his men had been tasked with capturing Ho Chi Minh and the Viet Minh leadership believed to be in the town. It was truly an impossible task, which made Bruno even more determined. Impossible was what made Bruno and his men extraordinary. Bruno would be the first to jump. He would land without a weapon. He wasn't worried. While not totally out of the question, the odds of landing near an enemy soldier were slim. But the show of bravado would boost the confidence of his men, and that was worth the gamble.

When the Viet Minh first heard the hum of the aircraft engines, they thought it was another bombing raid. It had started to rain, and visibility above the surrounding mountain ridges was negligible. When a Viet Minh soldier saw the first parachute descending through the clouds, he immediately ran to warn Ho Chi Minh and General Giap - the French were coming.

Giap naturally wanted to fight. How many men

could the French possibly land in the surrounding hills? The Viet Minh in the immediate area could easily surround and destroy them. But Ho quickly reminded his longtime friend that the French were not stupid. The paratroopers could be a diversion for a much more massive attack. The simple fact that they did not know the size of the enemy force they were facing meant that they should follow Mao's advice and retreat until they were sure they could win. "Fine," said Giap. "But I will send a blocking force to ensure your escape."

"Our escape," said Ho forcefully.

"Of course, Uncle. Our escape."

While Ho and his staff gathered the essential maps and intelligence reports, Giap issued orders to the commander of the blocking force - an entire brigade of Viet Minh. They were to find and destroy the French that parachuted into the mountains.

Because of the dense forest and steep hills, it took Bruno's company almost thirty minutes to rendezvous and secure the landing zone for the follow-on paratroopers. He assigned one platoon to guard the landing zone and the other two to follow him. He was anxious and wanted to advance into the village below in hopes of capturing his prey. He never got the chance.

The first company of Viet Minh made contact just as Bruno and his men started their descent. A firefight broke out. The sound of gunfire alerted the other Viet Minh units as to the location of the French, and they quickly made their way toward the battle. Twenty minutes into the battle, Bruno and his men were fighting for their lives surrounded by over 1,000 Viet Minh troops. These Viet Minh were the honor guard of General Giap, their ranks filled with veteran fighters known for their aggressiveness.

Bruno knew that the landing zone was compromised. He sent a radio call to warn the follow-on paratroopers of the danger. It would take several hours before he and his men would receive any relief. His position was not good. The grass was wet and slippery from the rain, and the hill was steep. The trees provided some protection against the enemy fire, but they were too few to make a real difference. Instinct told him that if they stayed, they would die. He went around to each of his platoon commanders to evaluate their situation and the strength of the enemy force they faced.

When he found one of the platoons facing a relatively light enemy force, he ordered his entire company to collapse back to that position. He would lead the breakout. He was tempted to pick up the rifle of a fallen paratrooper but decided against it. Confidence, he thought. It's all about confidence. When the other platoons were in position, Bruno ordered his men to follow him and ran toward the enemy line.

The Viet Minh were caught off guard by the French charge. It seemed insane. The paratroopers yelled their battle cry as they ran forward, firing their weapons. It was bone-chilling even for the veteran Viet Minh. Several paratroopers were hit and collapsed. Their comrades picked them up by the arms and continued running. There was no time to treat their wounds. The rest of the Viet Minh would chase them once they figured out what the French had done. The paratroopers leaped over the Viet Minh and shot several at close range. But the French did not stop. They needed to put distance between themselves and the enemy.

Once out of sight, the French stopped for a moment to catch their breath and tend to the wounded. The paratroopers started to dig in to face the Viet Minh they knew would be coming. "No," said Bruno. "We are going to the village."

"What?!" said one of the platoon commanders. "There may be hundreds, maybe thousands down there."

"Yes. They will never suspect such a bold move."

The paratroopers exchanged nervous glances. "Oh, come now," said Bruno. "Did you really think you were going to live forever?"

Bruno slid down the hill on the wet grass toward the village. His men hesitated for a moment. A platoon commander shrugged and said, "You heard the commander. Let's go."

The company followed Bruno down the hill slipping and sliding on the wet grass like novice Alpine skiers, some falling on their asses.

When the paratroopers entered the village, there was little resistance. Most of the Viet Minh were up in the hills looking for the French. "Search every house and building," said Bruno. "If we find Ho Chi Minh or Giap, we can use them as hostages to hold off the Viet Minh."

Two platoons took up defensive positions using buildings for cover while the third platoon searched the village. They found nothing. Ho and Giap were already gone. Bruno was furious and cursed like a French sailor. Ho and Giap had escaped his grasp for a second time. He vowed there would not be a third time.

He decided the village was the best defensive position he was going to find. It was better than having the paratroopers drop into a forest that he knew was crawling with Viet Minh. He organized his men into overlapping firing positions and prepared to meet the Viet Minh assault. It was all about buying time until he and his men could be reinforced by the paratroopers that were to follow. He radioed his commander that the square in the middle of the village would be the new landing zone.

When the Viet Minh attacked in force, Bruno called in airstrikes and marked his defensive positions with smoke to prevent friendly fire from the warplanes. Everything else was fair game for the French aircraft. The French artillery batteries had not been set up yet, and the heavy mortars of the approaching French strike force were still out of range. The French Air Force was their savior.

The fighter-bombers pounded the Viet Minh positions with rockets and bombs. Additional fighters from the French aircraft carrier Arromanches were called in to strafe the enemy positions in an attempt to hold them off. It worked. The Viet Minh veteran fighters recoiled from the fierce aerial assault and kept their distance beneath the safety of the forest canopy.

When the next group of paratroopers finally arrived, they parachuted directly into the village.

Some landed on thatched roofs and in pig pens, but losses were few considering the battle that was raging between the two enemies. As the day wore on, more and more French paratroopers arrived. The French aircraft continued their airstrikes well beyond sunset until it was too dark to hit anything. Fortunately, by that time, the French had over five hundred paratroopers on the ground and were able to secure the village.

The Viet Minh continued their attacks throughout the night. French scout planes dropped parachute flares to illuminate the battlefield.

By morning the Viet Minh had been ordered to withdraw by Giap. It was one thing to let his blocking force fight for an entire day, but it would be seen by Uncle Ho as disobedience if it went on beyond that. Giap did not always agree with Ho, but he did respect him and would do nothing to endanger Ho's mutual respect. The Viet Minh would save their resources and manpower to fight another day when the odds were more in their favor. Uncle Ho and General Giap had escaped unharmed. For that, the Viet Minh commanders were grateful. They had done their duty.

It was fortunate for the French that the Viet Minh had chosen the more conservative approach. The French ground forces were delayed by washed-out roads almost an entire week, and the river forces did not arrive until the very end of the campaign when they were of little use. The Viet Minh were indeed capable of wiping out the paratroopers, which would have been a heavy blow to the French. But then hindsight has always been more accurate than prophecy.

The war between the French and Viet Minh ground on for three years, each side having a few victories, but neither gaining a distinct advantage over the other. It was a stalemate. But a stalemate was more frustrating for the French, who wanted to withdraw victorious with their empire intact. The resources being expended were needed elsewhere. France's still struggling economy needed to be rebuilt. Not to mention, there were rumblings of rebellion in other parts of the French empire, including Morocco, Tunisia, and Algeria.

In the meantime, the Viet Minh grew in numbers, weapons, and training. The Viet Minh plan of never fighting unless victory was assured had worked well to conserve their strength. It also made the French look like the aggressor to the people of Indochina. Fed up with persecution, thousands of recruits flocked to Ho Chi Minh's rebel army in hopes of driving out the French before they once again became entrenched.

Ho still avoided help from both the Chinese and the Russians. But his hope of a reconciliation with the Americans was fading. It would soon be time for the Viet Minh to take the fight to the French, and to succeed, they needed weapons and supplies. If the Americans would not help him defeat the French, Ho would look elsewhere. Even so, he still desired that the Americans stay out of the war. His biggest fear was not the French military but American troops arriving on the shores of Vietnam.

In a village twenty miles southeast of Hanoi, Lieutenant Bernard De Lattre de Tassigny had just turned twenty-three and was taking a moment to write his father a letter. He had gone to great lengths, convincing his men to respect and help the Vietnamese living in the village. In between patrols, his platoon had cleared an acre of flatland and created a soccer field. He organized a team made up of French soldiers and Vietnamese and even convinced the elders of another village to put together a team so they could have competitions. The results were encouraging. The people once again trusted the French and even helped them identify Viet Minh agents in the two villages. The agents were dispatched quietly with knives or clubs and buried in the jungle to avoid any attention that might upset the villagers. He had won the hearts and minds of the peasants and destroyed the enemy.

Overall, things had not been going well within the French army. The men were discouraged by the lack of progress in defeating the Viet Minh. Discipline was lacking. When not on patrol or guard duty, many soldiers walked around with their shirts unbuttoned or without shirts. Most had beards, refused to bathe, and didn't wash their uniforms.

In his letter De Lattre told his father of the low morale and that the Army needed a leader that the men could believe in. Recent defeats had created a fear psychosis within the soldiers' ranks and was spreading like the black mold that seemed to cover everything in Vietnam. We need a leader who leads.

115

Fresh blood. No more niggling. No more small-arms warfare. We need you now more than ever. Without you, it will all go wrong, he wrote. You need to accept your destiny, Father. Then, with the morale we still have in spite of it all, we can win it. You can save everything.

Bernard's father was General Jean De Lattre de Tassigny, a retired war hero and considered the best military commander France had to offer. He was nicknamed King Jean because of his demand for protocol. He relished drama when not shown due respect for his rank or authority. He was, without a doubt, a brave man that often put himself in harm's way to lead his men and understand firsthand the progress of a battle. He had fought at Verdun during World War I and had been wounded five times, including a cavalry lance to the chest. In World War II, he commanded the 14th Infantry Division and tried to hold back the German Panzers near Rheims. He and his men fought fiercely but lost when the Germans broke through and surrounded his troops. He later escaped from a German prison and joined the Free French. He led the First French Army as they crossed the Rhine and captured Karlsruhe, Stuttgart, and Freudenstadt. At one point, he had 125,000 American soldiers under his command. He was a mix of MacArthur, Patton, and De Gaulle. The Americans respected him, and as France became more dependent on American aid in Indochina, that was important.

Reading Bernard's letter, General De Lattre grew concerned not only for his only son's safety but for the honor of France. Where will France's place in the world be if it loses Indochina? he thought. Which other of France's colonies will rise up and fight for freedom? He knew there were those in the Army and government that desperately wanted him to take the reins in Indochina. All that was needed was a rumor that he might consider the post. He would surely be asked. But this was not how he imagined his final years. He was tired, and his health was not the best. After such an illustrious military career, he had little to gain and everything to lose. He had served in two wars; need he lead a third?

York County, Virginia - January 12, 1950

Snow flurries at Camp Perry had driven all the tourists away. Granier was free to use the entire camp for training CIA recruits. In his mind, the rougher the weather, the better the training. Battlefields rarely had optimal conditions, and he wanted the new officers exposed to all conditions possible. It felt good to get out of the office and back into the wilderness.   Wilderness? he   thought. Hardly. At lunchtime, the officers would whine if they were not allowed to warm up while grabbing a bite to eat at a local restaurant. Granier hated whining. A three-day survival course had been approved by the director as part of the training for the recruits, but that was as far as he was allowed to push them. The officers were considered an investment, and the director didn't want to lose too many because they felt the training was too harsh. Bunch of pussies, thought Granier. Although he had to admit, they were smart. They picked up the techniques he taught them quickly and remembered them when tested later. He just didn't like how soft they were. They liked their wing-tipped shoes more than their hiking boots, and they were too picky about what they ate. Snake tastes like chicken when roasted correctly over a small fire, he thought. They should experience that. He made a note to himself to make sure to include roasted snake on the menu during survival training.

On that day, he had broken his recruits into two groups – the hunters and the hunters as he called them. The concept of the exercise was simple and similar to capture the flag, except the flag was a mannequin hidden in the woods, which one group was supposed to assassinate while the other group hunted them – both hunters. Everyone was a hunter in Granier's book. The officers wore winter camouflage over their fatigues. The white jackets had hoods that the officers were supposed to draw tight around their face masks, also white. When worn correctly, an officer in the snow was almost impossible to see... almost.

Granier was the joker in the game. He would track the officers and tap them with a stick or hit them with a rock if they were discovered. He preferred the rock. He was an outstanding hunter but usually chose to lay an ambush where he thought most of the officers might travel to get to the target. Most of the officers considered it cheating because only he knew the location of the target. When they whined, Granier would hit them with another rock to remind them that the enemy rarely played fair and used bullets, not rocks. It was a good lesson, and the additional rock helped them remember. After the exercise, they would gather together, and Granier would critique the performance of each officer. He would give them tips on how to improve and warn them of additional dangers that they had not identified. The officers didn't like their instructor and thought him unfair, but they all admired his experience, which was vast, and sought his praise, which was few and far between.

At the end of the day, as the frozen recruits scrambled for the bus that would take them back to Washington, a government sedan pulled up to the rendezvous point and parked. The windows were fogged from the cold air and the warm breath of the driver. Granier watched as his boss stepped out. "Little cold for a paper pusher. Must be important," said Granier as Colonel Patti approached.

"Who asked you, Officer Granier?" said Patti.

"Officer... I'm never going to get used to that."

"Would you prefer Commander?"

"No. That's worse."

"We need to talk."

"Okay. Step into my office," said Granier motioning to the woods.

"How about someplace a little warmer? I don't need to prove myself."

"Alright. How about some hot coffee and warm apple pie?"

"Now you're talking."

Patti and Granier sat in the corner of the camp café, sipping their coffee and munching on two pieces of warm apple pie, each with a scoop of melting ice cream. It was a rustic log lodge with animal heads hanging on the walls along with copies of the muskets that killed the critters. It was a place of hunters, and it made both men feel at home. "So, what do you know about Congressman Kennedy?" said Patti.

"Not much. He tracked me down in D.C. to ask my opinion about Ho Chi Minh. 'Sides that, I haven't heard from him," said Granier.

"And what did you tell him?"

"Whatever I knew, which wasn't much."

"Did you really tell him he should go over to Indochina and see for himself?"

"I don't know. Maybe. It was a few years ago."

"Well, whatever you said made an impression on him."

"Humph. I certainly didn't mean to."

"Word is that he's going to make a run for the Senate. He's heading over to Asia to spruce up his foreign policy credentials. He's decided to take a detour down to Indochina. He's requested you to accompany him."

"What?!"

"He wants someone that knows the lay of the land and the players."

"Well, tell him thanks, but no thanks. I'm not a tour guide."

"It's not quite that easy. The Kennedy family has influence in Washington, especially when it comes to appropriations. Kennedy will also need a bodyguard. The director has decided to accommodate the young congressman's request."

"Wait a minute. I'm a civilian. You can't order me

to go."

"No. But you've been complaining that you want to get back in the field. Here's your opportunity."

"Babysitting a congressman?"

"Granier, don't short change yourself. You are the only intelligence officer that has fought for both the Viet Minh and the French. Hell, you're probably the only living person that's fought on both sides of the conflict. You are uniquely qualified for this mission."

"It's hardly a mission."

"No. It's much more important than that. It's a chance to influence foreign policy at a very high level. Look, the French government has restricted the number of French nationals from operating in Indochina. Only officers are allowed, and most of those are paratroopers. Even with their colonial forces and the foreign legion, they're running out of soldiers. Up to now, the French have wanted America to stay out of the war so they can have a free hand in dealing with their colonies. That's changing. They are openly asking for financial support, and there are even discussions about American ground troops."

"American ground troops in Indochina?"

"Truman's considering it. He's convinced that if Indochina falls to the communists, there will be nothing stopping them from overrunning all of Southeast Asia. At the very least, he is talking about increasing financial support for the French. We still have huge stockpiles of weapons and aircraft leftover from World War II, and the French want 'em."

"So, give 'em the stockpiles. They're just rusting anyway."

"It's not that easy. If we give more weapons to the French, China and Russia may give more weapons to the Viet Minh. God knows what they will do if we send in American troops. One wrong move and this thing could turn into World War III."

"So, why me?"

"Like I said… you are uniquely qualified. Since the Deer Team pulled out of Indochina, we've had no contact with the Viet Minh, and the French have kept us at arm's length. We're blind."

"You do realize that both the Viet Minh and the French want my head on a platter?"

"Yes. We've considered that."

"Big of you, but it's my head."

"We don't think the French will do anything while you are with Congressman Kennedy. His visit is too important. They won't want to ruffle any feathers."

"The French are only going to show him what they want him to see. You know that, right?"

"Of course. But Kennedy can be quite persuasive. We are hoping he goes north to have a look around. The French have started the construction of a fortified line. The idea is to cut off Chinese supply lines coming across the border. It will also act as a buffer if the Chinese send in ground forces."

"Sounds like the Maginot Line. Look how that turned out."

"I didn't say it was a good idea. But the French are very proud of it, and we hope they will want to show it off to Kennedy. That could get you up North where you can get a good look at the French frontlines and troop readiness. That information could be very useful in making an assessment."

"So, that's it. Then I'm back to Washington writing reports again?"

"It's the best I can do at this point. I can give you a couple of days to think about it. But Kennedy wants an answer by the weekend."

"I don't need a couple of days. I'll do it."

Granier had to admit, he was anxious to get out of Washington D.C. and back into the field. He felt his skills and instincts were being dulled by the mindless reports he was asked to write and read for comment. Returning to Indochina was not his first choice, but it was his only choice at that point.

CHAPTER EIGHT

During World War II, the Chinese civil war between Chiang Kai-shek's Nationalists and Mao Zedong's communists had been put on hold so that both sides could fight the invading Japanese army that threatened to take over all of China. It was an uneasy truce at best. When World War II ended with the Japanese surrender, the civil war in China started again. Many of Chiang's best units had been destroyed in battles with the Japanese, and Zedong's army had grown in size and was now well supplied with Russian arms. Still, Chiang's Nationalists, with over 4.2 million troops, outnumbered the Mao's communists with only 1.2 million soldiers. Chiang was determined to fight a decisive battle and finish Mao's Army once and for all.

In the Autumn of 1948, Chiang committed his forces to Manchuria, and the Battle of Liaohsi began. To everyone's surprise, Chiang's superior army lost. It was a massive defeat from which the Nationalists never recovered. By October of 1949, Chiang's Nationalist Army had retreated to the island of Taiwan, and Mao declared victory with the founding of the People's Republic of China. The civil war was over, the communists had won, and Mao was ready to turn his attention to his neighbors - Korea and Indochina.

The problem with Indochina was that Mao wanted the French capitalists out, but he did not trust Ho Chi Minh. He saw Ho as more of a Nationalist than a communist. Mao wanted to spread the communist revolution throughout Southeast Asia, while Ho was focused on the independence of Vietnam alone. As much as Mao wanted an alternative to Ho that was more dedicated to the communist revolution, the people of Vietnam had chosen to follow Ho and his Viet Minh. Much to his displeasure, Mao was stuck supporting Ho.

The French and the Americans knew that Mao's victory in China could dramatically change the war in Indochina. To their surprise, arms and supplies did increase across the border, but not as substantially as General Giap and the Viet Minh had hoped. Like Ho, Mao did not want the Americans entering the war, so it kept China's effort to help the Viet Minh secret and, at a minimum. Both China and America wanted the war to remain a local conflict between the Viet Minh and the French. Both feared another global war.

Even though the Chinese leaders considered their support limited, in 1950 alone, China sent to the Viet Minh 14,000 rifles and pistols, 1,700 machineguns and recoilless rifles, 150 mortars, 60 artillery pieces, and 300 bazookas, as well as ammunition, medicine, communications materials, clothes and 2,800 tons of food.

The French were determined to curtail the Chinese arms and supply shipments across the border. While they would have preferred to seal off the entire border between China and Indochina, they simply did not have enough men and resources. Instead, the French concentrated their efforts on building a line of fortifications near the border. The most northern of these fortifications was the garrison at Bao Bang, where Ho Chi Minh had previously stationed his command headquarters. To supply the French fortresses along the border, the French rebuilt Route Coloniale 4 – a road that stretched from Lang Son to Cao Bang. In addition, the French added dozens of outposts with blockhouses and lookout towers to oversee the mountainous highway and defend against supply convoy ambushes by the Viet Minh. The string of fortresses and outposts worked and forced the Viet Minh to move their supply routes from China farther east away from Hanoi and Haiphong Harbor. Unfortunately for the French, the fortresses and outposts became tempting targets for the Viet Minh and were frequently harassed by enemy artillery and heavy mortars.

Route Coloniale 4, Vietnam - October 17, 1950

It was the dry season in Northern Vietnam, and that meant the Viet Minh and French military units could travel more quickly through the dense forests and traverse the steep hills. It was a constant game of cat and mouse, with both sides wanting to play the role of the cat. The idea was to find the enemy before he found you, then bring overwhelming force upon him. The French had their patrol planes that constantly flew over the green contours of the mountains, searching for signs of Viet Minh patrols, camps, and supply depots. The Viet Minh had the villagers, many of whom were sympathetic to their cause and reported the movements of the French units.

Bruno had once again been promoted and was now given a battalion of paratroopers to command. His first assignment was to search and destroy the Viet Minh units north of Route Coloniale 4. Reconnaissance planes had been combing the mountains for any signs of the Viet Minh. There were none. But just because the enemy could not be seen didn't mean it was not there. Every night, one or more of the lookout towers or outposts along the road was shelled by mortars and assaulted by Viet Minh ground troops shielded by the darkness. By morning, they were gone without a trace. Only the destruction they had created the night before remained.

Bruno's troops swept cautiously through the forest along a mountain ridge. His four companies were spread out in a long horizontal line, with the heavy weapons company taking the center position. It was a formation designed to find the enemy. The undergrowth was thick and often required machetes to cut through. Bruno refused to allow his men to use footpaths that could be easily mined or boobytrapped by the Viet Minh. Instead, they hacked their way forward. It was slow going, and even the paratroopers, who were in excellent physical shape, tired from the mountainous terrain. Bruno knew how hard he could push his men and when they needed to rest. Exhaustion could be lethal if a firefight broke out.

The paratroopers had been dropped on the northern side of Cao Bang and were working their way back toward the next fortress. The battalion provided a screen for the French engineers and troops building the outposts and watchtowers along the road called RC4. If the paratroopers came into contact with the Viet Minh, they could call in artillery from one or two of the four garrisoned cities along the 59-mile highway. The American-made M1 guns, nicknamed Long Toms, were stationed at each garrison. The 155 mm cannons had a maximum range of 13 miles, which allowed the entire road and surrounding area to be protected from two different artillery batteries. This was a welcome luxury for the paratroopers who were accustomed to fighting without additional fire support. The Viet Minh feared the French artillery almost as much as the French aircraft that flew overhead and strafed their troops and camps whenever possible.

Bruno's scouts returned and reported the location of an enemy camp. The paratroopers picked up their pace as they surrounded the position. When they closed in, they found no resistance. Whoever was guarding the empty camp had fled. The camp, which had a field hospital, looked like it had supported an entire battalion. By the number of flies on the recently cooked rice that had fallen to the ground, Bruno surmised that the Viet Minh had been there just a few hours before the paratroopers had arrived. That meant they were close. It was an eerie feeling looking out at the surrounding forest and wondering where the enemy might strike.

Seven miles away, French engineers were putting the finishing touches to a string of six watchtowers and four concrete blockhouses. Two bulldozers had cleared away the brush and trees paralleling the road on both sides, giving each fortification a two hundred yard overlapping field of fire. The blockhouses, which had eight firing portholes housed ten soldiers and were positioned between two watchtowers manned by light machinegun teams.

Civilians used the highway to transport their goods to nearby markets and the rail station in Lang Son, which connected to both Haiphong Harbor and Hanoi. Women set up small charcoal grills and sold skews of roasted chicken and pork to passersby. Children sold bottles of warm beer and used playing cards, usually missing a card or two, to the soldiers that were stationed along the road. The Vietnamese may not have cared much for their overlords, but that never got in the way of doing good business.

Two French soldiers set up their machinegun in their newly built watchtower while a third soldier lugged ammunition cases to a rope and pulley system tied into the roof of the tower. It was far easier to hoist the heavy cases up by rope than by climbing the ladder. With the engineers and support troops in the area, the soldiers were not too concerned that the enemy might attack. Plus, it was still daylight, and the Viet Minh almost always attacked at night when they were harder to spot, and the French couldn't use their aircraft effectively. "Hey, Robi. Do you want to play poker?" said Private Marchant.

"With that deck? It's missing the Jack of hearts," said Corporal Robiquet.

"Yeah, but it's still got one of the jokers, so that evens it out."

"Maybe after we're done setting up. How's Barreau doing on the ammo?"

Marchant looked over the railing and called down to Private Barreau, "Hurry up, you laggard. We're going to play poker."

"With that deck? It's missing a jack," said Barreau as he stacked another ammo case next to the tower's wooden leg.

"It's all we got. Now haul ass."

"Two more, and I'm done."

Marchant gave him a thumbs up. Barreau turned to retrieve the final two ammunition cases from a nearby supply truck. Marchant looked out as he wiped the sweat off his forehead. Below, he saw a Vietnamese man walking along the road holding his hat. "Will ya look at that? He ain't even got enough sense to wear his hat," said Marchant.

Robiquet stopped setting up the machinegun, turned to Marchant, and said, "Who ain't got enough sense to wear their hat?"

"That slope down there," said Marchant pointing. "He's got a hat, but he ain't wearing it. It's got to be ninety degrees out."

Robiquet didn't like what he saw. Marchant was

right. The man had his straw conical hat in his hand, not on his head, and he was nearing the blockhouse. "Hey, you! Stop right there," yelled Robiquet. "Barreau, get over there and check out that guy without a hat."

"He's got a hat, Corporal. He just ain't wearing it," said Barreau.

"Just do as your told and search him."

Barreau picked up his rifle and approached the hatless man. Seeing that he was about to be searched, the man sprinted toward the blockhouse. He dropped the hat in his hand, revealing a canvas bag with a metal ring and wire. It was a satchel charge.

"Oh shit!" said Robiquet reaching for his rifle while calling down to Barreau, "Shoot the bastard!"

The man pulled the wire, flung the canvas bag into the open door of the blockhouse, and ran toward the trees on the opposite side of the road. Barreau shot him in the back as ordered. He fell dead, but the damage was done. The blockhouse exploded, killing all those inside.

Robiquet hoped it was just another lone wolf attack from a disgruntled villager, and the attack was over. It wasn't. He heard several more explosions from the other blockhouses along the road and turned to see them burning. There were more gunshots as more sappers were killed. A chill ran down his spine. This is just the beginning, he thought. He instinctively looked out at the surrounding forest and chambered the first round in his machinegun. "Private, get your ass over here."

"What about the ammo?" said Marchant.

"Tell Barreau to carry what he can up the ladder.

I need you to feed the gun."

"You got a target?"

"No. But I will…"

Marchant yelled down to Barreau, then knelt next to the Corporal and prepared to feed the ammo belt into the machinegun's chamber once the shooting started. It didn't take long. Gunfire erupted along the tree line - hundreds of flashes from hidden shooters. Bullets tore into the wooden tower. Robiquet returned fire spraying the tree line at the base. He was disciplined. Three-second bursts so he didn't overheat the barrel. Laying down fire in one area, then moving to another.

Marchant was feeding the machinegun with one hand and readying the next ammo case with the other when he heard more explosions on the right side of the tower. He turned to see the tops of three watchtowers burning like a string of candles on a cake. It was a captivating sight.

He snapped out of it when Barreau reached the top of the ladder and set down another ammo case. "Should I go down again?" said Barreau.

"You damn well better. Bring everything you got," said Marchant continuing to feed the machinegun.

"You got it."

None of the three soldiers saw the Viet Minh bazooka until it launched its rocket from a hidden position in the tree line. It sailed across the sky, leaving a stream of smoke, and exploded when it hit the tower. Robiquet and Marchant were killed instantly by the high explosive rocket burst. Barreau was blown clear but broke his back when he landed on the road. He lived another five minutes wondering why he couldn't move his legs until a Viet Minh soldier put him out of his misery with his bayonet. The Battle of Route Coloniale 4 had begun.

It was mid-morning before Bruno and his paratroopers arrived at the section of highway where the attack had occurred. They had heard the distant explosions and the frantic radio calls of the embattled French soldiers as the Viet Minh poured out of the tree line and charged the remaining survivors. As far as the eye could see, there were the charred remains of the French defensive positions. The remains of the watchtowers, which weren't much, smoldered as did the blockhouses. The Viet Minh were gone, and the bodies of 200 French soldiers were strewn across the road. The weapons and ammunition had been taken by the enemy for later use. There were no Viet Minh bodies that were usually left after a battle. Their victory had been complete. Villagers looted the French corpses of anything of value; watches, rings, cigarette lighters, and even gold teeth and fillings that were pried free and removed with knives.

The paratroopers yelled and threatened the villagers to leave. It had little effect. For the villagers, this was a matter of survival. Bruno was more direct. He borrowed a submachine gun from the closest paratrooper, chambered a round, and fired into the road. He stitched a line of bullets across the road next to a small group of villagers picking over the remains of the soldiers around a smoking blockhouse. The villagers got the message and fled, disappearing into the surrounding forest on their way back to their homes.

Bruno ordered half his battalion to take up defensive positions. At the same time, the other half searched for any survivors and prepared the bodies for transportation back to the nearest garrison, where they would be buried. Staring out at the carnage and the destruction of the French fortifications and defenses, Bruno realized the flaw in the French plan. The Viet Minh's strategy had changed. They were no longer running away. They were coming for the French.

Boston, Massachusetts - January 19, 1951

On a Sunday afternoon in Boston, Granier walked into the Union Oyster House. At the front of the restaurant, there was an oak and marble-topped bar, shaped in a semi-circle where employees shucked thousands of oysters each day and served them up on chilled plates with thick slices of lemon. Most of the tables were booths with high wooden backs to create a feeling of intimacy. Granier moved to the back of the restaurant where he found Congressman John F. Kennedy at table 18 reading a newspaper and sipping a Bloody Mary with pepper sprinkled around the rim of the glass. "Officer Granier, good to see you again," Kennedy said, smiling broadly and rising to shake his hand. "I hope you brought an appetite."

"Always," said Granier as he sat down on the bench across from Kennedy.

"Good. The others should be along any minute, and we'll order."

"Others?"

"Yes. My brother Bobby and sister Patricia, who you've already met, have decided to join our little excursion."

"I see."

"I hope that's alright?"

"It's fine. I'm just not sure a war zone is a proper place for a young lady."

"Patricia will be fine. She's an experienced traveler and knows how to stay out of trouble. Besides, she's going to document the visit on film. Back in the late '30s, my father had a controlling interest in a movie studio - RKO Pictures. Patricia plans on following in his footsteps and becoming a producer."

"I didn't know that."

"Yeah. We Kennedys have a checkered past. There are rumors my father was a bootlegger during prohibition. He wasn't, but it makes a colorful story. I hope you don't mind me asking the director to assign you to be our guide. I feel your insight and experience with the country will be of great help."

"No. It's fine. It's just not what I normally do."

"Babysitting?"

"I didn't mean it that way."

"Well, I understand. In fact, I'd like to ask you a favor."

"What's that?"

"Watch out for Bobby and Patricia. I'd do it myself, but I tend to get distracted."

"So, I am a babysitter?"

"A highly-skilled babysitter."

"Alright. I'll do what I can."

Robert and Patricia Kennedy arrived together

and made a b-line for table 18, greeting the waiters and manager as they passed through the restaurant. Everyone seemed to know the Kennedys. "Sorry we're late," said Bobby. "Patricia insisted on driving."

"And what's wrong with that?" said Patricia frowning.

"Nothing, if you like the scenic route."

John and Granier started to rise. "Sit. No need for formality," said Patricia. "I'm famished. The sooner we eat, the better."

John signaled the waiter as he introduced Bobby, "Officer Granier, this is my brother, Bobby, and you already know my sister, Patricia."

They shook hands and sat. The waiter approached with menus, which were waved off. "I'll have the Shrimp Louise with the dressing on the side," said Patricia.

"Clam chowder and twelve oysters on the half shell with three extra slices of lemon," said Bobby.

"Do you like lobster stew, Granier?" said John.

"Never had it before," said Granier.

"Trust me. It's the best in Boston, and that's saying a lot."

"Alright."

"Two lobster stews," said John to the waiter.

"And drinks?" said the waiter.

"Unless somebody objects... a round of Bloody Marys."

Nobody objected, and the waiter left to get their orders. Granier seemed a bit unsure and said, "Never had one of those either."

"A Bloody Mary?" said Patricia, surprised.

"Nope."

"Great drink for the morning and afternoon. Quite refreshing with a little kick of spice. You like a little spice, don't you, Granier?"

"A little, sure."

"So, Patricia. Officer Granier and I were just talking about you. He's not sure Indochina is the best place for a young lady," said John with a grin, knowing that he just got Granier into hot water.

"Oh, really?" said Patricia. "Bit old fashioned, don't you think?"

"I just meant that the entire country is a war zone," said Granier.

"I can handle myself."

"I'm sure you can. I regret bringing it up already."

Everyone chuckled.

"So, let's get to the nitty-gritty," said John. "Where do you plan on taking us, Officer Granier?"

"Well, first of all, it'll probably be safer if we drop the titles. Especially for you, Congressman."

"Agreed. Everyone goes by first names."

"You can just call me Granier if it's all the same."

"You don't like Rene?" said Patricia teasing.

"Granier will do just fine."

"Moving on," said John.

"Saigon should be the first stop, and if the French have their way… our only stop," said Granier.

"What do you mean?"

"I'm guessing the French aren't going to be too thrilled with any American poking around their business. The shorter your visit, the happier they are going to be."

"Well, that's too bad. They want our help. We get

to poke."

"Look, even if you want to leave Saigon and visit the countryside, it's not going to be easy or safe. The Viet Minh are everywhere. The farther you get from Saigon, the more aggressive they'll become."

"That's why we have you, right?" said Patricia.

"Sure. And I'll do my best to protect you, but you gotta be smart and not take unnecessary risks."

"This is a fact-finding mission. We can't learn much sitting in a Saigon hotel. Besides, it was you that suggested I go and see for myself," said John.

"I did. But I hardly thought you'd take me up on it."

"Well, now you know."

"Alright. It is what it is. The French are going to want to give you a dog and pony show that they have firm control of the country. You should let them. It'll put them at ease and give you a good lay of the land. Just don't expect to see anything shocking. They're not gonna let that happen."

"What about the Vietnamese units?" said Bobby.

"They are only going to allow you to see units loyal to the French."

"Are they that afraid of what they might say?"

"I think the French are less worried about what the Vietnamese say to you as what you say to them."

"How's that?"

"Right now. The Vietnamese in the South believe that the Americans are backing the French."

"But we're not. We're neutral for the most part."

"Yeah, but that's not what the French are telling them. They're saying America is 100% behind the French and will step in if needed. The French are going to keep you as far away from the Vietnamese army as possible. Especially, the military commanders."

"That's outrageous."

"That's Vietnam. As long as the French control the Vietnamese military, they can do and say whatever they want. They're not going to let an American congressman infect the military with the truth."

"So, what are we supposed to do? How do we find the truth?" said John.

"You need to go North. The French are building a new line of defensive fortifications to defend Hanoi and Haiphong Harbor. They're very proud of it. They are sure to bring it up. When they do, ask to tour it. If they take the bait, you can fly to Hanoi. The farther from Saigon that you go, the less control the French wield, and the more you'll see of how things really are. The important thing is to let it be their idea."

"Alright. We can do that. But you also said the farther we go from Saigon, the more dangerous it will be."

"That's correct. So, how much are you willing to risk to find the truth?"

"There's a great deal at stake if America enters this war. Better we know what we are getting into. The truth is worth the risk."

The waiter returned with their meal. Everyone was about to dig in when Boddy and Patricia stopped to offer a silent prayer. John ignored them by buttering a roll and sprinkling pepper on his stew. Granier was unsure what to do. It had been many years since he had prayed and never in a restaurant. He waited until the two Kennedys finished and crossed themselves. They started eating with relish. Granier chewed the first spoonful of Lobster stew. "Well? What did I tell you?" said John. "Good, huh?"

Granier nodded. It was a lie. The flavor was overpowering. He had been impressed with the Kennedys' desire to find the truth about Indochina. This trip wasn't just a publicity stunt to get John elected to the Senate. The problem was that Granier wasn't sure how he felt about what was happening in Indochina. He had always been a soldier and didn't need to worry about the politics behind American military operations. Now, working for the CIA, things were different. What he said and did affected the decision-makers. He had to be more careful. He had influence, and influence was a two-edged sword. He liked simple things, mechanical things. This was neither.

When the meal was done, everyone gathered their coats in preparation of leaving. John and Bobby were excited about the trip and talked to each other rapidly. Patricia took advantage of the moment and moved over to Granier. "I hope this isn't going to be a problem… me tagging along. I didn't exactly make a good impression the first time we met," she said.

"I won't worry about it. I rarely make a good impression anytime," he said. "You're a strong woman. I'm sure you'll do fine."

"Anyway, I'm glad you're going. I would do anything to protect my brothers," she said with a caring smile.

CHAPTER NINE

Ho Chi Minh was suffering from another cold brought on by the rainy season in the mountains. Living in the northern villages did not suit him. He needed a city where he could get a variety of fruits and vegetables to strengthen his aging body. It seemed he would get over one illness only to be plagued by another. "How are you feeling, Uncle?" said Giap as he entered Ho's quarters.

"We have far more important matters to discuss than my health," said Ho wiping his nose with a well-worn handkerchief.

"I can think of nothing more important than your health."

"I'm fine. You have news?"

"I have thoughts and conclusions."

"Let's hear them."

"It is time to change our strategy from defensive to offensive. We should attack the French in strength."

"We have already discussed this. Our men need more training before they grapple toe-to-toe with the French."

"Uncle, I understand your caution, and I appreciate it. But our men are ready. A major victory will show the Chinese and the Soviets we are worthy of their support. It will demoralize the French and show them that their defeat in Indochina is inevitable."

"And what about the Americans?"

"The Americans are the biggest reason we should strike now. We must show them that supporting Colonialism is a doomed strategy. Even with American weapons, armor, and aircraft, the French will fail."

"And if they decide to commit troops?"

"The Americans will not commit troops while the Chinese side with us. They do not want to see the war expanded."

"You don't know that."

"And neither do you, Dear Uncle. You fight a ghost that doesn't exist. It prevents our victory."

"And our defeat."

Giap took a moment to calm down before continuing. He knew Ho wasn't feeling well, and he didn't want to put undue strain on him. "I know you hold the Americans in high esteem. But they are humans just like we are. They are not invincible. If they come, we will defeat them. But no matter what, let's get on with it while we have the momentum. It is our time."

Ho sighed. He felt tired and worn out. He knew his weariness was affecting his judgment. Giap, a

143

younger man, seemed to have all the energy in the world and was ready to fight. "Where would you attack?" said Ho, resigned.

Giap had won, but he felt far from happy about it. He felt ashamed that he had raised his voice against his mentor. Ho, more than anyone, was responsible for Giap's success as the leader of the Viet Minh. He knew he must press his attack against Ho even though everything inside him wanted to defend the man. "The French fortresses in the North along Colonial Route 4. We will break them so weapons and supplies can flow from China. Our initial assault was met with great success. We should finish them before they change their strategy."

"Promise me you will not fight unless you can win," said Ho, reminding Giap of Mao's philosophy.

"I promise, Uncle. I promise."

"Very well. Set our nation free, General. Destroy the French and the Americans be damned if they try to stop us."

Lieutenant Colonel Pierre Charton was a short but serious officer much loved by the men under his command. His no-nonsense approach, combined with his foul mouth, often put him at odds with his fellow officers and commanders. He had been placed in charge of one of the most challenging posts in all of Indochina – the fortress of Cao Bang. It was the northernmost point on Colonial Route 4 and represented the end of French civilization in Southeast Asia. Anything beyond the fort was considered enemy territory. The 2,600 soldiers that made up the garrison were a combination of colonial troops, mostly Moroccans, and Foreign Legionnaires. The Legionnaires were made up of a large number of German recruits fleeing Allied justice for war crimes.

Earlier in the year, the fortress at Dong Khe had been attacked and overrun by Viet Minh forces annihilating the 300-man garrison and cutting off Cao Bang's supply line. Fortunately for the French, a battalion of paratroopers was able to quickly retake the Dong Khe fortress and resupply Cao Bang before it fell. But the writing was on the wall – Cao Bang was too vulnerable to defend against a sustained Viet Minh attack. While the French inflicted more casualties on the Viet Minh in most of the battles they fought, the Viet Minh could replace their losses with new recruits. The French, on the other hand, were running low on replacements. The more the French fought, the weaker they became. More and more, the French forces turned to defense rather than offense. They hedged their losses as much as possible, but it wasn't enough. They simply did not have enough troops to control all of Vietnam, especially in the north.

In September, Dong Khe was again attacked by an overwhelming force of Viet Minh – five infantry battalions and one heavy weapons battalion. The fortress fell in less than a day. Only twelve of the 300 soldiers in the garrison survived. Cao Bang was again cut off. The French believed that Giap would attack with the full weight of his army as soon as his troops and artillery could be repositioned. The French Air Force could pin down the Viet Minh for a short time, but even the aerial bombing and strafing could not hold back the red tide indefinitely. The Viet Minh were coming, and the French knew it.

The orders to abandon the garrison came in late September. "So, that's it. They're pulling the plug," said Charton handing the message to his Executive Officer, Major Pelletier. "We need to move out before the 30th. We are to rendezvous with Colonel Page's relief column from Lang Son."

"We're not taking RC3?" said Pelletier surprised.

"RC3 is not capable of supporting heavy equipment."

"I don't understand the problem. The orders say we are to destroy our artillery and vehicles and to proceed on foot."

"Damn the orders. Napoleon did not give up his cannon. I shall not give up mine. The men will travel by truck with the artillery in tow. It will be faster than going on foot. We will take as many of the Thai partisans as wish to go with us."

"And their families? They will slow us down."

"Nobody is to be left behind."

"Of course. So if we are to travel on RC4, what will we do when we come to Dong Khe? The Viet Minh have overrun it."

"We'll retake it and wait for the relief column. Once they arrive, we'll head back to That Khe and then Lang Son. We'll be over eight thousand strong at that point. I doubt even Giap will want to mess with us. And if he does, we'll be happy we brought our artillery with us."

The column of vehicles and pedestrians stretched more than two miles. It took almost three hours to leave the protected walls of the Cao Bang garrison. The French left the fortress at Dong Khe and its stores ablaze, leaving nothing of value for the Viet Minh. Unfortunately, the smoke rising from the fort revealed the French retreat to the Viet Minh watching from the surrounding mountains. The Viet Minh stayed hidden in the forest as they paralleled the column on both sides of the road.

Although the rainy season was over, the roads between the two fortresses had not yet been repaired. The trucks struggled with the heavy loads, and many got stuck in the mud. They were quickly abandoned, and the artillery gun barrels were destroyed with high explosives, making them useless. Charton had given strict orders that the column must keep moving. Stragglers were to be left behind once the trek began. The French and the civilians knew that the Viet Minh were near and watching. Unprotected, stragglers would not last the hour once the tail of the column disappeared in the distance.

Page's relief column from Lang Son held 3,000 Moroccan and Tabor colonial troops, plus 500 paratroopers from the Foreign Legion's 1st Parachute battalion. Before starting, Page sent out intelligence units to capture prisoners in hopes of discovering what they might face. The news was shocking and consistent. Giap had a massive force assembled and planned to attack before the relief column could reach the protection of That Khe fortress. They were advancing into a trap, but they had little choice. They were the cavalry expected to save Charton's garrison. It would be rude to be late.

Instead, Page requested air support to pave the way between the fortresses. He also used the 155mm guns at Lang Son to lay down an artillery barrage in the forest that paralleled the road. The trees made aerial recon photos almost useless. They had no idea what kind of damage, if any, they had inflicted on Giap's forces. But they couldn't wait any longer. Using the early morning mist as cover, the relief column set out for That Khe.

The aerial and artillery barrages had done the trick, or at least, so it seemed. The relief column made it to That Khe just before sundown and entered the protection of its walls for the evening.

In the meantime, Charton's column had suffered multiple assaults from Viet Minh ambushes along the road. The French forces fought to protect their artillery, while the Thai partisans fought to protect their families. The assaults were short in duration but heavy in effect. Machineguns firing from the tree line raked the column, killing and wounding dozens. With the injured needing medical attention, the column slowed to a crawl. Charton was seeing his command destroyed piecemeal as the Viet Minh continued to spring their ambushes and harassing assaults that nipped at the rear guard.

Unable to retreat to Cao Bang and still too far to reach Dong Khe, Charton's column was forced to spend the night on the road. They slept little as the Viet Minh used the darkness to carry out a series of assaults. Tracer rounds streaked across the open road, and Viet Minh mortar shells exploded, lighting up the sky. French aircraft flying over the battlefield dropped parachute flares all night long. Unfortunately, they had a negative effect as they lit up the French positions, creating targets from their silhouettes. Charton finally called off the aircraft, believing that his unprotected soldiers were better off shielded by the darkness like the Viet Minh. It was a hellish night for the French and Thai partisans on Colonial Route 4.

Around midnight, just as everyone inside the garrison at That Khe was dozing off, the Viet Minh opened fire on the garrison with their heavy mortars hidden in the trees. The French in the fortress could not determine the location of the enemy mortars. There was little the garrison could do except take the punishment. Shells rained down all night. Casualties were unusually heavy because of the cramped conditions inside the walls. It seemed that wherever a shell exploded, it found a body to pepper with shrapnel.

When morning broke, the devastation on Charton's forces was revealed. Hundreds of French troops had died in the night. Many of the Thai partisans and their families had abandoned the road and made their way into the surrounding forest. The Viet Minh were waiting for them. Young and old were massacred, and their bodies were displayed to remind the survivors still in the column that there was no way out. Morale plummeted.

Charton had had enough. He gave the order to destroy his precious artillery and burn the trucks.

The column would leave the road and go west into the hills on foot. He figured it couldn't be any worse than traveling on the road, and it would put distance between his forces and the Viet Minh. They would move in the same direction toward Dong Khe. Hopefully, Page's relief column could retake the fortress, and Charton's column could emerge from the hills and join them. They would have time to tend to their wounded and rest before starting toward That Khe and eventually, Lang Son.

Giap ordered his troops to hold their assaults on Charton's forces. "Never interrupt your enemy when he is making a mistake," he told his commanders. The Viet Minh watched from the eastern tree line as Charton's column left the road and disappeared over the first hillside to the west. The Viet Minh knew where they were headed, and they would be waiting. The Viet Minh troops had learned to travel light and move quickly, even in the densest forests and jungles. Catching up with the French column would be less than challenging. What Giap wanted now was for the two French columns to combine so that he could concentrate his forces. With luck, the French would oblige.

By morning, the soldiers in Page's relief column were exhausted from a sleepless night in the That Khe garrison. Once again, they set out early in hopes of reaching the garrison at Dong Khe by the afternoon. With luck, Charton's column would arrive before nightfall, and they would be able to attack the fortress from two sides.

Less than a mile out of That Khe, Page's relief
column was assaulted by wave after wave of Viet
Minh troops emerging from the forest on both sides
of the road. Air and artillery strikes were immediately
called in. The Viet Minh had learned through
experience, that the only way to defeat the French
aircraft and artillery was to grab the enemy by the
belt. If the Viet Minh fought close, the French troops
couldn't use their aircraft and artillery for fear of
being hit by friendly fire. It leveled the playing field.
Page's column took heavy losses and was forced to
fall back toward That Khe. But unlike previous
battles, the Viet Minh did not disengage. Instead,
they pushed harder and stayed entangled with their
enemy. While the artillery and aircraft could attack
any enemy forces that had not yet closed the gap with
the French troops, they could not drive a wedge
between the two combatants once entangled. Page's
soldiers continued to take heavy losses until they had
reached the That Khe fortress. The riflemen inside
were able to fire from the walls and pick off the Viet
Minh. Now it was the Viet Minh's turn to take heavy
casualties. They broke off and retreated toward the
safety of the tree line. French aircraft strafed and
bombed the fleeing enemy, increasing the body
count until the Viet Minh disappeared under the
forest canopy.

Once safely inside the fortress at That Khe, Page and
his officers quickly revamped their strategy. The Viet
Minh had overwhelming numbers and seemed much
more willing to fight the French forces. Even if they

151

could reach the fortress at Dong Khe, retaking it would be nearly impossible. Page also received a radio call from Charton advising Page that Charton's column had abandoned their vehicles and were now on foot west of the road. Page decided to link up with Charton's column in the hills west of the fortress, then escort them back to That Khe, where they would spend the night under even more crowded conditions.

In the early afternoon, there was a lull in the fighting. Page decided to use the opportunity to leave the fortress and head west into the foothills. His force had been whittled down to less the 2,500 troops still capable of fighting. Unrestrained by the need to stay on the road, his men spread-out in three-wide sweeping lines. It was safer and ensured that their force could not be overrun by the Viet Minh. If they came into contact with the enemy, Page's troops could quickly consolidate their forces, and the lines could support one another. Surprisingly, the Viet Minh assaults were few and far between. More like reconnaissance skirmishes meant to collect information, not to hurt their enemy in any meaningful way. Page did not understand why Giap had broken off his attack, but he was grateful he had.

Giap was keeping a close eye on the progress of both columns approaching each other. He demanded constant radio reports from his units in the area. He had picked the spot where he wanted them to meet. He used his troops to prod one column while slowing the other. He pushed his enemy in the direction he wanted while directing his own units. He gave strict orders to his commanders that they were not to engage the enemy or reveal their position or size of their force. The Viet Minh was like a boa constrictor, using the trees for cover while encircling the two columns with a mass of force.

The silence was unnerving for both Charton and Page. They could feel the enemy was tracking them, but there was little they could do to prevent it. They were in survival mode. They needed to link up and get back to That Khe as fast as possible. Each commander could see the exhaustion on the faces of their men, and they felt it in themselves.

As the sun set, they found each other. The men were relieved, as were their commanders. Even with their losses, which were heavy, they still had a sizeable force that could fend off the enemy. The only question was whether to attempt to travel during the night. Both commanders knew what it meant to sleep in the open, but they also knew that traveling at night would mean multiple ambushes before they reached the fortress at That Khe. There was even a quick discussion of attempting to take back Dong Khe, which was only a few miles away from their position. It was the Viet Minh that were trapped in a box this time. The French could call in artillery and airstrikes to drive the Viet Minh from the fortress. If they could retake it, their men would be far safer inside the fortress walls even if the conditions were crowded. When surveying their men and seeing the fatigue on their faces, both commanders realized that retaking Dong Khe was wishful thinking. It could end up as a deadly trap when the Viet Minh consolidated their forces and closed in.

The decision was made to let the men rest until the first crack of dawn. They could dig in on the ridgelines and create a natural fortress like a giant foxhole. The artillery at That Khe was still within reach and could protect them if there was a significant attack. The men fortified their positions as much as possible, ate a quick supper, and quickly fell asleep.

The Viet Minh waited patiently. The last battalion moved into position and kept out of sight. It was the Viet Minh that would light up the sky with flares tonight. Giap set the time of the assault to be midnight. He issued extra rations of rice with fish sauce to all the men. He wanted them ready when the final attack came. No fires were allowed. Giap did not want to alert the enemy to their presence. He had ten infantry battalions and one artillery regiment surrounding the French.

A few minutes before midnight, Viet Minh sappers crept up on the enemy outposts a hundred yards from the French perimeter. The explosion of grenades tossed into the French foxholes signaled the start of the attack. The outpost guards were all killed. A barrage of heavy mortar rounds followed. There were so many explosions, so close together, Page wondered if Giap had brought ever heavy mortar in his entire army. He had. Lighter mortars launched flares over the French position. It was the Viet Minh that wanted to see clearly as they advanced on the French. The Viet Minh artillery barrage of Chinese 75mm and American 105mm howitzers, captured during the Chinese civil war, devastated the French as the shells arced over the hills and landed within their lines.

The French called in artillery strikes and radioed for air support. The French commanders would throw everything available at the Viet Minh and vice versa.

The earth was torn as fountains of dirt and rock were flung into the air by the exploding shells. The French troops covered their mouths with wet bandanas to keep from choking on the dust. The only defense against the flying shrapnel was to keep one's head down, which prevented the French from seeing the Viet Minh advancing on their perimeter.

The battle continued for two days without stop. The lines undulated back and forth as the Viet Minh overran the French positions, only to have the French drive them back with a counter-attack. The paratroopers that had traveled with Page's relief column were the most experienced and aggressive fighters. They were used as a reserve assault force to plug holes in the French lines, striking the enemy before they could entrench. It was an effective strategy at first, but the paratroopers took heavy casualties during the counter-attacks. As the numbers of dead and wounded mounted, it became more difficult to fight off the Viet Minh, which seemed to have an inexhaustible supply of troops.

The French believed they had brought enough supplies and ammunition with them to fight off any Viet Minh assault. After the second day of battle, they were running dangerously low on ammo, and even water was becoming a problem. Charton and

Page decided that they must make a break for the fortress at That Khe or face annihilation. The dead were buried in place. The wounded that could travel were placed in the center of the breakout force. Those that were too injured or exhausted to move were left behind. They would man the machineguns and continue the fight while their comrades made their escape.

At the end of the second day, the French waited until sundown then made their move. Less than 1,500 French troops attempted to make it back to the fortress, and most of those were wounded.

Giap had been expecting such a move and had moved the bulk of his forces between the French breakout column and That Khe. At the same time, he assaulted the fortress, weakening its defenses and reducing the numbers of its defenders. Even if the French made it to the fort, they would find no respite. Giap had the French in a death grip, and he had no intention of letting them loose.

As the sun broke the next day, the Viet Minh attacked the breakout column near the Coc Xa gorge. The French were quickly overrun. Those that were still alive scattered and ran for their lives. Only 130 paratroopers out of the original 500 were able to escape by climbing down a 75-foot cliff carrying their wounded on their backs.

Over the next few days, surviving French troops straggled into That Khe. The French attempted to reinforce the garrison with 268 paratroopers from the 3rd Colonial Commando Paratrooper Battalion. It wasn't near enough to withstand Giap's overwhelming force. The fortress fell, and the battalion was annihilated. Only 14 paratroopers survived.

In all, only 700 of the original 6,000 French soldiers survived the Battle of Colonial Route 4. It was a devasting loss for the French. Even Lang Son, with its major fortifications and rail supply lines, had to be abandoned within the month. The Viet Minh victory was complete, and the French blocking strategy had been demolished.

Giap had revealed the strength of his army. For the first time in the Indochina War, the Viet Minh had stood toe-to-toe with the French and won. They had learned how to fight and fought well. French artillery and aircraft were not as effective against the new 'grab-them-by-the-belt' strategy used by the Viet Minh. To say it was unexpected was an understatement.

The French were in shock. There were significant concerns among the French leaders about the Viet Minh's ability to attack Haiphong and Hanoi. If Hanoi fell or the French lost the use of the Haiphong Harbor, all of Tonkin was in danger of falling. A general retreat back to Hanoi was ordered for all French forces in the Northern outposts. Hanoi is where the French forces would make their stand.

Unlike the fortress cities along the border where the Viet Minh could attack from all sides and quickly cut off lines of communication, Hanoi was different. French control of the surrounding area was much stronger. The lines of communication were much shorter, allowing reinforcements within hours rather than days or even weeks. There were developed roads and railways that were well-guarded by the

French. Many blockhouses and watchtowers had already been built, restricting the movement of the Viet Minh. While the distance between Haiphong Harbor and Hanoi was somewhat of an issue, it was a far shorter distance than Hanoi to Lang Son or Cao Bang. French aircraft could be quickly called in on any assault. Both the Air Force airfields in Hanoi and the Navy aircraft carrier in the Gulf of Tonkin could be used for air-to-ground support. The shorter flying distance and the ability to quickly rearm doubled the French airstrike capacity. Even though they were now greatly outnumbered by the Viet Minh forces, the French had many advantages in defense of Hanoi.

The French had bigger problems than the loss of 3% of their entire fighting force in Indochina. Morale was at an all-time low. The French troops and Parisian politicians had lost confidence in General Georges Carpentier, the Indochina military commander.

But the biggest problem for the French was the Americans. The Americans had signaled that they were ready to vastly increase the weapons and supplies the French needed to fight the communists. But the French knew that the aid was conditioned on their capability to defeat Ho Chi Minh and his Viet Minh army. The losses sustained during the Battle of Colonial Route 4 would need to be 'adjusted' for American eyes, at least until the new French commander could gain control of the situation. The less said about the convoluted battle, the better.

The French hated asking the Americans for aid. But even worse was the advice the Americans would offer as part of that aid – the strings of a puppeteer were not welcome.

With the French blocking line now gone, the Viet Minh were free to import weapons and supplies from China. Viet Minh battalions were sent for additional training in the Chinese camps across the border. Ho Chi Minh's fledgling Viet Minh army was now becoming a finely tuned war machine capable of taking on the Western Powers. The more they fought, the more they learned how to fight.

CHAPTER TEN

The loss of Route Coloniale 4 was the straw that broke the camel's back for General De Lattre. He could no longer deprive France of its best hope – himself. As he suspected, a whisper that he might agree to take the top position in Indochina was enough to have France's leaders come calling. He accepted. Many saw this as a step down for the general, but he only saw his duty to his country. He was made both Commander-in-chief of the French Army in Indochina and High Commissioner of Indochina. As a condition of accepting the post, he had ensured that he had the control that he needed to "win it all," and that is what he intended to do.

Driven to Orly Airport in Paris, De Lattre exited the vehicle to see two thousand of his old comrades waiting to cheer him on and wish him well. They still trusted the old general to lead France to victory.

It would take five days to reach Vietnam. It gave

the general time to think and devise a strategy to turn the war around. Morale won or lost wars, not numbers or technology. If you think you are beaten, then you are beaten. He would make sure France had the upper hand by merely changing the attitude of the men under his command.

The war had been raging for exactly four years when his plane touched down in Saigon. He stood at the top of the stairs as a military band struck up "The Marseillaise," and the crowds cheered. It was quite the show, and De Lattre, wearing white gloves, took full advantage of the moment to demonstrate that he was here to clean up the mess. He walked down the stairs and over to the bandleader, where he proceeded to berate the officer because one of the instruments was out of tune. He ripped into the officer in charge of the honor guard because it appeared slovenly and not up to his standards.

Inside the terminal, De Lattre confronted a co-pilot wearing a beard and ordered him to shave in the next five minutes or spend the night in the brig. The message was clear and spread like wildfire through the ranks, King Jean was here, and everyone better clean up their act or face his wrath.

A few months later, in Boston, Granier and the Kennedys prepared for their departure. The Boeing 377 was an oddly-shaped plane with its double-bubble fuselage that divided the passenger cabin into a main deck seating area and a spacious lower deck lounge. The commercial version of the aircraft was based on the Boeing C-97 Stratofreighter, which in turn, was developed from the Boeing B-29 Superfortress used to drop the atomic bombs on Japan. It was considered the most luxurious airliner at the time, so naturally, the Kennedys chose it for the transatlantic leg of their overseas fact-finding tour.

The Kennedys weren't just visiting Indochina. There were additional stops planned for Israel, Iran, Pakistan, India, Thailand, Japan, and Korea - all communist hot spots of potential and actual conflict. The international tour would take seven weeks in total. For most of it, Granier was just along for the ride and to provide security if needed. In each of the countries they visited, the government and militaries were cautious with the Kennedys. It would not be a good diplomatic move to have a U.S. Congressman killed or wounded in their country. As Granier had suggested, the Kennedys were only allowed to see what the foreign officials wanted them to see - a diplomatic bubble. John was especially frustrated by this but didn't want to cause an incident. It was Indochina that most interested him. It would be there that he made his stand.

The flight from Boston to Saigon had sixteen different stops and took almost two weeks. But the food was very good with main courses that included roast beef and lobster, and the alcohol was free. While the Kennedys flew in the first-class section, Granier, who had only flown in unpressurized military aircraft, had insisted on traveling economy class. He had no interest in mingling with the rich people in First Class with which he had nothing in common. Even economy-class seemed extravagant. Although, he liked the tight skirts worn by the stewardesses who fed him constantly and tucked in his blanket when the lights dimmed for the evening.

Granier had his hands full during the Kennedys' visits to Israel, Iran, and India. There were ample police and military units provided by each country's government, but Granier didn't trust anyone's motives. He stayed close to the Kennedys and, at times, requested that they leave an area when his intuition warned of potential danger. The police and military officers in charge were often insulted at the insinuation that their protection was substandard, but Granier didn't care. He did his job, and to hell with their feelings. The Kennedys felt reassured that a man with Granier's experience was watching their backs, and they rarely ignored his suggestions when it came to security.

Two days after the Kennedys' routine visit to Pakistan, Pakistani leader Liaquat Ali Khan was assassinated in front of 100,000 people while giving a speech. The assassin was an Afghan national who was killed by the Pakistani police during the shooting. A clear motive for the killing was never determined. Many Pakistani believed that America was secretly behind Khan's murder because he had established diplomatic relations with China and had accepted an invitation from the Russians to visit Moscow. Others believed that the Kennedys' visit was just poorly timed, and opposition forces were most likely responsible. The one thing that could not be disputed was that John F. Kennedy was a political and diplomatic lightning rod as he and his siblings visited some of the most dangerous countries in the world.

When De Lattre had arrived in Indochina, discipline was waning, and some troops were flat-out refusing to leave the protection of the French outposts to find the enemy. The more soldiers from the massacre of Colonial Route 4 that retreated to Hanoi, the more the rumors spread of Giap's unstoppable red wave. De Lattre knew he needed to correct the situation quickly if the army was to defend Hanoi and Haiphong from the Viet Minh successfully. He also knew the best medicine for morale was a victory. He needed to win a major battle against the Viet Minh no matter the cost.

In addition to the 3,000 French soldiers preparing defensive positions around Hanoi and Haiphong, De Lattre had four mobile forces – GM1, GM2, GM3, and GM4 - each containing about 3,000 men. His plan was simple… wait. He knew Giap would attack soon with a large force to break the French defensive line around Hanoi, and when he did, De Lattre would hit him with everything he had, including a new weapon that had never been used before in a major battle – napalm. If his men could hold the line against the Viet Minh, French morale would be restored.

Feeling invincible after the border battles, Giap unknowingly obliged. He assembled two divisions – 308th and 312th, with 10,000 men each - along the Tam Dao ridge above the city of Vinh Yen, 30 miles northeast of Hanoi. Tam Dao was the last mountain before the flatlands leading to Hanoi. Covered with trees and bushes, it was an excellent refuge to assemble a large force without the French aircraft spying. The Viet Minh were anxious to get at the French once again, and there was talk of ending the war within the year. Morale had never been higher. The mountain ridge was steep, but it was the dry season, and the rains had stopped. The footing was stable. It was cold at night, and frost often formed on the trees and grass in the early morning.

Giap wasted no time. As soon as all his forces were assembled, he gave the order to attack. The 308th made a diversionary attack on the small French outpost at Bao Chuc two miles from Vinh Yen. The fifty French soldiers held their ground, which was surprising considering they were outnumbered almost 200 to 1. Giap had given specific orders to harass but not to overrun the outpost. He was fishing for something bigger.

Hearing the distress call over the radio, GM3 moved quickly to rescue the besieged French garrison. As they approached the outpost, the Viet Minh 312th division moved from their hidden position on Tam Doa ridge and attacked. With both the 308th and the 312th hammering the French expeditionary force from both sides, the French were quickly surrounded. Human waves of Viet Minh infantry were sent in to destroy the French troops. But unlike the attacks in the hills and forests around Colonial Route 4, the Viet Minh were assaulting the French positions over flatland. The Viet Minh had over 20,000 soldiers surrounding the French – a dense, unprotected mass.

Any Viet Minh troops not in close combat with the French troops were subject to artillery barrages and airstrikes.

Artillery from Hanoi was moved to within range and opened fire with devastating effect. Shells rained down on the Viet Minh. To protect themselves, they tried to move closer to the French troops they were attacking, but that just made the mass of Viet Minh troops denser and the casualties heavier. Any shell that found its target within the mass was sure to kill or wound a half dozen men.

Then came the warplanes — American-made Grumman Hellcats from airbases around Hanoi and the French aircraft carrier Arromanches off the coast of Haiphong. The fighter/bombers were a recent addition to French Air Force and Navy, as were the bombs they carried. They were a welcome part of the growing military aid package from America to France. Hellcat squadrons swooped down over the Viet Minh caught in the open. It was the first time the Viet Minh had been attacked by the fast-moving, heavily armed aircraft, and the first time they had been exposed to the horrors of napalm. When the napalm canisters hit the ground and ignited, anyone in the path of the fiery explosion was instantly consumed. There was no time to run. Initially developed for flamethrowers, the gelatin substance stuck to the skin and clothing immediately, raising the temperature to 800 degrees Celsius, eight times the temperature required to boil water. Facing incredible pain, the victims tried to brush it off with their hands, which only resulted in spreading the burning chemical over more of their bodies.

The Viet Minh were horrified when each bomb explosion ignited an area of 2,500 square feet, consuming their comrades in a solid wall of flame. But what frightened them even more was the waves of Bearcats approaching from the distance. The Viet Minh lines broke into pieces, some soldiers staying engaged with the French troops while others ran for their lives. But there was nowhere to run. The French aircraft continued chasing after the Viet Minh using their machineguns to strafe the fleeing soldiers. Wherever the French pilots found a clump of Viet Minh, they attacked dropping napalm, then strafed any survivors that had avoided the flames. The psychological effect of napalm was far more debilitating against the Viet Minh forces than the actual damage. No matter the threat of disciplinary action, the Viet Minh refused to attack the French on open ground. They would rather die than suffer the ravages of the French firebombs.

Once the commanders had calmed their troops, the Viet Minh returned to the fight. But it was too late. The French had disengaged and returned to the defensive lines around Hanoi. Giap had failed to break the French and lost nearly 8,000 of his best soldiers in the process.

De Lattre had his victory. It worked like a charm. Morale among the troops rose quickly as word spread of the new secret weapon – napalm. De Lattre would follow the victory with a rigorous return to discipline. The French were to regain their respect and honor. The general would also continue construction on the De Lattre defensive line, which stretched from the northern coast of Haiphong to encircle Hanoi to the west, then back to the sea in the south. Hundreds of fortified bunkers designed to reinforce one another. It was his castle wall on which he would break the Viet Minh.

When the Kennedys' plane landed in Saigon, Patricia was first out the door. On exiting the air-conditioned cabin, a wave of heat and humidity hit her in the face. It was a shock, but it didn't slow her down. She was determined to document every stage of her brothers' trip. Tucked under her arm was a new Bolex 16 mm movie camera with a lens turret. It was a hefty 5 lbs. and awkward to hold. The spring that drove the camera was already wound, and she had pre-selected the lens she wanted to use for the arrival. Her first shot was a quick pan of the crowd of French officials and military officers in front of the Saigon Airport terminal. It seemed like half of the entire French government and army had shown up to greet the young congressman.

On the tarmac, there was a military band of Vietnamese soldiers conducted by a French officer patiently waiting for the first signs of the American Congressman. A pool of foreign press and photographers waited with their cameras. In the distance were row after row of French soldiers that John would be asked to inspect before leaving the airport. Patricia finished her shot then trotted down the stairs while rewinding her camera. Not an easy move.

John, still on the plane, waited as Patricia found a good angle and readied the handheld camera. She signaled Bobby, peaking out the aircraft window, that she was ready. Bobby cued John.

John, who had served in the Pacific during WW II, knew what to expect and was prepared for the heat when he exited the air-conditioned aircraft. The band played The Star-Spangled Banner to welcome the American congressman. John grinned and waved to the dignitaries and reporters as he stepped down the stairs.

Bobby, who was not prepared for the heat, quickly peeled off his jacket and slipped on his sunglasses. He followed John down the stairs, careful not to draw attention away from his brother. Granier followed Bobby along with the rest of the passengers.

Patricia decided to perform a handheld dolly-style move so she could get a better angle on John as he moved past the reporters and shook hands with the dignitaries. While looking through the viewfinder, she took long sideways strides to prevent camera jiggle. Sweat was pouring down her face and dripping off her chin and earlobes. Her hands were wet with sweat, and it made it difficult to hold the camera steady. She let the camera loose with one of her hands and wiped the sweat on the back of her skirt as she continued to move sideways. Condensation fogged the camera's viewfinder making her job even more difficult.

Granier saw the empty baggage cart in Patricia's path even though she didn't. He thought about yelling a warning, but he knew that everyone would look in her direction. It was too late anyway. A disaster already in motion. He kept his mouth shut and hoped for the best. It didn't go well. Patricia's knee hit the edge of the cart, and she fell. Her slippery fingers fumbled the camera, which was still rolling, finally releasing it to find its own fate and freeing up her hands to cushion her fall. She landed on the cart. Her hands reached out, trying to regain balance. Instead, they found the stainless steel bed of the cart that had been sitting in the sun for almost an hour. Her palms burned like fried eggs. The camera also landed on the bed of the cart but slid off the opposite side and hit the tarmac with a loud crack.

Granier reached the bottom of the stairs and ran over to check on her. "Are you okay?" he said.

"Nothing a few squirts of Bactine won't cure. Forget me. How's my camera?" she said as he helped her up.

Granier walked around the cart and picked up the camera - the long lens on the turret mount had broken off. "I don't think it's supposed to work like this," he said, holding up the broken-off lens and the camera.

"No. It's not," she said. "I hope the film wasn't exposed."

"You're worried about the film?"

She turned to look at John, still shaking hands, and said, "My brother is going to be president of the United States one day. That film is the history of his rise to power."

"I suppose. But this camera probably ain't gonna do much shooting until you get it fixed."

"I doubt I'm going to find a Bolex repair facility in Saigon. Would you mind taking me camera shopping first chance we get?"

"Sure. I'll ask around, see where we can pick one

up. Do you mind used?"

"I don't mind anything as long as it's reliable."

"Alright. Look, I need to get back to your brother."

"Do you think he could be in danger?"

"Here… with all this Army brass? I doubt it. But I don't want to take any chances. I think you can probably find some Bactine for your hands at the shop inside the terminal."

"Honestly, I'd rather find a room with air-conditioning."

"Heat getting to ya?"

"I think it's more the humidity."

"Yeah, it's a bit much. You're in luck. The terminal is air-conditioned."

"Okay. I'll see you inside."

"Just do me a favor. Once you find some Bactine, stay by the window so I can keep an eye on you."

"I told you I could take care of myself."

"Humor me."

"Fine," she said, turning to walk toward the terminal, acting angry but feeling flattered that Granier was showing concern for her.

Granier walked back over to John, continuing to shake hands accompanied by his grin. Granier's eyes combed the crowd searching for threats. There were none as he suspected. Still vigilant like a wolf in a pack protecting the alpha male, he would stay in the background, far enough away to not draw attention, but close enough to make a difference if needed.

Standing behind his brother, Bobby was the same, but in a different way. Bobby was incredibly shy and awkward, but a hard worker that could be counted on when the going got tough. He rarely complained. He knew his place. He was never seen as having potential for public office, especially by his father, Joe Kennedy. Instead, Bobby would support the others that did have potential like his brothers, John and Ted.

As the French commander of Indochina forces, De Lattre was at the airport to greet John. The general was impressive, decisive, and well respected by those under his command. When John asked if it would be possible to view his troops in action, De Lattre immediately offered to personally escort the congressman and siblings on a tour of the battlefield outside of Saigon in the Mekong Delta. John eagerly accepted the offer, and the general's staff began to make the required transportation and security arrangements.

In a newspaper darkroom under the glow of red lights, a French lab technician and his Vietnamese assistant finished their shift by hanging a group of photos to dry on a line. The images were of the Kennedys departing the plane and greeting the French officials. The technician grabbed his cigarettes and lighter and headed out the double revolving door designed to keep light out. With the technician gone, the assistant pulled what seemed to be a handful of duplicate photos from the line and placed them in an envelope which he carried out of the darkroom.

The first night, the Kennedys were invited to stay in the palace of Vietnam's Head of State and former

Emperor Bao Dai. Upon meeting him, Patricia whispered to Bobby that the man's skin looked like it had been recently fried in oil. John was given the only bedroom with air-conditioning in the entire palace. When asked by Bobby and Patricia if they could sleep on his floor, John offered to swap with Patricia and give her his bed so he could sleep on the floor. "Your back?" said Patricia knowingly.

"It's a bit stiff after the long flight," said John understating the seriousness of his affliction.

John had chronic back pain most of his adult life. It had gotten so bad that the year before the international tour, John had undergone experimental back surgery and spent four months in the hospital. The surgeon had botched the operation, and John was left with a metal plate in his back and an eight-inch open wound that refused to heal. His health was always fragile. He had lied his way into the Navy, knowing that he would never pass the physical. Even with his afflictions, John seemed the picture of health, and his family did what was necessary to promote that image. Anytime John's pain overwhelmed him in public, the press was always told it was an old war wound from the sinking of PT 109 and his heroic rescue of the crew. It wasn't. It was something far more severe. John had Addison's disease, an insufficiency in adrenal production that left its victims fatally vulnerable to infection like slow-motion leukemia. His doctor felt it was improbable that John would live beyond the age of 45. He was almost right, but for the wrong reason.

Granier thought it a bad idea to accept Bao Dai's offer to stay in the palace. The former emperor was well known for his Machiavellian mischief and was not above murder if it suited his political purposes. John had overruled him and accepted the offer, figuring he might have a good conversation with the Vietnamese leader at some point during his overnight stay. He didn't. Bao Dai had little interest in impressing the American congressman and retired to his bedroom shortly after dinner. The Kennedys' French tenders did not leave until the Kennedys retired to their bedroom. They did not want any side conversations between the Vietnamese leader and the congressman. They trusted neither. The French were determined to stay in control of the situation no matter what the Kennedys wanted.

Granier slept in a chair just outside John's bedroom. He would have stayed awake the whole night, but John was a ball of energy during the day, and Granier needed his sleep to stay alert. At the slightest sound, his eyes sprang open, and his hand reached for the .38 revolver in his pants pocket. I'll be lucky if I don't blow my dick off, he thought when he had grabbed the gun the wrong way and almost pulled the trigger. Usually preferring to have his weapon hot at all times, he decided to make an exception and put the safety on.

The next morning, De Lattre had the Kennedys picked up by a small military convoy and shuttled his American guests to a South Vietnamese army base. All of the officers at the base were French, while the soldiers were Vietnamese nationals. Just like at the airport, companies of crack troops, Vietnam's best, lined up in file, and John was asked to inspect them.

When John wanted to ask a question of one of the soldiers, a French translator provided by De Lattre was used. By the expression on the soldiers' faces, John was unsure he was getting the straight scoop. Later, Granier, who was fluent in French, told John that the translation had been changed to reflect the French point of view. John suggested that Granier translate from that point onward.

After the inspection, a briefing on enemy positions was held by the French commander of the base and his staff. Maps showed the French making progress in containing the Viet Minh forces. But Granier had informed John that the threat was not just from the Viet Minh. There were also large gangs, communist cadres, and religious militias that could be potential threats to Vietnamese and French forces. When John asked about these additional forces, the French commander shrugged them off as if they were nothing.

A litany of inspections and briefs continued throughout the next several days with visits to motor pools, Navy yards, supply depots, and military airfields. Everywhere they went, the maps and charts showed the French were winning. John was feeling fatigued by the third day. He was discouraged that he might not find the truth of what was really happening in the war. But unlike most men, John took stock and became even more determined. He liked General De Lattre and thought him a strong commander well-liked by his troops. But that didn't mean John was going to let him pull the wool over his eyes. Liking the general was one thing. Trusting him was another.

Ho and Giap stood over a map in the Viet Minh command center. A messenger entered, saluted, and handed the general the envelope containing the photos stolen from the newspaper darkroom by the Vietnamese assistant. As the messenger left, Giap pulled the pictures from the envelope and laid them on the table so Ho could also see them. "Photos from the American delegation in Saigon," said Giap.

"Yes. Kennedy is here to evaluate the war effort by the French," said Ho studying the photos. "His recommendation for additional aid will carry great weight with the American people and President Truman."

Ho picked up one of the photos and studied it more closely. Kennedy was walking down the stairway from the plane, smiling and waving to the crowd. Appearing in the plane's doorway above him was Granier. "Granier?" said Ho, surprised.

"That's impossible. He's dead," said Giap examining the photo. "My men lied to me. I will see that he is dealt with immediately."

Ho contemplated the photo and said, "No. He is close to Kennedy. Leave him be. He may still be of use."

It was Sunday in Saigon. Both Patricia and Bobby wanted to attend mass. John wanted to sleep in, but Granier wanted to keep everyone together. John acquiesced.

French colonists built the Basilica in Saigon in the late 19th century. Located in Paris Square in District 1, the church was impressive. With a red brick facade, stained glass windows, and two bell towers, the structure looked as if it was lifted from the streets of Boston and set down in the heart of Saigon. Serene gardens for contemplation surrounded the basilica with plenty of open space so as not to block the view of the stately structure. It was a proud symbol of western culture in Southeast Asia.

The service was in French and Latin. Granier did a lousy job of translating for the Kennedys. He was too busy identifying potential threats, of which there were many. It didn't matter. The Kennedys were accustomed to the Catholic rituals and needed little help in understanding what was going on.

When the service was finished, and parishioners were filing out, the Kennedys stayed behind to greet Archbishop Paul Nguyen Van Binh along with several dignitaries. It was not easy being a devote Catholic in a country where most of the people were Buddhists, and the Kennedys felt they needed to commend the clergy for its efforts.

When the Kennedys finally headed for the exit, Granier was suspicious of a well-dressed Vietnamese man waiting in the narthex next to the front doors. Granier stepped between the Kennedys and the man as they passed. "Congressman Kennedy?" said the man.

John stopped and turned, "Yes?"

"Be careful. Remember who might be watching," whispered Granier.

177

John nodded and stepped toward the man, so they were away from the doorways and the eyes of those outside. "My name is Ngo Dinh Diem. I was formally interior minister for Emperor Boa Dai," said Diem.

"Formally?"

"We had a parting of the way when he elected to become a French puppet."

"I see," said John knowing that it was one thing for him to have conversations with other westerners, but the French would be wary of any discussion with an ex-government official that they did not set up. He proceeded with caution, "How can I help you, Mr. Diem?"

"I think it is I that can help you, Mr. Kennedy."

"How is that?"

"America cannot possibly wish to see the French return to power in Vietnam. They are colonialists, just as the British were over America before your revolution. It would go against the very roots of your independence."

"Times have changed, and so have circumstances."

"You are referring to the communists."

"America does not wish to see Indochina fall into the communist orbit."

"Nor do I. And I am not alone. There is another way... if you are willing to hear it."

"Mr. Diem, I do not want to offend you, but I am being hosted by the French, and they are watching me closely. What you suggest is a dangerous discussion. Some would say treasonous... or, in my case, subversive."

"I am well aware of the risk. One must be willing

to fight for one's beliefs."

"I agree, but one would need an army to fight. Do you have such an army?"

"No. Not yet."

"You see my need for caution."

"Of course. But our cause is growing... with your help, it would grow faster."

"Unfortunately, I'm not sure Indochina has the time to wait. The communist threat is very real and now."

"You will back the French?"

"I didn't say that."

"Then, there is hope."

"There is always hope. Mr. Diem, I am interested in hearing what you have to say, but not here and not now. Perhaps we could communicate next time you are out of the country. It would be safer... for both of us."

"Yes. The French guillotine is kept very sharp."

Kennedy handed Diem his Congressional business card. "This has my phone number. Just give my receptionist your name. She will be expecting your call and know how to get ahold of me. I shall be returning to the United States in about a month."

Diem placed the card in the inside brim of his hat to hide it from French searches. They shook hands, and Diem disappeared out a side door. "If the French find your card on him, it could mean trouble for you," said Granier.

"I have found through experience that progress does not usually come without some risk," said John. "Let's just hope the French want American aid more than my head."

Granier grunted as they exited the church.

CHAPTER ELEVEN

After leaving Boa Dai's palace and for the remainder of their time in Saigon, the Kennedys checked into the Hotel Continental located on Rue Catinat a few blocks from the Saigon River in the French quarter. The Continental was owned and run by Mathieu Franchini, a reputed gangster from Corsica. Nicknamed Radio Catinat, the Continental was considered the social and political hub of Saigon filled with tourists, businessmen, politicians, and foreign journalists. The restaurants and lounges within the hotel were bustling dens of gossip mixed with the news of the day. If one wanted to know what was happening in Saigon, the Continental was the place to be.

Even with the hotel being open to the public, Granier was more comfortable with the Kennedys staying at the Continental rather than Bao Dai's palace. They were free to come and go as they pleased, and the common areas were well-protected with teams of private security guards. Just being away from Bao Dai's secret service agents made Granier feel more at ease. But even in such a public place, Granier still needed to be aware of potential threats. The Prime Minister of Pakistan's assassination following the Kennedys' visit was a stark reminder that no one was safe in the Third World, even when well-guarded.

French intelligence agents tailed the Kennedys and reported on whom they were meeting to the government and military officials. The French needed American military aid to continue fighting the Viet Minh. It was essential that the Kennedys return to the U.S. with glowing reports of the French efforts to fight the communists. But the American congressman was known for being an independent thinker. They feared John would be difficult to control.

Keeping with the meaning behind its name, Saigon, with its languorous allure, was indeed a "gift to the foreigner." Just outside the hotel, slender Vietnamese girls wearing white ao dai - a long silk dress open on both sides and worn with pants - plied their trade along the tree-lined boulevards under the yellow glow of gaslights. A few blocks away, opium dens with their dark interiors, oil lamps, and long pipes provided guests with the ultimate escape from the violence and tension of the city. Pleasure and entertainment never stopped. Whatever one wanted could be found at the right price in Saigon.

As promised, Granier located a motion picture

camera dealer for Patricia. Early the next morning, while John and Bobby slept in their air-conditioned rooms with a hotel security guard posted in the hallway outside their doors, Granier and Patricia went out in search of a replacement camera. Always looking for an adventure, Patricia wanted to take a trishaw. Granier wanted to take a cab, which he felt would be safer. She dug in her heels. He decided to offer a compromise; they would take a trishaw to the edge of the French Quarter, then take a cab into downtown Saigon where the camera shop was located. Accepting his compromise, she eagerly climbed into the closest trishaw - a cycle-driven rickshaw. In Indochina, most of the trishaws were designed to carry the passengers in the front with the cycle-driver pushing from the back. The trishaw was a relatively new invention of a Frenchman in 1939. Nicknamed xich lo in Vietnamese, the trishaw had become more popular than the infamous rickshaw because they were faster and required less effort on the part of the driver. However, they did have a bad reputation of launching their passengers through the air if the driver was ever required to come to a sudden stop. Fortunately, their short trip through the French Quarter was uneventful, and Patricia loved it.

Saigon's French Quarter looked more like a street in Paris than Southeast Asia. Billboards and business signs were all written in French with little regard for Vietnamese customers. There were concrete sidewalks with streetlamps, iron trashcans, and postal boxes. Vietnamese nannies pushed baby carriages and escorted toddlers around the parks, while residents window shopped at the boutiques and sipped their morning coffee at the many sidewalk cafés. It was all so... French. One hardly knew there was a war on except for the occasional bomb blast or machinegun fire in the distance.

When they arrived at the Camera shop, it was still closed. The sign in the window said 10:00, but Granier knew that was only an approximation of when the shop might open. The Vietnamese had a very loose definition of time. While they waited, Granier took Patricia across the street to a small café where he ordered them both Vietnamese coffees.

Unlike American coffee, which was usually brewed beforehand and served with cream, Vietnamese coffee was prepared tableside using a small metal container set on top of a glass. The container which held the ground coffee had little holes in the bottom that let the coffee drip down into the glass when hot water was poured. A half-inch layer of sweet, condensed milk rested at the bottom of the glass, waiting to be mixed with the brewed coffee by a brisk stir of a spoon. When the two liquids combined, it created a sweet drink similar to hot chocolate but with a distinctive coffee flavor and kick of caffeine.

While the waiter went to get the coffees, Patricia set her purse on top of the table. She retrieved her compact and began to powder her nose. Granier surveyed the surrounding area. At the end of the block, he saw two teenagers next to a motor scooter looking their way. He knew they were going to attempt to snatch the purse. One would drive with the other on the back of the scooter. The passenger would simply lean over and grab the purse as they sped past. Patricia was oblivious to the danger. Granier did not want to make a scene. It was simpler to reach into his pocket, pull out the revolver, and set it on his knee where the two young men could see it. He turned toward them casually and shook his head as if to say no-no, boys. They flipped him off French-style and drove off. Patricia finished powdering her nose, replaced her compact, and set her purse on the floor between her and Granier, where it would be safe. Their coffees were served moments later.

Granier knew that the Kennedys were naïve about the dangers of Saigon. John was better than Bobby or Patricia, but even he had lived such a sheltered life growing up that he was oblivious to the dangers of the street most the time. Granier didn't feel the need to continually lecture them on the potential dangers. Instead, he handled things quietly whenever possible. He was their faithful guard dog and knew his place sitting quietly in the background, watching… always watching.

By the time they finished their coffees, the owner of the camera shop had arrived and was open for business. They walked across the street and entered his shop.

The owner had a surprisingly wide selection of cameras and lenses plus an electric refrigerator full of film stocks. Patricia did not ask about the price. She was more concerned about finding the right camera. She was lucky. The owner had the same make and model as the camera she had broken. He even took the broken camera and lens in trade. Granier knew the owner would take advantage of Patricia, who seemed entirely too pleased when it came to negotiating the final price. He was right but again decided not to interfere. It wasn't his job, and besides, the Kennedys were rich, really rich. A few hundred extra dollars would not make a difference to their pocketbooks, whereas it might feed the owner's family for an entire year and then some. She also purchased some extra film stock. Granier gave the owner the eye when it came to pricing the film stock, and the owner got the message. He threw it into the deal at no extra cost. Patricia insisted on paying for the film, but Granier said it was a culture faux pas and that the owner would feel insulted if she did not accept his special gift to her. She complied, paid the owner, and they exited the shop.

As they walked out, Granier's eyes kept a constant watch on passersby while Patricia looked for a cab to flag. As Granier scanned the surrounding area, he saw something in the distance that caught his eyes – a woman crossing the street at the corner of the block. He recognized her face and her slim figure. It was Spitting Woman, a Viet Minh scout and his former lover. She had betrayed him and almost got him killed by the Japanese. He could feel his heart rate increasing and his face flush. He felt profound emotions – love and hate in equal proportions. She did not look in his direction, and he wondered what she was doing in Saigon. As a Viet Minh, this was enemy territory for her. She disappeared as she walked past a building. He wanted to run after her. He wasn't sure what he would do once he caught up with her, but it didn't seem to matter. He just wanted to talk to her and to ask her why she did what she did. He desperately wanted an explanation. He desperately wanted to forgive her.

As he started to walk toward where he had last seen her, it suddenly dawned on him why she was here. She was meant to draw him away from Patricia. A possible kidnapping or assassination attempt? It was the only logical explanation. By why her and not John? He looked around for potential threats. Everything seemed normal. But it couldn't be. Why was Spitting Woman here if not to tempt him? It pained him greatly, but he returned to Patricia's side. He stepped next to her like a shield. "Is everything alright," said Patricia.

"I don't know. But we should go," said Granier, his eyes darting back and forth.

"Alright. You're the boss."

"Stay close. If something happens, hit the deck."

"You're really spooked. What did you see?"

"I'm not sure anymore. Someone I knew. She shouldn't be here."

"She?"

He ignored her question as he placed his hand around her arm to keep her close to him. He slid his other hand into the pocket in his trousers and felt the grip of the pistol he was carrying. Six bullets in his revolver and another six rounds in his other pocket. That's it. He would need to be careful not to waste a single shot. He looked for escape routes. He and Patricia would stay away from the alleys where they could get blocked in or, worse, ambushed. He imagined the adrenaline pumping through his veins, preparing his body for the assault. He wasn't afraid.

He had learned that fear was not his friend, and it wouldn't help him in a situation like this. His senses were heightened. He noticed everything. But still, there was nothing that looked even remotely like a threat. Patricia saw a taxi and flagged it down. They ran over to it and climbed in. Granier looked out the back window for any sign that someone was following them. There was nobody. He felt stupid, like he imagined things. "So who was she?" asked Patricia as the taxi sped away.

"Nobody. Just... nobody," said Granier, lost in thought.

"Now you really have my curiosity. A mystery woman."

"Yeah, well... let's just leave her in the shadows. Trust me. It's better that way. Do me a favor and don't mention this to your brothers, especially John. He's got enough to worry about."

"Alright. I can keep a secret."

"Thanks."

That evening the Kennedys dined in the hotel's main restaurant, which specialized in international cuisine. The waiters and the chef were French while the cooking staff was Vietnamese – a European facade of sorts. This was a typical setup throughout Southeast Asia - the foreigners taking charge and interfacing with western customers while the nationals did all the real work. The meal was excellent.

After dinner, Granier and the Kennedys retired to the roof of the hotel, where a bar served international drinks topped with local flowers. There was a cool breeze that made the humid night more bearable. A

Vietnamese cigarette girl was wearing a traditional violet ao dai with colorful handsewn flowers. She seemed to glide from table to table, offering the hotel's guests French cigarettes and Cuban cigars along with packs of gum. The waiters wore black and white tuxedos while the busboys wore dark blue ao dais to hide the stains from clearing tables.

Across the river, there were distant flashes of light, followed by deep rumblings like thunder follows lightning. Tracer rounds arced across the night sky like red tongues of fire. Patricia and Bobby, neither familiar with war, looked out with fascination. "French artillery and machineguns," said Granier.

"That close?" said Bobby.

"It's on the outskirts of the city, a good ten miles from here. We're safe."

"Is it the Viet Minh?"

"Could be. Could also be religious militias or gangs fighting for turf."

"Religious militias?"

"Yeah. Some religious leaders form their own militias from their followers."

"Why?"

"To protect their temples from looters and gangs. Their statues are covered with gold-leaf, but the people think they're solid gold and worth a bundle. Even the Catholics have militias, especially in the smaller cities. They are used to protect their parishioners and schools. They don't rely on the government troops to protect them."

John sat, keeping to himself, deep in thought, processing all that he had seen and learned throughout the day. Granier kept an eye on him but wasn't too concerned. The French army had guard units permanently stationed in and around the hotel. The hotel also had its own private security force that was not afraid to toss out anyone that even looked suspicious. Discord was not permitted at the Continental. The guests were shielded from the world outside its walls.

Seven blocks from the hotel, just outside the French Quarter, there was a bright flash followed immediately by a loud crack. "Fireworks?" said Patricia, hopefully.

"Grenade. Probably a local café or nightclub frequented by French soldiers. Beyond the French Quarter, the streets aren't safe at night."

"Why is the French Quarter safe?" said Bobby.

"The French army has roadblocks and checkpoints going in and out of the quarter plus roaming patrols that check I.D.s. It doesn't completely stop the terrorists, but it does slow them down."

"How can the French live with all this violence? Why not just go home to France where it is safe?"

"The French colonists believe this is their home, and they're willing to fight for it. It's like the West in America. It wasn't an easy life, and the settlers faced constant danger, but the West was where there was opportunity. A man could grow rich if he survived. The same is true with Indochina. It doesn't take much to start a business or plantation here. Labor is cheap, and the soil is fertile. The French government keeps taxes low to encourage colonists. Besides, the colonists have hope that once the Viet Minh are defeated, things will calm down."

"Will they calm down?" said John.

"Probably, for a time, at least. But defeating the Viet Minh is a big if. They're an elusive bunch. Good fighters too."

"You fought alongside them… the Viet Minh?" said Bobby.

"I trained some of them. In hindsight, that was not the best move, but at the time, I was following orders."

"So, you know their tactics?"

"Some of them. But the most important thing to remember about the Viet Minh is that they evolve. What was true yesterday may not be true today and may change again tomorrow. They don't have a rigid command structure or training procedures like western armies. They are far more flexible, and that makes them unpredictable."

"So, how do you fight an enemy that is ever-changing?"

"Very carefully."

Early the next morning, Granier and the Kennedys escorted by General De Lattre flew over the Mekong Delta region of Southern Indochina in a French-built, twin-engine NC702 Martinet. Patricia had insisted on riding in the rear of the aircraft, where the passenger windows were unobstructed by the wings and engines. She wanted to try out her new camera. John rode on the opposite side. De Lattre offered a verbal tour yelling above the noise from the engines in the unpressurized plane. "The battles in the Mekong Delta have mostly been hit and run type operations by the Viet Minh. Few have been larger than a company," said De Lattre. "They are really more of a nuisance rather than a threat to Saigon. The Mekong Delta is flat, which allows us to use our aircraft and artillery to great effect. We keep the pressure up, patrolling the villages and surrounding rice paddies. The most common attack is by mortar. It usually lasts two or three minutes then subsides when the culprits disappear into the countryside. They ambush our soldiers when our forces give chase. We lost a squad of sixteen just last week. But that is rare. The more likely outcome is that the Viet Minh lose more men than we do. That's been true with almost every battle in the war so far."

"Then it would seem it is just a matter of time until you wear their forces down?" said John.

"I wish it were that easy. The Viet Minh are replacing their losses far faster than we are. In fact, their army is growing each year, while we are restricted to the troops we already have in-country."

"I don't understand."

"The French government has placed a moratorium on French troops coming to Indochina. All replacements must be from the colonial troops."

"You mean from Indochina?"

"No. We can draw from any of our colonies. Our Moroccan, Tunisian, and Algerian troops are quite good fighters, but they do not have the experience or training of the French troops. Officers are the most difficult to replace."

The plane landed at Can Tho military airfield without incident. Another military band played as the Kennedys deplaned. "You French sure do love your bands," said John.

"Very much so," said De Lattre. "They lift the spirit."

"And draw attention," grunted Granier.

A convoy of soldiers and vehicles, including three armor cars, was waiting. "Monsieur Granier, you will ride with me," said De Lattre.

"And where do we ride?" said Patricia.

De Lattre motioned to one of the armored cars. "You've got to be kidding," said Patricia. "How am I supposed to shoot the countryside from within that tin can?"

"You are welcome to shoot through the gun portal. I had the machinegun removed for you," said De Lattre.

"Whose brilliant idea was this?" said John perturbed.

"Mine," said Granier. "A month ago, French General Chanson and the provincial governor were traveling in the area when a terrorist got close enough to throw a grenade through an open window of their car. They were both killed instantly along with their driver and bodyguard when the grenade exploded. The terrorist escaped unharmed. It's a bit overkill, I agree. But you'll be safe as long as you keep the hatches closed."

"Why aren't you going with us?" said Bobby.

"There is only room for three passengers," said Granier. "But I will be close."

"Arguing isn't going to get us there any quicker. Let's go," said John.

The Kennedys climbed into the armored car, and the driver started the engine. It was a very tight fit with little ventilation, making it more like an oven on wheels. All three Kennedys sweated profusely. The stiff suspension did not help John's back, and every pothole in the road sent a streak of pain up his spine.

Granier rode with De Lattre in a staff car. A mechanized platoon of colonial troops with a French officer escorted the convoy.

The convoy made its way across bridges and elevated roads that allowed vehicles to travel through the knee-deep marshes and rice paddies that dominated the Mekong Delta. Patricia was able to capture some footage of the countryside through the empty gun portal, as De Lattre had suggested but not without objection from John and Bobby. The portal was the only hole big enough to provide ventilation, and Patricia blocked the air whenever she put her camera in the portal. She kept her film shooting to a minimum.

The convoy stopped at a protected hamlet surround by a cocoa plantation. The trees were lined up in perfect rows and carefully tended by the villagers. The trees were their livelihood. Unfortunately, the orchard restricted the field of fire from the protected walls of the hamlet and made the enemy's approach more obscured. The French platoon took up defensive positions and checked the hamlet thoroughly before the all-clear was given, and the Kennedys were allowed to depart the armored car. Granier was waiting with three canteens of water and said, "They're safe. I drew the water from the hotel before we left."

The Kennedys drained the canteens in less than a

minute.

A watchtower protected the hamlet, and rows of wooden spears dug into the ground with the sharp points upward. It gave it a primitive, menacing look. There was only one road into the hamlet, and it was always guarded by two villagers armed with French submachineguns. One of the guards was roasting his lunch over a small fire - three skinned rats on wooden sticks stuck in the soil at an angle, so the meat was near the coals. Eating rats was widespread in the countryside. The rats mostly ate the farmers' crops, not garbage like the city rats. They were unusually healthy and without disease. The meat was dense, moist, and rich, almost sweet. A meal of roasted rat provided free protein to the villagers and reduced the damage to the crops.

Armed with modern Chinese weapons, the Viet Minh could easily overrun the village if determined, but it was safer just to go find another unprotected village to raid. In that sense, the program worked. But the hamlet could not protect the villagers that needed to get their harvest to market in Can Tho. The Viet Minh would wait until after the harvest, then attack the villagers on the road. That was why the Kennedys were brought to this particular hamlet. The previous week, the Viet Minh had ambushed three families traveling in a caravan along a dike. Three fathers, a mother carry a child, and a teenage boy, were killed. The harvest of cacao, a valuable commodity, was stolen, leaving the families without money for food.

Patricia filmed the interview performed by a translator as John and Bobby listened to the survivors. A woman holding a child spoke, and the translator told her story, "In the morning, my husband tried to convince more families to travel with us to market, but they were too scared. We had a late start. It was close to dark, and we had not reached the next village yet. That's when they attacked. My husband had a bow and arrows, but they were no match for the Viet Minh rifles. He was shot in the shoulder and could not fight. The other families ran away but were chased down by the Viet Minh. My children and I stayed with my husband. We were surrounded. They took my two sons for their army. I don't know if I will ever see them again."

"And your husband?" said the translator.

"They cut him with their knives until he died. They removed his head and stuck it on a pole to warn other villagers not to resist when the Viet Minh attacked. They took our harvest. Now, we will starve."

"What happened to the other families that ran off?"

"The fathers were killed like my husband, then they took the sons and raped the mothers and daughters."

Patricia was shocked by what she filmed. John and Bobby were uncomfortable and disturbed. Granier had heard it all before. This was the true face of war. The one that the politicians failed to mention when the war drums started beating.

As the interview wrapped up, De Lattre received an urgent radio call. When he was finished, he turned to John and said, "We have an opportunity if you wish. Our scouts report that a platoon of Viet Minh is approaching one of our outposts. If we hurry back to the plane, you may be able to see the battle unfold."

"Yes, we would like that very much," said John.

Granier was suspicious. It was very convenient that a battle was being fought so close and in broad daylight so the Kennedys could see it. He decided to keep his mouth shut until he could talk with John alone. The Kennedys thanked the villagers, and Patricia gave the woman who had lost her husband all the money she had in her purse. It was more money than her husband had made since they were married seventeen years ago. Without knowing it, Patricia had just made the woman the wealthiest person in the hamlet. Everyone piled back into the vehicles, and they took off for the airfield.

The battle was already in progress when the plane flew over the outpost. The French forces were well-entrenched with strong defensive positions along the road. A machinegun fired from a watchtower into a series of rice paddies between the road and the jungle where the Viet Minh were advancing. "We are in luck," said De Lattre. "It is very unusual for the Viet Minh to attack in daylight. They usually wait until dark when they can approach without being noticed. It could be the Viet Minh are a reconnaissance unit probing our defenses."

The battle was one-sided, with the well-protected French winning decisively as the Viet Minh charged from the tree line across the open rice paddies. Patricia filmed as much as she could, but it was difficult because of the plane's altitude. "Can we fly lower?"

"I am afraid not. The outpost commander may call in artillery strikes. We need to stay clear of the shells' trajectory," said De Lattre.

Granier watched through the window as two Viet Minh broke from the tree line and ran into the rice paddies. He was surprised to see them turn and fire back into the trees like an unseen enemy was chasing them. A well-placed French mortar shell killed both men when it slammed into the knee-deep water and exploded, sending a cascade of brown water and mud into the air along with deadly shards of shrapnel. Granier looked over at John, who was also watching through the window, and saw the two men die. Granier wondered if John understood the implication. John turned and looked at Granier like he was confused, trying to figure out what was going on. Granier just shook his head briefly, and John understood… it was a setup.

A French recon company had tracked the Viet Minh platoon in the jungle. Like a big game hunt, the French soldiers acted as beaters driving the Viet Minh in the direction of the outpost. When they exited the tree line, the Viet Minh came under fire from two sides - the outpost and the jungle. They never stood a chance and were gunned down to demonstrate French superiority to the Kennedys who were sure to report their finding to Washington.

CHAPTER TWELVE

The mist hanging over the Saigon River was breaking apart as the morning sun rose. Edmund Gullion, a veteran diplomat, and luminary working at the American embassy ate breakfast with John and Bobby Kennedy on the rooftop of the Majestic Hotel. The Majestic was considered the best hotel in Southeast Asia and offered its patrons a spectacular view of the Saigon River. Patricia, who kept her breakfast to a cup of coffee in an attempt to watch her figure, studied a sampan maneuvering its way upriver. Granier kept one eye on the doorway as he patrolled the edge of the patio, searching for trouble. There was none. It was too early. Terrorists rarely attacked before noon in Saigon.

John had wanted a candid conversation with Gullion away from the embassy. He had met Gullion previously and was impressed with his knowledge of foreign affairs. He was a fountain of information and seemed to have a handle on the real issues that faced

199

each country he served in. He was considered one of the few American experts on Indochina. John had a multitude of questions. No sooner would Gullion finish his thoughts on one subject than John would bombard him with the next question. John felt no guilt about interrupting Gullion if he didn't understand something he had said, or he wanted to dig deeper than what Gullion was offering on a subject. Gullion was delighted to see John so curious about Indochina and patiently answered his questions. "It's not that the French have done nothing during their stewardship of Indochina," said Gullion expanding on one of John's questions. "They've created an immense amount of infrastructure throughout the territories - railroads, highways, bridges, harbors, and airports. They built hospitals, schools, and hundreds of factories. But all of these benefits the French far more than the Vietnamese, Cambodians, or Laotians. What good is a highway if you cannot afford a car to drive on it? Or a hospital that charges more for a one night stay than the average citizen makes in a year? What the people of Indochina really want is land reform. Most are farmers and just want to make enough to support their families. The French have drained Indochina of its resources while leaving little behind for the people. It's no wonder they're losing the war."

"You believe that… that the French are losing?" said John.

"It's inevitable. The French are too few and the Indochinese too many."

"But not all the people of Indochina are against the French. There are many Vietnamese,

Cambodian, and Laotian soldiers fighting on the French side."

"Yes. For money. Money is the great equalizer in the third world. A man will do just about anything to feed his family, and that includes joining the army no matter what his loyalty to the government. Those soldiers don't want the French here. Nobody does except the Indochinese politicians and military leaders getting rich as the French turn a blind eye to their corruption."

"So, how do we stop the communists from taking over?"

"That's the real trick, isn't it? America doesn't want to see Colonialism or Communism prevail, and yet the French and the Viet Minh are the only ones with armies."

"Are you proposing that America get involved deeper and commit ground troops?"

"Oh, god no. That would be like throwing kerosene on a fire. In twenty years, there will be no more colonies. The French have lost. If we come in here and do the same thing, we will lose, too, for the same reason. There's no will or support for this kind of war back in Paris. The Homefront is lost. The same thing would happen to us. Once the French finally leave, one way or another, the real civil war will begin. It must be fought by the people that live here and not by outsiders looking for a proxy war. The people must decide their own fate if there is ever to be peace in Indochina."

"You make it sound like this war will go on for a decade or more."

"It will most likely."

"There is no hope for these people but war?" said Bobby, distraught.

"There is always hope," said Gullion.

"What might that be?" asked John.

Gullion studied the two brothers for a long moment as if he had a secret that he was determining if he should share. "A third force," said Gullion. "An army that is not beholden to the French and is anti-communist."

"Does one exist?"

"No. But many Indochinese soldiers and officers want to see an end to Colonialism but fear the communists. I believe they would fight for an independent Indochina if given the opportunity."

"Are you talking about a military coup against the French?"

"No. Not as such. Corruption is so ingrained in the Indochina military leadership. I doubt you could find anyone above a major that is not receiving money to keep things just the way they are."

"So, if not a coup, how does one form such an army?"

"I'm not sure. I suppose America could support such a movement instead of throwing millions of dollars down the French army's bottomless pit. But we would need to find a leader that the people would follow. I can certainly tell you that leader is not Boa Dai. He is far too closely associated with the French and not trusted by the populace."

Patricia watched as the family in the sampan frantically pushed something in the water away with their paddles as they passed. "Granier, have a look at this. Those people in the sampan... What are they pushing away with their paddles?" said Patricia.

Suspicious, Granier moved quickly and put himself between Patricia and the view of the river. "Patricia, do me a favor and go sit by your brothers," he said.

"What? Why?" said Patricia forcing her way past him and again looking out at the river.

With a final push from a paddle on the sampan, a headless torso bobbed to the surface of the river. Patricia gasped, "It's a man. Where's his head?"

"You don't need to see that," said Granier trying again to keep her from watching.

Bobby, John, and Gullion rushed over and looked out at the river. "Barbarians," said Bobby.

"Who would do such a thing?" said John.

"There are many. Could be the French secret police found another person suspected of being a communist or the Viet Minh assassinating a government official. But if I had to guess, I'd say it was a gang contract killing. The head is removed and presented to the person that paid for the murder," said Gullion.

"This happens a lot?" said John.

"Nightly, I am told. We are in another world where the rules of civilization do not always apply. You must be careful what you say in public and keep in mind who might be listening."

As they watched, five more headless bodies floated downriver. Bobby lost his breakfast.

As the Kennedys were leaving the Hotel Majestic, Patricia noticed a crowd gathered around a man in the lobby. She moved off to see who was behind the commotion. Granier, who often felt like he was herding cats, saw her moving away as John and Bobby were already heading out the front door. He decided the danger to John and Bobby was greater on the street than to Patricia in the well-guarded lobby. He called after Patricia. She turned. He pointed to the front door, hoping to coax her into rejoining the group. She smiled, nodded, and then proceeded to the crowd around the mysterious man as if ignoring Granier. Granier grunted and went outside.

As Patricia approached the small crowd, she saw the man, who she recognized as Graham Greene, the novelist. She pushed her way through the crowd and offered her hand to Greene as she said, "Mr. Greene, so good to see you again."

Greene, not recognizing the attractive American woman, looked slightly confused as he shook her hand. "I apologize, young lady, but I don't remember your name," said Greene.

"Patricia Kennedy. You may remember my father, Joseph Kennedy. His movie company, RKO Pictures, distributed your film The Fugitive."

"I remember. But it was hardly my film. I wrote the book that the studio screenwriters and executives massacred. In fact, I think your father still owes me a royalty check."

Patricia laughed, "He probably just forgot. Checks and birthdays are his Achilles' heel."

"How convenient."

"I would be happy to look into it if you wish?"

"No. I have an American law firm on retainer. It makes me feel more frugal when they actually earn my money. So, Patricia, what are you doing in Saigon?"

"I'm here making a documentary about my brother John's fact-finding tour of Indochina. He's a U.S. congressman."

"Fact-finding in Indochina? I wish him luck. Are you staying at the Majestic?"

"We're at the Continental."

"With the journalist riff-raff?"

"I'm surprised a journalist such as yourself refers to his colleagues as riff-raff."

"Ex-journalist. And I assure you, I too was riff-raff when I was a journalist. It goes with the territory."

"I'll remember that."

"Is this your first visit to Saigon?"

"Yes. It's fascinating. But I haven't had a chance to get out much because of security issues."

"Well, that's a shame. Saigon is the Pearl of the Orient. A young woman privileged enough to be here really shouldn't miss it."

"I'm doing my best."

"If you would allow me, I would be happy to show you around."

"Really?"

"Of course. I have a knight-in-shining-armor complex, and I always enjoy the company of intelligent young women. I'll ring you at the Continental once I have set it up."

"Thank you. That would be great. I'd love to stay and chat, but I imagine my brothers are waiting."

"It's been a pleasure. I hope to see you soon," said Greene kissing her white-gloved hand. Patricia blushed at the attention, then trotted off through the hotel's front door.

The Kennedys sat in the Continental's patio café, having lunch. The walls were painted pale yellow, and the shutters green. Shades made of thin bamboo strips blocked the sun's rays. The tables and chairs were made of wicker, allowing air to flow while keeping the guests cool. Waiters in white served tall glasses of iced tea and club sandwiches. Busboys in black cleaned the dirty tables. Electric fans spun slowly overhead. The café was buzzing with conversations of business and gossip. Only the journalists staying at the hotel talked about the latest battles and military strategies. Everyone else just wanted to forget there was a war on.

Palm trees planted in porcelain pots lined the café's perimeter, separating the guests from the surrounding street and sidewalk. Women stood on the other side of the palm tree barrier, hoping to interest the guests with their tourist trinkets and color postcards. Their merchandise was hung on long poles that could be slipped through the palm tree barrier for the guests to see if they even glanced in the vendor's direction. The hotel security force did regular rounds outside of the hotel and chased off the vendors every half hour. The vendors would return once the security guards were out of sight, and their sales efforts would continue.

Granier didn't like any of it. They were too close to the street. An easy grenade-toss away from a terrorist. His eyes surveyed the street and sidewalk for threats. He had argued his point, but John had insisted they all needed a change from the rich food served on the rooftop restaurant. The veranda café served simple lunch plates, and the drinks were refreshing, not too sweet like the fancy cocktails on the rooftop restaurant. Granier considered admonishing John about security but decided it would do little good. It was hard to argue with a well-known war hero. "I feel like we are wasting our time," said John. "The French are not as forthcoming as I had hoped. We need to find the truth behind what is happening here before we leave."

"I've got an idea about that," said Bobby. "I've been developing a list of foreign journalists working in Saigon. I thought we could track them down and get their opinion on the war."

"You think they would talk to us?"

"Maybe. Especially if you could give them material for a story of their own."

"Quid pro quo?"

"More like swapping baseball cards."

"Alright. But we should look for journalists with different opinions. I'm not looking for parrots spouting the French government's agenda. We want the best of the best."

"I can do that."

"I think we should try and find them in their homes rather than their workplace where they might be watched."

"What do you think, Granier?"

"I suppose it would be okay as long as you meet them inside away from the street," said Granier, not bothering to look over at John and the others, keeping his eyes on the surrounding area and passersby.

"It's settled then."

"Let me see if I can set up some interviews," said Bobby excusing himself from the table.

"John, I just want to let you know that I will be gone tomorrow," said Patricia.

"Gone? Gone where?" said Granier jumping in.

"Graham Greene has offered to take me on a tour of Saigon."

"Why wasn't I told about this?"

"I'm telling you now."

"Did he give you some sort of itinerary?"

"Nope. It's a surprise."

"What kind of security has he arranged?"

"He didn't. I did. One of the hotel's private security guards is going to accompany us."

"I wouldn't call that security."

"I'm sure you would do a much better job, but you need to be with Bobby and John. I can take care of myself, remember?"

"Let me at least talk to the security guard."

"Of course. But I'm going. How often does a girl get an invitation from an author like Graham Greene?"

"You know, he has quite a reputation as a lady's man," said John.

"Look who's calling the kettle black."

"She'll be fine, Granier. She's got claws and knows how to use them."

"I still don't like it," said Granier with a grunt, and he once again surveyed the surrounding area. He turned his head slowly like a submarine's periscope and suddenly stopped... And there she was again –

Spitting Woman – standing in the park across from the hotel staring straight at him, unmoving, her eyes beckoning him like a wolf calls for her mate.

Granier was frozen. Emotions flooded his mind, confusing him.

She waited a long moment, then turned and walked deeper into the park. "No. Not again," said Granier panicking.

"What's wrong?" said Patricia looking in the direction he was looking, seeing the woman walking away. "Is that her?"

"Stay in the hotel. Make sure nobody leaves until I return," said Granier squeezing past the palm tree planters around the café perimeter.

"Good luck catching her," said Patricia.

"Catching who?" said Bobby watching Granier run across the street. "Where's he going?"

"Never mind, Mr. Noisy," she said. "You wouldn't understand anyway."

Granier ran into the park and spotted Spitting Woman on the opposite end, walking across the street into an alley. He ran after her. She moved into the alley and disappeared between the buildings. He picked up his pace, his leg pumping. He ran across the street. A trishaw passed in front of him, blocking his way. The driver slowed his bike and turned his head, thinking the American wanted a ride. Granier leaped into the empty passenger area and out the other side.

He ran into the alley. It was filled with food vendors and customers, grabbing a bite to eat. He pushed his way through the crowd, searching for

Spitting Woman. She was nowhere in sight. Just when he was about to give up hope, he saw her again turning down a side alley. He picked up speed, pushing madly through the crowd, knocking people over as they ate. He turned down the side alley and saw her again further in. The alley was like a snake with uneven curves and bends. She turned again and again. Each time he lost sight of her only to regain it after a few moments. "Wait," he yelled.

She didn't respond but turned down yet another alley. He ran after her. When he turned the corner down the alley, he saw a man standing with a pistol aimed straight at his head. Spitting Woman was behind the man starring straight at him. "You, bitch," said Granier, frozen in his tracks.

There was no place to dive for cover. The gunman had him dead to rights. Granier slowly reached into his pocket, holding the pistol. The odds of him drawing and firing before the gunman fired were slim to none. Two more men moved up behind him. They grabbed him by the arms. His instinct took over, and he struggled with them. Spitting Women yelped as if not wanting him to get hurt by the men. The gunman stepped forward and hit Granier on the forehead with the butt of the pistol. Granier went limp in the men's arms, out cold. They dragged him deeper into the alley.

Granier woke. His head was throbbing. He was lying on the wooden floor of a room devoid of furnishings. A man holding a pistol was standing in front of him. "I apologize for the bump on your head," said the man. "My men had firm instructions not to hurt you."

"Yeah, I guess they didn't hear you," said Granier getting up slowly, wincing as he touched the bump on his forehead. "That's gonna bruise."

"I imagine. Again, my apologies."

"Where is she?"

"Safe."

"I wanna talk to her."

"She doesn't want to talk with you. Besides, you were brought here to talk to me."

"And who the hell are you?"

"My name is Zhou Youyong."

"That ain't a Vietnamese name."

"No, it's not. It's Chinese. You may call me Mr. Zhou."

"Why don't I just call you Shithead if it's all the same?"

"If it is your pleasure."

"It is... my pleasure. So, Shithead, why the elaborate game of cat and mouse?"

"We needed to speak."

"So, speak... Shithead."

"I work for Ho Chi Minh."

"I figured as much. How is Uncle these days?"

"Alive and well... and concerned."

"Concerned?"

"For you, in fact. He said he once considered you a friend... an ally even."

"Yeah, well... he has a strange way of treating friends."

"I have heard the story of your capture by the Japanese."

"Let's leave out the recap and cut to the chase.

What do you want? Or what does Ho want?"

"To warn you."

"Warn me. That's rich. Warn me about what?"

"Your life and the life of Congressman Kennedy are in danger."

"Really? By who?"

"By those that have the most to gain from Kennedy's death."

"Why does Ho want to kill Kennedy?"

"He doesn't. He has nothing to gain and everything to lose from the death of Kennedy, especially if it appears that the Viet Minh killed him. I ask again… who has the most to gain from Kennedy's death?"

"You're telling me the French want to kill the Congressman?"

"If Kennedy is perceived to be killed by the Viet Minh, the American President will have no choice but to seek revenge. Your people will demand it, and America will enter the war on the side of the French."

"Bullshit."

"Perhaps… perhaps not. Either way, I have done my duty and delivered the message. It is up to you what you do with it. Uncle Ho now feels he has offered amends for the misunderstanding between you and him."

"He's saying we're even?"

"Yes."

"Not hardly."

"Nevertheless, our business is concluded. You may go."

"I want to see the woman."

"No. She has done what was asked of her. I will

not oblige her further."

"Fine. Just tell her… just tell her I'm sorry things worked out the way they did."

"I will deliver your message."

"Thanks, Shithead… I mean, Mr. Zhou," said Granier leaving the room.

Granier, Bobby, and John rode in a taxi through a quiet neighborhood. Granier had a bandage over the lump on his forehead. He wasn't sure if he was going to tell the Kennedys about Mr. Zhou's warning. He wasn't sure if the threat was real or what more could be done if it was real. He needed time to think it through and decide on a strategy.

The driver pulled up to a small bungalow-style house surrounded by a well-trimmed garden and a pond with floating lilies and purple flowers. Orange and white koi swarmed in the green water, thinking it was feeding time as Granier and the Kennedys passed. "Sorry, guys. Maybe next time," said John.

Bobby knocked on the front door. Ngoc, a young Vietnamese woman dressed in a yellow ao dai, answered. "I'm sorry. I think we have the wrong house," said Bobby.

"Want Anderson?" said the woman in broken English.

"Yes. We're looking for Bill Anderson. Does he live here?" said Bobby.

The woman stepped to one side and motioned with a sweep of her hand that they should enter. They walked in and followed her into another room where Bill Anderson, an Associated Press journalist, was talking on a phone with his editor. "Tom, this is definitely front-page stuff. The French are saying they killed several thousand Viet Minh in the battle, and that's not counting wounded or prisoners. It's the first time the French used napalm. Yeah, it's that fiery gelatin developed for flame throwers. Sticks to anything. Hard to put out. We've got photos of a couple of prisoners. Damn near made me lose my lunch when I first saw 'em," said Anderson seeing Granier and the Kennedys waiting. "Tom, let me call you back. I've got Congressman John F. Kennedy standing in my den. Yeah, that John Kennedy."

Anderson hung up the phone and said, "Congressman Kennedy, it's a pleasure to meet you. It's not often I have a war hero visit my home."

"I was just doing my duty like everyone else," said John shaking his hand. "This is my brother Bobby and our advisor Rene Granier."

"We spoke on the phone," said Bobby shaking Anderson's hand. "Thanks for giving us some of your time."

"No problem. I hope you like finger sandwiches. Ngoc's been cutting the crust off bread half the morning."

"Ngoc is your cook?" said Bobby.

"Ah, no. Ngoc is my Congaie," said Anderson. "She lives here with me like an arranged girlfriend. I take care of her, and she takes care of me. She keeps the house spotless and makes the best pho you've ever tasted, plus she cooks a few western dishes."

Anderson turned to Ngoc and said a couple of sentences in Vietnamese. She bowed to Anderson, then to Granier, Bobby, and John. They bowed back. "Ah, you're all older than her. You're not supposed to bow," said Anderson. "It'll just confuse her."

"Oh, sorry," said John.

"Don't worry about it. I made hundreds of mistakes when we first started living together. I gave her some perfume, and she burst into tears. She thought I was saying she smelled bad. Have a seat and make yourselves at home."

They sat. "If you don't mind, I know your time is limited. I'd like to jump right in with some questions," said John.

"Sure. Go right ahead."

"You were embedded with a French engineering company?"

"Yeah. Just outside of Hoi An. They were rebuilding a bridge that the Viet Minh had blown up. They also built a watchtower to prevent future attacks."

"Do they work... watchtowers?"

"Sure. The Viet Minh won't blow up the bridge. They blow up the watchtower instead, anything to get even with the French soldiers. Both sides can be quite vindictive and ghastly in their revenge. I've seen it firsthand. I don't need to see it again. Not ever. War is the stuff of nightmares."

"Amen," said John. "You were attacked at your base camp?"

"Yeah. An entire Viet Minh company against a platoon of French engineers. They came at us in the middle of the night so that we couldn't call in an airstrike. Fortunately, we were within the range of an artillery battery of 105's. We just hunkered down and let the arti-boys hammer 'em. That's the way the French like to fight. Defensive. Let the big guns wear down the enemy, then counter-attack when they're too stunned to fight back."

"And that's an effective strategy... hunkering down?"

"It is if you're trying not to get killed. But it ain't gonna win the war."

"So, you think the French are going to lose?"

"Yeah, I do. But it'll take some time. The French are stubborn and hate to lose face. Of course, everything could change if America decides to get involved."

"If America gets involved, you think the French and the Americans together could beat the Viet Minh?"

"Sure. As long as the Chinese and Russians stay out of it."

"And if they don't?"

"Well then... we've got World War III, and everybody dies."

"Let's say for the moment that the big nations stay out of the fight. Is there any way the French can beat the Viet Minh?"

"I doubt it. No matter what the French commanders tell you, the Vietnamese people are against them. The Vietnamese want the French out, and they refuse to follow Bo Dai. He's a French puppet, and the people know it. If there were a national election today, Ho Chi Minh would win it by 70% or better. How do you win a war when 70% of the country is against you? It's not possible. Eventually, the French are going to withdraw. It's just a matter of time and pain."

"So, why do you think America entering the war

would make a difference?"

"The Vietnamese like Americans. They see them as kindred spirits. Revolutionaries like themselves. But that will change soon enough. You can already feel it. You can see it in their eyes when you walk down the street."

Ngoc entered with a tea tray and a plate stacked with enough finger sandwiches to feed a small army. Bobby couldn't help but stare at her face as she set the tray down on the serving table in front of him. She was so beautiful and young. She couldn't be more than sixteen or seventeen. Her skin was smooth without blemish and her slender figure like that of a young woman. He couldn't figure out if he was more disgusted or jealous.

Greene was disappointed when Patricia showed up in his hotel lobby with a bodyguard in tow. It wasn't that he, twenty years her senior, planned to seduce her. It was that Patricia, like most young women, could be easily impressed, and one never knew where that might lead. Patricia explained that her brother had insisted on extra security. Greene had no choice at that point and decided to make the best of it. He had arranged for one of the hotel's limousines to take them around the city. The bodyguard rode next to the driver while Patricia and Greene rode in back. Patricia seemed quite accustomed to riding in a limousine. After all, she was the daughter of a multi-millionaire.

Just outside the French Quarter, a crowd gathered around a portable shadow-puppet theatre. The patrons waiting for the show blocked part of the busy street, snarling traffic. Only trishaws, motorbikes, and bicycles forced their way through by gently tapping pedestrians with their front wheels until they moved aside, creating a path. Once the small vehicle passed, the hole closed back up as the crowd surged forward. The car that Greene had arranged was stuck behind a delivery truck stacked with sacks of rice well beyond its wooden side-gates, giving it the impression that it could tip over during a sharp turn or emergency swerve. They were not moving.

Seeing that their car would be unable to drive past until the show was over, Greene and Patricia decided to join the audience. They exited the vehicle with Patricia's bodyguard. The bodyguard pushed his way through the crowd, followed by Greene and Patricia until they could see the theatre.

The theatre's tiny stage was deep, blocking out the sun. There was a thin rice paper screen in the back. The puppeteers stood behind and to each side of the screen. Four candles a few feet back from the screen produced the required illumination to create the shadows.

The scenery was cut out of paper and fixed in place on a stand directly behind the screen while the paper puppets were fixed on the end of sticks and operated by the puppeteers. The puppets were extremely detailed, giving them distinct personalities and character traits. A single character had several paper puppets, each showing action or holding an item such as a sword or lantern. At the end of each scene, the curtain would close, and the scenery would be swapped out. Speed between scenes was essential so as not to lose the audience. A small three-piece band accompanied the performance and entertained the crowd between the scenes. When the curtain opened, new characters and scenery would appear, and the story would continue.

Patricia was delighted watching the shadow puppets come to life. The storyline was easy to follow; no understanding of Vietnamese was required. Near the end of the performance, two women pushed their way through the audience, soliciting tips by carrying conical hats flipped upside down.

A man in the crowd removed his hat and moved through the crowd collecting tips as if he was part of the performance. "I think he's stealing their tips," said Patricia. Greene motioned to the bodyguard and said something in Vietnamese. The guard grabbed the man by his shirt as he went by and punched him in the face until he surrendered his hat. The bodyguard took the hat and handed it to another audience member. "Wait," said Patricia, opening her purse and placing several large Vietnamese bills in the hat. "Okay."

The hat was passed overhead until it reached one of the women collecting tips. She poured the contents into her hat and handed the empty hat back to the audience. She smiled and bowed her head at the American lady that had given the performers such a big tip. Her tip would feed them well for a month and pay for several boxes of candles. The hat was passed back to the thief, who then slunk away grateful that he still had his hat. The angry audience slapped and kicked him as he passed. The few police that patrolled outside the French neighborhoods rarely interfered in the daily lives of the Vietnamese. The citizens dealt out their own brand of justice. It was fast and surprisingly effective. As long as nobody was murdered, the police stayed out of it.

When the performance ended, everyone clapped and cheered as the performers emerged from behind the curtains with their paper puppets in hand. Those that wished examined the intricate puppets up close and praised the performers that dedicated their lives to the ancient art form.

As the audience broke up, Greene and Patricia followed the bodyguard as he made a path through the crowd. They climbed back in the car and were on their way once again.

The car pulled up in front of a temple complex, and the passengers stepped out. The roof was multi-layered and covered with green tiles, while the walls were pink. Paper lanterns hung from the building's beams and on wires strung across the front courtyard like a legion of red jellyfish with golden tentacles. "This is Chua Ngoc Hoang nicknamed the Jade Emperor Pagoda. It's Taoist," said Greene as they passed through the front gate.

"Is it made of jade?" said Patricia.

"Heavens, no. That would be too costly and would probably be pilfered. The jade refers to the green ceramic tiles on the roof and used to decorate the interior walls."

Inside the outer walls, the complex was beautiful but felt cramped, swamped with praying worshipers holding candles and incense as they bowed toward the stone statues of legendary Taoist monks.

Worshippers touched the statues, then tapped their foreheads for luck. A large brass cauldron filled with sand and capped with a stone pagoda gave the parishioners a place to plant their burning incense sticks. There was a thick layer of heavily-scented smoke that choked the two Americans and made them constantly cough during their visit.

Toward the front of the complex, Patricia leaned over the wall of a tortoise pond and fed the reptiles bits of bread from a bag Greene had purchased for her. The pit stank of turtle shit as if it had not been cleaned in a year, but the turtles didn't seem to mind.

Two stone lions guarded the actual temple. The walls were scenic carvings retelling the ancient legends of the Taoists. The front doors of the temple were brass that had turned a dark brown over time. Greene and Patricia removed their shoes and entered the temple. The bodyguard kept watch at the doorway. The interior of the temple felt even more claustrophobic, with walls dividing the space into separate rooms, each with a specific function and filled with statues and glass-caged relics. The layer of burning incense was even heavier inside, and their eyes watered.

In one room, worshippers petted a lacquered statue of the emperor's horse, touching the horse's head, then patting their own heads as if transferring the good luck that emanated from the statue.

In another room, dozens of ceramic dolls surrounded a small statue of the emperor who built the temple. The dolls were covered with colorful handmade robes and adorned with fresh flowers.

In the main room, the Buddha statue in the center

of the altar was covered with a glass enclosure to prevent pilfering of the gold flake that covered it. Worshippers knelt and bowed to touch their foreheads on the wooden floor as they prayed. Some wept in supplication for sick relatives, hoping their god would hear their pleas.

Next, Greene took Patricia to an umbrella factory. The umbrellas were made of bamboo stripes covered in colorful lacquer. The workers, mostly women, painted the strips of bamboo first, then assembled the bamboo into stunning designs that would sell like hotcakes to the Western tourists. When completed, the umbrellas were placed in a courtyard to dry in the sun. Hundreds of umbrellas covered the ground and made a vivid scene. At the tourist shop inside the factory, Patricia bought umbrellas for each of her sisters and her mother. She knew that her mother would not approve because the gift was Asian, but Patricia didn't care. In her mind, it was the thought that she had brought a beautiful, handmade craft halfway around the world that counted.

Greene and Patricia ate a late lunch at Dong Bac Dumpling House. It was a local hangout being taken over by Westerners. Before sitting down, they watched two ladies gossiping and laughing as they made dumplings near the front of the restaurant. The dumplings were stuffed with duck, pork, crab, and flavored soy paste, then steamed, sautéed, or boiled depending on the customers' orders.

Sitting down at the wooden tables covered with plastic tablecloths, they each ordered a beer with their dumplings. Greene ordered a variety of dumplings so Patricia could try the different types. Her moans of pleasure after each sampling told Greene he was on the right track. As they ate, Greene asked, "So, how am I doing as a tour guide?"

"Great. I loved the umbrella factory," said Patricia.

"I imagine. I think you bought half their inventory."

"One cannot travel to Asia without gifts for the family. It would be beyond rude."

"Well, we can't have that."

"I must admit, I thought you would take me to some of the darker parts of Saigon."

"And are you disappointed that I haven't?"

"A little, I guess. I feel like one cannot understand the Vietnamese or the French without seeing what they do after the sun sets."

"The day is still young. What would you like to see?"

"I don't know. I've traveled quite a bit, but usually with a member of my family or girlfriends from school."

"I see. A sheltered life."

"Exactly. I'm twenty-one now, and I feel like I'm ready to stretch my wings a bit."

"Let me see what kind of trouble I can drum up."

"Within reason."

"Of course. I'm sure you will tell me when I cross the line."

"Great!" said Patricia popping a dumpling in her mouth.

Granier, John, and Bobby stepped from a taxi. A French nun led a group of young girls, both Vietnamese and French, past them. Several of the girls giggled on seeing the handsome Americans. The nun at the end of the line snapped her fingers. The girls immediately stopped giggling and averted their eyes as they continued past the Americans.

With the sidewalk clear, the Kennedys entered an apartment building. Granier stayed outside and kept watch.

John struggled as they climbed two flights of stairs, fighting the pain in his back. He was far from being a weak man and looked as if he was in great shape. As always, he ignored the pain.

Seated at the kitchen table in her Saigon apartment, Brigitte Friang banged out an article for her employer, a French magazine, on her portable typewriter. In the corner by the window was an elaborate wooden cage containing an exotic bird that fluttered its wings, hoping to find an escape. There was none.

There was a knock at the door. Brigitte continued typing until she had finished her thought. She walked to the front door and placed her foot six inches behind the door before opening it to prevent anyone from forcing their way in.

In the hallway stood the Kennedy brothers. "Mademoiselle Friang, my name is Bobby Kennedy. We spoke on the phone earlier. This is my brother Jack," said Bobby motioning to John.

"Yes, yes. The American congressman. Please come in," said Brigitte stepping aside.

"It is a pleasure to meet you, Mademoiselle," said John with a big grin and hearty handshake.

They sat in the living room where Brigitte served coffee and biscuits. "I understand you have just returned from Paris where you were training with the paratroopers," said John.

"Yes. It seems these days, if one wishes to see the beginnings of a battle, one must jump."

"Bit dangerous, isn't it?"

"Parachuting?"

"No. Reporting on a battle."

"It is a job like any other."

"I've seen battle. It is hardly just another job."

"Perhaps, but it is important that the people know the truth about war and why our soldiers are fighting."

"I'm glad you said that. I feel the same… about the truth."

"Ah, we get right to the point."

"Were you expecting more pleasantries?"

"Expecting… yes. Desiring… no. I appreciate your frankness. And since we are being frank, I must tell you that I am a patriot. I love my country, and I believe in what we are doing here in Indochina."

"I would not value your opinion if it was otherwise."

"Alright. So, how may I help you, Congressman?"

"I was hoping to get your perspective on the French opinion of the war," said John.

"The French are sick of war, just as you would expect. The Nazis left my country in ruins, our wealth and treasures plundered. But the French will not shirk from the task at hand – rebuilding our country and our empire."

"Even at the cost of more French blood?"

"It is never easy to see one's countrymen die, especially in a land so far from home. But yes, the French know the cost of war like no other people. We understand the sacrifices that must be made to retain one's honor."

"And that is the way the French see it – a point of honor?"

"Indochina is part of France. We cannot just surrender something so precious and expect the world to respect our nation. One must fight for the things one believes in. May I ask you a question, Congressman?"

"Of course."

"Why does America not support its oldest ally?"

"We do. But there is great need all over the world, especially in Europe with the Soviet threat of expansionism. Our resources only go so far."

"You give money to rebuild Germany and Japan, the very countries that caused all the destruction. Why?"

"To prevent the next war. You're an intelligent woman, Mademoiselle Friang. Surely, you understand the mistakes of World War One and the Treaty of Versailles."

"Avoiding punitive damages is one thing, but rebuilding their countries before those of your allies?"

"We are helping France too."

"You give almost nothing to help us fight the communists in Indochina."

"That's not true. And I am sure America would

give a lot more if France would agree to grant Indochina true independence."

"You speak of independence. America would not even be a country if it wasn't for France coming to your aid during your fight against the British."

"And France would still be under the German thumb if it wasn't for America coming to your aid."

"Let's call it even, shall we?" said Bobby jumping in.

"No, no. I am happy to debate Mademoiselle Friang on American policy."

"Yes, but that is not why we are here, Jack."

"Of course. You're right."

"I am happy to see an American with such passion," said Brigitte. "The French love to discuss such things. It is part of our culture."

"Americans too, but perhaps not with such zeal. We Kennedys are Irish. Zeal is in our blood."

Brigitte smiled. "Look, you want to know how the French feel about the war in Indochina. The truth is most don't even know where Indochina is located on a map. The politicians do their best to keep the people focused on other issues. They have passed a law that prevents more French soldiers from being sent overseas to fight. They bury the cost of the war deep in the defense budget, so not even an accountant can find it. Any news from the war zone is heavily censored to only show success on the battlefields. You would learn more about the French war from picking up the London Times than Le Monde."

"As a journalist, that must stoke your ire."

"No. I agree. The French people have suffered

enough. Let them be oblivious... for a while, at least. To catch their breath, if you will. In the meantime, our leaders must do what is necessary to save our empire and return our nation to its rightful place as a world power."

"No matter the cost?"

"Unlike the Americans, the French do not see money as the most important factor. Honor and duty are held more dear than the franc and dollar. Besides, as I understand it, America is increasing its financial and military aid substantially."

"So far, yes."

"So far?"

"America sees Indochina as an investment to stave off Communism and keep Southeast Asia free. But like all good investments, we must ensure its stability. That is why I am here. To find the truth."

"So it is you that will determine the fate of France?"

"Nothing so grandiose. I'm a congressman. One voice in a house full of very loud men and a few women. But like you, I am a patriot, and I will do my best to serve my country."

They continued to talk for several more hours. Brigitte was a human encyclopedia of French policy and culture. She also knew a considerable amount about French military strategy and tactics. John and Bobby gulped down the information like hungry children eating ice cream. They wanted to know everything. It was only when their minds were so full that they couldn't think straight that they finally relented and allowed Brigitte to get back to her writing.

Outside Brigitte's apartment building, Granier stood near the front doorway, eyeing anyone who entered the building to determine if they were a threat. John had insisted on his brother and him talking with Brigitte alone. He didn't want it to seem like the Americans were ganging up on the woman and thought a more intimate setting would be more conducive to the truth. It was getting late in the afternoon, and Granier was growing concerned about the Kennedys traveling at night. Even in the French quarter, Viet Minh terrorists passing on motorbikes were known for attacking westerners. Grenades were their weapons of choice, with semiautomatic pistols a close second.

As the Kennedys exited the building, Bobby saw a taxi in the distance. He whistled loudly and waved his hands. The driver saw him and turned down the street. Granier didn't like the attention but thought the sooner they were out of the area, the safer the Kennedys would be. They climbed into the cab and took off.

It was past sundown, and Saigon came alive with paper lanterns and streetlamps. The limousine was moving slowly down a side street in a bottleneck of trishaws, handcarts, and pedestrians. Impatient, Greene barked out orders to the driver as if it would help speed things up. It didn't. "I'm sorry about this. We seem to be going nowhere fast again," said Greene.

"It's fine. I'm enjoying the culture like a goldfish in a glass bowl," said Patricia staring out the car window.

"We're fairly close to our destination. I'd say let's get out and walk, but this isn't the best neighborhood. The war has made a real mess of things."

"About that… the war. Do you think the French are right protecting their empire?"

"No. Of course not. Their empire is dead. The French just refuse to accept it."

"And the British empire?

"Completely different. Alive and well."

"Really? That's a bit hypocritical, isn't it?"

"Of course. I'm British," he said with a grin.

"So, you think the French will lose?"

"Eventually. Soldiers can only go so far to keep order. If the majority of the population wants freedom and are willing to fight for it, it's impossible to stop them. Simple numbers game, really - 28 million Vietnamese against 1 million French colonists. Of course, all bets are off if you Americans get involved."

"You think we will get involved?"

"It is your nature to stick your nose in other people's business."

"That's a bit harsh."

"But true."

"We sure saved the British bacon against the Nazis… France too."

"You make my point. I don't doubt that America is exceptional. I just get tired of Americans going around and reminding everyone in the world of that fact."

"So, what are we supposed to do, just sit back and watch the communists take over the world?"

"It wouldn't be so bad, would it? Americans fear what they don't understand, and they do their best not to understand anything. They just do what they think is right and bully everyone else into going the same way."

"So, you think Ho Chi Minh is right?"

"I don't know the man, so how can I possibly have an opinion about what he is thinking? However, if you are asking if I think Communism is right for Vietnam, then yes. Look at what Capitalism has done to them. The people are starving."

"Colonialism is not Capitalism."

"Now, you're just being naïve. Colonialism is the ultimate form of Capitalism. The rich and powerful preying on the poor and weak."

"You honestly believe that the French have done nothing to help the people of Indochina?"

"No. But roads and bridges are a bad tradeoff for starvation, wouldn't you say?"

"What about culture and religion?"

"What about them? The Indochinese had been getting along just fine without them before the French came to their shores. Western countries always assume their culture is the best because they are more advanced. But is it really? Look at the Crusades and the Inquisition. Hardly examples of humane ethics."

"I've heard that argument before. It lacks context."

"Alright. How about this? The Indochinese are mostly Buddhist and seek harmony and peace. That's why they were so easy to conquer by the French in the first place. Why do we want to change

231

that? In the name of progress? No. We want to subjugate them. Changing their culture and religion is the best way to do that."

"I think subjugation was far from the minds of the first Catholic missionaries that came to Indochina. Their intentions were pure. They wanted to bring Indochina into the fold of Christianity."

"Perhaps in the beginning. Now, the Catholic priests create their own armies to protect their treasures and churches."

"…and their parishioners."

"If you say so. But if you look closely, I think you will find it is more of the former and less of the latter."

"Your vision of the world is filled with a great deal of skepticism."

"I'm a writer. I think about things."

"And I don't?"

"You're young. You are still finding your way. It's natural to believe what our parents taught us. It's where we all start, but not where we must end up."

"I will never be a communist… or a Buddhist for that matter."

"Good. The world needs different points of view."

The car pulled to a stop in front of a well-worn building without windows. "Ah, we're finally here," said Greene opening the door and stepping out.

Patricia didn't move. "Are you coming? You wanted to see the dark side of Saigon."

She still didn't move. "Just because we don't see eye to eyes doesn't mean I don't like you. On the contrary, you're an intelligent young woman with an opinion. I think you have a lot to learn and experience. But we all do when we start our journey of trying to understand the world."

"And you are condescending."

"Yes. But I still like you."

Greene offered his hand, inviting her to join him. "What is this place?" she said, surveying at the building.

"Only one way to find out," he said, raising an eyebrow.

Patricia was more curious than she was mad. Greene was an intellectual bully, but he was fascinating. She took his hand and stepped out of the car. They walked to the front doors, and Greene knocked. The door opened, and a large Vietnamese man blocked the entrance. Greene simply smiled. The man recognized him, bowed, and stepped aside. They entered.

It was a gambling parlor. The interior was completely different from the exterior. It was posh, decorated in a Chinese-style with lots of dragons, cranes, and koi on the walls and ceilings. Blue porcelain vases with gold inlays were placed around the rooms. Silk lanterns hung from the beams. The furniture was beautifully carved from exotic wood and covered with golden silk fabric. It was a two-story building with balconies overlooking betting tables where gamblers on the second floor could lower their bets with baskets on strings to the dealers below. The patrons were a mix of rich Asians and Westerners, most dressed in suits and long dresses. It was loud, which forced people to shout to be heard and only added to the noise. "It's like Monte Carlo," said Patricia.

"Yes. Do you gamble?" said Greene.

"I'm not sure. I just turned 21."

"Well, if you place a bet, then you gamble."

"How do I do it... bet?"

"First, you have to pick a game of chance. I suggest Bau Cua Tom Ca. It's simple," said Greene pointing to a table. "There are six images - a fish, a prawn, a crab, a rooster, a calabash gourd, and a stag – on the table. You put a bet down on one or more. The dealer rolls three six-sided dice with matching images. If your image comes up, you win. It's a Vietnamese version of fish-pawn-crab originally from China."

"I gave away all my money at the puppet theatre."

"Here. Let me contribute to education in debauchery," he said, handing her some French coins.

"Is this legal?" she said, placing a bet.

"No. But it is allowed."

The dice rolled. Patricia won. She was hooked. It gave Greene great pleasure to see the young woman enjoying herself. When she lost, he gave her more money. It wasn't that he wanted to corrupt her; he just wanted her to see the other side of the world where polite company dare not tread. He believed it would make her more interesting and introspective, especially for the daughter of American tycoon Joseph Kennedy and the sister of a congressman.

It was late, and the curfew was approaching. The crowds and traffic had thinned out considerably. The limousine drove through another Vietnamese neighborhood. The bodyguard kept watch for threats as they traveled. "I could have done without the cockfight. Those poor chickens," said Patricia.

"Roosters, actually," said Greene. "Your conscience didn't prevent you from picking the winner."

"No. I spent a lot of time on our horse farm when I was young. I learned to be a good judge of animals."

"A handy skill, especially in Saigon."

"I should give you the winnings. It was your money anyway," she said, opening her purse and pulling out a wad of French bills.

"Please keep your winnings. I insist. Buy something to remember the experience. That's the important thing... remembering."

"Alright. So, where to next?"

"You will be going back to your hotel for a good night's sleep."

"That's it? That's the dark side?"

"Not all of it, no. But enough for today. We malefactors must pace ourselves."

The car pulled to a stop in front of another nondescript building. Greene opened the door and stepped out. "I hope you've enjoyed your tour."

"I did immensely. Thank you."

"Anything for a fellow evildoer."

"Where are you going?"

"Dreamland," said Greene with a smile.

"Can I come with you?"

"Not this time. I am sure I shall see you again. Perhaps breakfast before you leave."

"That would be lovely."

"Well, goodnight," said Greene closing the door and moving off to a doorway.

The car drove off. Patricia watched through the

back window as Greene knocked on the door, and a woman appeared. She recognized him and stood aside. He walked in, and the door was closed. "Wait," said Patricia.

The car rolled to a stop. Patricia got out. The bodyguard also got out. "No. I'll go alone. Stay here. I shall only be a few minutes," said Patricia.

She walked to the door and knocked. The woman answered and looked at her through the doorway. The woman shook her head and started to close the door. "Wait," said Patricia reaching into her purse and pulling out her winnings to show the woman.

The woman thought for a moment, then stepped aside and let Patricia enter.

The interior was thick with a greyish-brown smoke that hung like a layer of mountain fog. It was dark. The only light came from small lamps sitting on bedside tables. Men and women laid on beds, some sleeping, some smoking from long pipes. Patricia wasn't sure what to do and thought about leaving, but she was intrigued and continued farther into the opium den.

She watched a man prepare a pipe for a woman reclined on a bed. He spooled the sticky opium on the end of a long wooden needle, then rolled it against the ceramic pipe-bowl until it was in the shape of a cone. He used the needle to place the dark brown cone inside the mouth of the pipe-bowl, then moved the needle in a circle to spread open the center of the opium so air could flow smoothly into the pipe once the opium was lit. With the pipe ready, he helped the woman lift her head from the Asian-style pillow. This was clearly not her first pipe of the night. He moved the opium lamp closer and lifted the pipe to the woman's lips. She sucked on the tip as he guided the pipe-bowl over the flame. It lit. She inhaled. Her eyes rolled back. The man removed the pipe from her lips and let her head gently lower down on the pillow. He placed the pipe on a stand next to the bed. He would come back later and relight it for her until all the opium was spent.

Patricia was fascinated. It occurred to her that she was staring at the woman, and the woman was staring back at her. The woman's eyes were lost someplace else. Patricia moved deeper into the den.

She found Greene reclined about to smoke his first pipe. He said nothing when he saw her. He wasn't angry at the intrusion. He simply smiled. The woman preparing his pipe was ready. She handed Greene the pipe and moved the bowl to the flame. The opium lit. He inhaled, keeping his eyes on Patricia. His eyes rolled back, and he was gone. The woman that prepared the pipe raised it toward Patricia, offering it to her.

Patricia realized that this could a turning point in her life. An awakening of sorts. She was more than curious, drawn to the pipe, but afraid at the same time. The woman smiled. Her teeth were rotted away. Her skin was wrinkled and cracked. Her hair was brittle. Grotesque. Patricia shook her head, refusing. She took one last look at Greene, lost in a dream. She turned and headed for the door. She was done.

CHAPTER THIRTEEN

Located 39 miles southwest of Hanoi, Hoa Binh was the capital of the Muong people. Terraced rice paddies scaled the lush green hillsides, while bamboo waterwheels provided year-round irrigation for the young rice plants in the valleys. Limestone karsts, some hundreds of feet tall, shot up from the ground like a giant's fingers ready to scoop up the rice fields. Slow-moving rivers cut through the flatlands twisting and turning as if unsure where to go.

It was the caves cut deep into the limestone mountains that first attracted the Muong. A refuge from the weather and other warring tribes. But it was the rice that kept them in the valley and helped their population grow. Now hundreds of villages dotted the valley floors.

Ho Chi Minh wanted Hoa Binh. He wanted the rice to feed his followers, and he wanted the caves to keep his troops safe from the French planes. He wanted the Day River, which he could use to smuggle more Chinese weapons and supplies deep into the country. And he wanted the Muong who he knew were ferocious fighters and were familiar with the land. The Muong had been neutral in the war so far, but Ho hoped to change that once he controlled their territory.

Since his loss at the Battle of Vinh Yen, Giap had been itching for another fight. Morale among his troops was still high, but nothing gave his men more confidence than victory. He wanted to show General De Lattre his army could stand toe-to-toe against French forces even with their airpower and armor. Giap ordered the Viet Minh 164th Regional Battalion into the area around Hoa Binh in preparation for the upcoming offensive.

De Lattre and his staff considered Giap's troop movement as an opportunity to fight the Viet Minh on French terms. While there were many mountains in the area in which the Viet Minh could hide, there was also a great deal of flatland, especially near the rivers, that the Viet Minh wanted to control. If the French could lure the Viet Minh into battle, De Lattre believed that French airpower and artillery could do significant damage to Giap's forces.

To get the Viet Minh to fight, De Lattre needed the right bait. He chose the 1st Colonial Parachute Battalion commanded by Little Bruno. De Lattre surmised that Giap knew that the paratroopers, while fierce fighters, were lightly armed. It would be a great temptation to destroy such an elite unit and demoralize the French. De Lattre believed that if he dropped the paratroopers right in Giap's lap, he would have little choice but to attack. An assault against the paratroopers would pin down the Viet Minh and allow the French to bring in a much larger ground force and air power to pummel their ranks.

Directing the final briefing, Bruno stood in front of a map of the area around Hoa Binh, reviewing the plan. "We will drop 2 miles west of the Cho Ben Pass," said Bruno. "Then make our way into the pass and secure it. There are limestone caves in the mountains that overlook the only two ways in and out of the pass. We will use these caves to protect our rear flank. The caves will also allow us protection against our artillery and air-to-ground assaults. Our job is not to destroy the Viet Minh units that will hopefully attack us. Our job is to keep them occupied while the rest of our forces move up and attack their flanks. We are the pinning force. They are the hammer that will grind the Viet Minh into dust."

"How do we know the Viet Minh will attack us?" said a captain.

"The Cho Ben Pass is a major supply route for Chinese supplies and weapons coming in from the north. Without it, Giap will be unable to support his troops in the area and will be forced to withdraw. He will not let that happen. He will attack."

"Any update on how long we will have to fight before the task force arrives?" said a lieutenant.

"One day. Two at the most. Mobile Group 2 will be coming from the south. Their armor will block the Viet Minh at the mouth of the pass. Our air force and artillery will do the rest. You are going to want to keep your heads down for this one. I am informed it is going to be quite a show."

"Will the bombers be using napalm?"

"I would imagine."

Everyone exchanged nervous glances. "I sense you are worried about our pilots' aim?" said Bruno.

"There have been mistakes in the past," said a lieutenant. "Napalm is unforgiving."

"True. But it will also destroy your enemy with great efficiency. The planners picked this spot specifically for the limestone caves that will protect us. Make sure you bring plenty of colored smoke to mark your positions. One last thing before we dismiss. Brigitte Friang, a French correspondent, will accompany us."

"A woman?"

"Yes, a woman. Brigitte served in the French underground with me. She is very capable and para qualified. I expect everyone to be on their best behavior."

Bruno asked if there were any more questions, then closed with, "Gentlemen, tomorrow we will tickle the dragon. Good luck and try not to get eaten."

Operation Tulipe began just before sunrise when sixteen Douglas C-47 transport aircraft took off from a Hanoi airfield. The C-47s, nicknamed Dakotas, were war surplus hand-me-downs from the United States as part of their military aid package. Holding 28 paratroopers in each plane, the fleet would require two trips to carry the entire battalion to the Cho Ben Pass.

Brigitte, wearing a jumpsuit and parachute, sat next to Bruno in the lead aircraft. It was only her third jump, and she still felt the need to rehearse the procedure to ensure she did everything correctly. It was less about dying and more about looking bad in front of the other paratroopers who seemed relaxed. "Are you nervous?" said Bruno.

"No. No. I just want to make sure I do it right," said Brigitte.

"Well, take comfort in the fact that if you do it wrong, you will only need to worry about it for twenty to thirty seconds," he said, smacking his hands together to create a smacking sound.

Brigitte slugged him as hard as she could in the arm. It hurt her fist more than it hurt him. He laughed, "Don't hurt yourself. We're days away from a hospital."

"You can be such an asshole, Little Bruno."

"Listen. When we land, you stay close. I won't have time to look for you, and I would hate to see you captured on the first day of the operation."

"That's sweet."

"Of course. Who would write about me?"

"Asshole."

He laughed again. Brigitte was grateful. Bruno's warped sense of humor took her mind off the jump and helped her relax. They were ten minutes out from jumping into Viet Minh territory, and there was a genuine possibility of being killed before the day was done.

Unlike the British and the Americans, the French paratroopers carried their weapons strapped to their bodies so they could be used mid-jump if required. Leg bags dangled from a strap attached to their harness and held everything they would need until they returned to their base, sometimes weeks later. As was his custom, Bruno jumped without a weapon. Brigitte and the paratroopers landed on a terraced rice field. It was not an ideal landing site because it was on the side of a hill, but there were no trees or large rocks. Each paratrooper gathered his parachute and placed it in a central location for reuse at another time. Bruno was the rally point. They moved to surround him, found their platoon commanders, and checked their gear.

With only half the battalion on the ground, the paratroopers were particularly vulnerable. Bruno sent out scouts in all directions. If the enemy was coming, he wanted to know about it first. He wasn't afraid. He had no time for fear. But he did believe in being prepared as much as possible.

Having spotted the hundreds of parachutes falling from the sky, the Viet Minh commanders had sent their reconnaissance units to determine the size and position of the French force, but they did not attack. They, too, believed in being prepared before making any sort of assault.

The Muong also sent scouts to find out what was happening. Much to the dismay of the younger tribal members, the elders had no interest in taking sides in the conflict between the Viet Minh and the French. Their scouts stayed hidden and watched as the battle unfolded.

Three hours later, the second wave of paratroopers arrived. With the entire battalion safely on the ground, Bruno ordered his men to advance into the pass. It was a steep climb through dense undergrowth and tangled vegetation, but the paratroopers were in excellent shape and made easy work of it. Brigitte, on the other hand, was huffing and puffing. "Do you want me to carry you on my back?" asked Bruno.

Brigitte gave him the French finger and marched ahead like it wasn't a big deal. It took everything she had left, but it was worth it.

After two hours, the battalion reached the pass — still no major contact with the Viet Minh. Bruno began to wonder if the intelligence was wrong and if the Viet Minh were even in the area. The silence was unnerving. The paratroopers took up positions at the mouth of the limestone caves Bruno had told them about. Some of the caves were massive, capable of holding a hundred men, while others were quite small enough for a four-man fireteam. What all the caves had in common was that attack from the rear was impossible. The caves' rock overhangs also made mortar fire less effective, a significant component of any Viet Minh assault. Bruno had elected to use caves on both sides of the pass. It was a risky move because of the danger of crossfire, but it allowed the superior French positions to support one another during enemy assaults.

The paratroopers used their foldable shovels to dig themselves foxholes in the loose soil. They gathered up loose rocks and fallen logs and stacked them up in front of their firing positions for extra cover. All in all, they were in a strong defensive position. The paratroopers were trained to fight anywhere and at any time. They were the point of the spear for the French army. They had earned their elite reputation and admiration of their fellow soldiers.

Once their firing positions were finished, the paratroopers took time to grab a quick bite to eat, and some even slept. The men had learned to sleep whenever possible because they never knew how long it would be until they could sleep again after the battle started.

Brigitte went around interviewing the soldiers, asking about where they were from, if they had a girlfriend or wife, and which battles they had participated in. Bruno took the time to radio into headquarters and gave his commander an update. He also inquired about the progress of the mobile group that would eventually link up with the paratroopers. He was careful not to say rescue. Paratroopers never needed to be rescued. All was going according to plan… so far.

General Giap immediately recognized what the French were doing. He knew the paratroopers were bait. He considered the situation and realized that this could be a great opportunity to turn the tables on the French. He had several divisions within striking distance. Annihilating the paratroopers before the French could reinforce their position was a real possibility and would be a great boost to the morale of his men who hated the paratroopers. But he also wondered if there wasn't more to gain than just a battalion. After careful consideration, Giap decided to throw out some bait of his own – an entire Viet

Minh regiment. With luck, the French would attack the 64th Regiment when it reinforced the 164th Battalion, and the Viet Minh would be ready for them.

The Viet Minh waited until nightfall to begin their probing assaults. The skirmishers were meant to pinpoint the enemy positions and gauge their strength.

The commander of the 164th Battalion was a young major and wanted to prove his worth to his leaders. He had been informed that the 64th Regiment was on its way to reinforce his position. He had been ordered to pin down the paratroopers and not let them escape until the reinforcements had arrived. He didn't want to wait. When he arrived, the commander of the regiment would take over the operation and receive all the credit. As soon as the major determined what he was facing, he would attack with his entire battalion. If he could destroy the paratroopers before the regiment arrived, there would be little doubt that it was he that won the battle.

When the probing skirmishes started, the French were careful not to expose all their positions or reveal all of their strength. They did not see the Viet Minh skirmishers as a real threat. They sent out fireteams to fight back the Viet Minh units and to hide the actual location of the majority of their forces. It worked.

When the skirmishers returned to their lines, they

pointed to the locations where they had encountered the French units near the mouth of the pass. In fact, the French were much deeper and near the top of the pass. When the Viet Minh artillery barrage started, it was way off target. The bombardment was followed by a general assault. The Viet Minh ran up the hill, wearing themselves out and encountering nothing. The soldiers looked around, surprised. No French. Some claimed the French had run off when they saw the Viet Minh charging up the hill.

With the Viet Minh huffing and puffing to catch their breath, the French counterattacked, charging down the hillside, firing their weapons. Now it was the Viet Minh that were unable to use their artillery for fear of hitting their own men tangled up with the paratroopers. When the paratroopers ran out of bullets in their weapons, they kept charging instead of reloading and used their guns as clubs to bash the surprised Viet Minh.

Almost one hundred Viet Minh were killed in the initial attack. The French paratroopers did not take prisoners because they had no way to care for them. No quarter was given, and none was expected. It was a small victory considering what the paratroopers were expecting in the coming days. That was the key for them; fight the battle in front of you, and don't worry about the future. It will get here soon enough. They retreated to their defensive positions inside the caves.

Bruno was careful to rotate his men. He only kept half his men on the line at any one time. The paratroopers were known for their aggression. It was difficult to be aggressive when you were exhausted.

The men that assaulted the Viet Minh were taken off the line and given time to rest. This switching back and forth kept morale high. The soldiers knew that they were only expected to fight for a prescribed amount of time and would be allowed to rest in the safety of the caves. They also kept up their strength by eating and drinking plenty of water. Unlike the other French commanders, Bruno did not allow his men to drink wine in the field and discouraged it in the base camp. It was not a popular rule, but his men trusted him to keep them safe even if it meant sacrificing their precious ration of wine.

Another hour passed without an attack by the Viet Minh. That's good, thought Bruno. The more time he could chew up without fighting, the better. The odds of victory or even survival would vastly increase once the Mobile Group arrived. He felt like they were in a good position and could hold out until relieved. He received word from his reconnaissance unit that the 64th Regiment had arrived and was now united with 164th battalion, vastly increasing the number of enemy troops his men must now fight. He knew his men could hold them off for a time, but how long he wasn't sure. It all depended on the aggressiveness of their assault against the paratroopers. If an entire regiment and battalion attacked at the same time in a full-on push, it would be hard to hold them back.

Artillery whistled into the French positions and exploded, shaking the ground and showering the paratroopers with bits of rock and flying dirt clods. The Viet Minh had brought up their artillery and would attempt to drive the French out of their positions. Bruno thought himself smart for having chosen the caves to protect his men until an artillery shell slammed into a rock cliff directly above a platoon. The shell exploded, and the rock face broke free, raining chunks of limestone down on the French. Three of his men were crushed to death, and several more were seriously wounded.

Bruno ordered his men to move deeper into the cave and reform their defensive lines. Many voiced their concern that they could be buried alive if there was a major landslide caused by the shelling. After seeing their comrades crushed to death, the paratroopers seemed more afraid of the falling rocks than the Viet Minh bullets. Bruno reassured them that the other paratroopers would come to their rescue and dig them out if needed. It did little to still their fears, but they obeyed his order. It was not ideal, but the rocky overhangs were still the best protection against artillery and mortar fire.

While French artillery vastly outnumbered Viet Minh artillery, the Viet Minh gunners had become more and more effective as the war progressed. They still could not calculate the trajectory of indirect fire but had become proficient on direct firing of their weapons. The Chinese had begun training the Viet Minh, but it was a slow process since most of the gunners had poor math skills. Spotters with radios had been instructed on how to walk-in the gunner's shells. It was a crude but effective method and was taking its toll on the French. Like most things, the Viet Minh made use of what was available.

Bruno radioed air support and asked for the first

249

of many air assaults. The target was not the Viet
Minh troops but rather the artillery in the valley
below the pass if it could be spotted from the air. It
was difficult. The Viet Minh were masters of
camouflage and used the local foliage to augment
their camouflage nets. The only time a pilot could
spot an artillery gun was when it was firing. There
was no way to disguise the sheet of fire and smoke
from a 105mm cannon. When a cannon was spotted,
the French descended on it like a swarm of wasps and
continued their air assault until it was destroyed. Viet
Minh artillery was considered a high priority for the
French.

The Viet Minh continued to assault the French
positions in the pass throughout the night and most
of the next morning. Outnumbered, the
paratroopers took a beating and lost almost ten
percent of their fighting force to death or severe
wounds. The French medics struggled to keep up
with incoming wounded. As always, the French
paramedics were well prepared and had brought
extra medical supplies. They got little sleep during
the mission. There were too many wounded for the
luxury of sleep.

By the next morning, the French were exhausted and
starting to run low on ammunition. They had
brought as much ammunition as they could carry,
but it wasn't enough to fight off the continuous
human waves the Viet Minh sent up the hill. Water
was also becoming an issue. It was the hot season in
Vietnam, and that meant the men needed to drink

regularly to stay hydrated. Bruno had sent scouts out to find the springs that he knew would be in the mountains, but they came back empty-handed. Either the springs were too well hidden, or they were in Viet Minh territory. Either way, he and his men went thirsty. This was especially difficult for the wounded, who tended to become dehydrated quickly from the loss of blood. Even though the paratroopers gave up part of their ration, several of his wounded men died from lack of water.

But thirst or no thirst, the Viet Minh kept coming. Just as one assault would end, another would begin. There was no time to rest in between the battles, and it took its toll on the French. It was hard to focus when exhausted and even harder to fight hand-to-hand if it became necessary.

The Viet Minh had far more men than they could rotate in and out of the battle, giving them time to rest and build up their strength before once again charging into the pass.

The paratroopers were running on adrenaline. Many would take short catnaps in between the assaults, then snap awake just in time to fire at the Viet Minh charging their position. Catnaps were an art mastered by the veteran paratroopers and the envy of the younger recruits.

With the sun up, Bruno called in more airstrike, this time against the Viet Minh troops. The French marked their positions with colored smoke to prevent friendly fire from the fast-moving aircraft.

Grumman Bearcats armed with 1,000 lb. bombs hammered the Viet Minh, who moved slowly up the steep hillside and made easy targets. Although the destruction of their ranks was significant, it was more damaging to Viet Minh's morale. It was one thing to face French paratroopers known for their ferocity, and quite another to have French fighters dropping bombs that shook the very ground on which they ran. The Viet Minh regiment had little in the way of anti-aircraft weaponry, which made them entirely at the mercy of the French pilots. But the pilots were not in a merciful mood that morning. Once the bombs were dropped, each Bearcat returned for a strafing run — four 5-inch unguided rockets and hundreds of shells from their four Hispano 20mm cannons, which tended to disintegrate the enemy troops they hit. The Viet Minh took massive losses from multiple airstrikes. It seemed the French Air Force and Navy were the only reason the paratrooper positions had not yet been overrun.

It was a little past noon when the artillery guns of Mobile Group 2 could be heard in the distance. The cavalry had arrived on time, for once. The paratroopers cheered. Knowing that their reinforcements had arrived made the paratroopers anxious to fight. They were jealous of their victory and wanted to ensure history recorded their deeds.

When the Viet Minh turned to face Mobile Group 2 advancing on their rear flank, the paratroopers attacked once again — running downhill — killing anything that stood in their way.

Sandwiched between a hammer and an anvil, the Viet Minh broke and fled the battlefield. Although it was far from an orderly withdrawal, the Viet Minh were remarkably disciplined and had been ordered not to surrender their weapons no matter what happened. Because of the shortage of supplies and the plethora of volunteers for Ho Chi Minh's army, the Viet Minh soldiers were less valuable than their weapons and ammunition. They retreated into the surrounding forests and hills. It would be several days until the regiment commanders could gather all their troops and become an effective fighting force once again.

Bruno and his men have once again accomplished their mission… with a little help from Mobile Group 2.

When word arrived, Giap was not wholly disappointed at the outcome of the battle. Even though it broke, the Viet Minh regiment had served its purpose in bringing more French into the battle. He knew the regiment would heal itself in time and fight again.

In the meantime, Giap brought up the 304th and 312th Divisions from the Red River, where they had been putting pressure on Haiphong Harbor and Hanoi. They would slam up against the French Mobile Group and paratroopers trapping them in the pass. With no exit, the French would be forced to surrender or face annihilation. It was a victory that Giap needed to boost the morale of the Viet Minh and prove to Ho and the politburo that he indeed was the right man to lead the Viet Minh forces.

The Viet Minh 88th Regiment moved against Tu Vu in an attempt to cut off French supply lines. In a swift lunge, the Viet Minh forces tangled themselves into the French lines. The French Air Force was helpless without risking the lives of its own troops. Outgunned and outnumbered, all looked lost for the French supply post until two companies of Moroccan colonial troops, accompanied by a squadron of tanks, took up the fight against the Viet Minh in a furious battle. Neither side wanted to give up their ground. The French tanks, armored cars, and half-tracks poured fire on the Viet Minh line. The Viet Minh fought back with heavy mortars, artillery, and bazookas. Lunge mines were used whenever possible, sacrificing the Viet Minh sappers that detonated them. The French armor took its licks as it advanced on the Viet Minh. The Moroccan troops fought intensely to keep the Viet Minh sappers away from the sides of the tanks, which were vulnerable to the lunge mines. The Viet Minh were exhausted, battered, and low on ammunition. They had no choice but to break off their attack, and when they did, the French Bearcats took their toll dropping napalm and strafing the fleeing troops. French armor and airpower once again showed their superiority on the battlefield, and it was the Moroccan troops that carried the day.

As De Lattre received reports of the 304th and 312th advancing on French positions, he ordered a full assault against them, including air, artillery, and armor. Destroying the highly regarded Viet Minh divisions would deal a mortal blow to Ho Chi Minh and his followers. The veteran fighters were the best the Viet Minh had to offer. De Lattre saw it as a unique opportunity to turn the direction of war and potentially seek peace on favorable terms. Mobile Group 4 was brought in to support the attack and keep the Viet Minh pinned down while the air force and artillery batteries did their work.

Taking off from Cat Bi Airfield in Haiphong, several squadrons of B-26 Invaders headed into battle. Each carried six 1,000 lb. bombs, four internally in the bomb bay, and two on wing hardpoints. In addition, the bombers carried ten HVAR rockets under their wings and six M2 Browning machineguns in their nose turrets. A single bomber carried a powerful punch, but a squadron was capable of taking out an entire battalion of enemy troops if caught in the open.

When the Viet Minh heard the drone of approaching aircraft engines, they scattered, seeking whatever cover they could find. Their leaders would have thought this cowardly had they not seen for themselves the damage a squadron of bombers could reap on their troops. Even if the shrapnel didn't kill its targets, the concussive wave from a 1000 lb. bomb could turn a soldier's insides into jelly.

Surprisingly, the soldiers in the 304th and 312th did not break. The took the punishment from the French aircraft and held their positions. When the squadrons were finished and headed for the horizon, the Viet Minh rose and continued their assault. They left behind the dead and dying for the medics and support personnel. They knew great sacrifices were needed to overthrow their French overlords. Every bomb that dropped and artillery shell that exploded may have decimated their ranks but left the survivors more resolved that their cause was righteous and more determined to achieve victory. Their deepest desire was not to survive but to get at the French.

The two Viet Minh divisions split; one continued the assault against Mobile Group 2 and the paratroopers while the other turned to face Mobile Group 4 nipping at their flanks. The French armored cars and tanks smashed against the human wave attacks. While the Viet Minh had no armor, they did have Chinese bazookas and lunge mines that could take out steel beasts if they could get close enough. Many Viet Minh fireteams waited in ambush for the French armor to advance past their hidden positions before opening fire. The result, more times than not, was that the Viet Minh fireteam would be wiped out by a spray of machinegun fire. But there were victories, and those victories cost the French dearly.

The Viet Minh ground against the French like a sandstorm. They seemed to be everywhere at the same time. No place was safe.

For their part, the French fought mightily. Never giving an inch without extracting a price in blood. But in the end, it was the French that decided the cost was too high. They could not afford the losses like the Viet Minh. Replacements were hard to come by and were usually inexperienced. The longer the French fought, the weaker they became. It was not a rout by any stretch of the imagination. The French performed a disciplined fighting withdrawal making the Viet Minh pay for their new territory. After a week of fighting, both sides were exhausted. The soldiers just wanted the battle to end so they could sleep once again and maybe have a decent meal. After three days of constant battle, the Viet Minh stopped their advance and let the surviving French return to the safety of their defensive line.

The Viet Minh claimed victory. They had driven the French from the battlefield, but the cost was high on both sides. Over five thousand French Union soldiers were killed or seriously wounded. The French generals were grateful it wasn't worse.

The Viet Minh suffered about the same but were better able to absorb the loss, although many of their veteran fighters had been killed and would no longer be available to instruct the recruits and give them confidence.

De Lattre's biggest concern was to prevent the Americans from finding the actual results of the campaign. He was unable to stop the French and foreign press from reporting what they had seen and heard to their readers out-of-country. Brigitte had been part of it, and there was no way to stop her. She wrote the truth of how the battle unfolded and the final results even though it reflected poorly on the French army as a whole. Revealing the truth, even when painful, was her duty to France and her readers.

But in Indochina, De Lattre was the man in charge of both the army and the government. He threatened to shut down the local publishers if he didn't like what they reported. When they complained, he reminded them that the communists would do far worse if they took control. Journalists would be the first killed. They shut up and reported light French casualties. The whole affair was swept under the rug. De Lattre's only real problem was the Kennedys. They were still in-country and digging for the truth. Now more than ever, he needed to steer them away from the Battle of Hoa Binh.

CHAPTER FOURTEEN

John sat next to De Lattre as they were driven to yet another troops inspection with a full band and dignitaries. John was peeved. He wasn't interested in the dog and pony show De Lattre was offering. "So, Congressman Kennedy, what do you think of our military strategy so far?" said De Lattre.

"Honestly, General, and I mean this with all due respect, I'm not sure I see a strategy," said John.

"What do you mean?"

"Your forces control the cities and patrol the main roads during the day. Except for a handful of hamlets, the Viet Minh control the countryside and take over those same main roads at night. In America, we call that a stalemate."

"I admit it. It has been difficult to take the offensive. We are short on manpower and weapons. If President Truman were to commit ground troops to guard the cities and roads, my men would be free to attack the Viet Minh and end the war once and for all."

"We can help with the weapons. Lord knows we have plenty of surplus left over from the war. But to be honest, American ground troops are wishful thinking. The American people think Europe is where our military should focus its efforts, not Southeast Asia. We might be able to send some advisors to help train your men."

"Advisors will help, of course, but it takes time to train men, especially colonial troops. The language is always a problem."

"I don't think language is the problem. I think it's leadership."

"What do you mean, Congressman?" said De Lattre, offended.

"Not you, sir. The Vietnamese government. Nobody in the Vietnamese army seems very excited about supporting Bao Dai as a leader of the people or the army. They don't believe he has their best interest at heart. They believe he is a self-serving French puppet. Just another tool used to control them."

"They are soldiers. They will do as they are told."

"I wish that were true. I know you have far more experience at leading men into battle than I. I was only a lieutenant in charge of a PT boat. But I knew, from the day I set foot on that boat, my men would only fight for someone they believed cared about their wellbeing. And I'm not talking about someone who mothers them. There were times they needed a sharp kick in the ass. I'm talking about leading from the front. Not asking them to do something you are not prepared to do yourself."

"We are doing what we can to help our young officers become better leaders. But frankly, leading does not come naturally to the Indochinese. Most are Buddhist and take a 'what will be, will be' attitude. They just don't have the drive that it takes to lead. Perhaps your American advisors can do better."

"Have you considered giving them something to fight for?"

"Such as Independence?"

"Well... yeah."

"We've granted them independence."

"Limited independence. France still controls Vietnam's finances, diplomacy, and military."

"Only until the country is stabilized and the government can take on the additional responsibilities required."

"And when will that be?"

"I imagine when the war is over, and the communists are no longer a threat.

"The Vietnamese don't believe you will keep your word."

"We cannot be responsible for what they think. And frankly, independence will not solve Indochina's problems. Destroying the communists will solve Indochina's problems."

"And yet, you have no real plan for doing that."

"A plan? Of course, we have a plan. The De Lattre line will be the bastion that crushes their spirit."

"You mentioned that before. I'd like to see it."

"It's difficult. The Viet Minh continue to attack our outposts in the north on a nightly basis. I fear it would be too risky."

"Risky, for whom?"

"Are you inferring that I am hiding something?"

"General, I respect you as a leader. Your men are loyal to you. That says a lot. But you talk about this mythical defensive line like it's the solution to your problems, and yet you won't show it to me. What am I supposed to tell the president when I get back?"

"That we are America's allies and deserve his support."

"He already knows that. What he wants to know is, can you win?"

"Of course, we can win."

"Then show me. Let me take that message back to my president."

De Lattre considered for a long moment and said, "Alright. We will go. But I warn you that it is dangerous. Hanoi is not Saigon."

"I understand. I have one other request."

"Yes?"

"No more dog and pony shows."

"Dog and Pony?"

"No more military parades or inspections of your crack troops. You put on an impressive show, but I've seen enough. I want to see the real French Army in action. If you truly have faith in your men, you'll let me see them as they are. You will let me see them fight."

"Very well. No more dog and pony. You may go where you wish and talk with whomever you please."

"I appreciate it, General. Do you mind if we skip the current inspection?"

"The men will be disappointed."

"Well, I don't want to be responsible for lowering

morale, now do I?"

"I would hope not."

"Lead on, General. Lead on."

Granier sat on the Continental patio café waiting for John's return like a dog waiting impatiently for his master. John had asked to travel alone with De Lattre on this day so he could have a frank discussion with the general. Granier didn't like the idea but wasn't given a choice. One of the things he liked about John and all the Kennedys was their independence. They did what they thought was needed and right.

Granier watched the streets around the hotel. Everything seemed normal – taxis carrying westerners, pedestrians strolling around the park, a man selling newspapers to passing businessmen, two policemen patrolling on foot, and checking identification of Vietnamese in the area.

Patricia walked into the café and sat down next to him. "Penny for your thoughts," she said.

"That's about all they would be worth," said Granier. "You really shouldn't be out here... on the patio. It's too exposed."

"Yes, mother hen. I am risking my life for a coffee and... to tell you something."

"What's that?"

"I'm going back to the states tomorrow. I've got an early morning flight."

"Why is that? I thought you loved Indochina."

"It's fascinating for sure. But it's like you said... you've got to pace yourself. And for now, I've had enough. Besides, I've accepted a job in Hollywood."

"Hollywood, really?"

"Before we left, I was offered a position as a television producer for NBC."

"Did your father pull some strings?"

"What makes you think I couldn't get the job on my own?"

"You're twenty-two, Patricia. I don't think NBC hands out management positions to kids just out of college."

"Well, I'm sure father was instrumental behind the scenes, but I never asked him for help."

"I wouldn't imagine you would need to. So, what's the show?"

"Don't laugh. It's a cooking show called I Love to Eat with the chef James Beard."

"A cooking show. People will actually watch that kinda thing?"

"I don't know. I suppose we are about to find out. It's the first of its kind. The folks at NBC are excited. They've got lots of sponsors lined up."

"I wish you luck. What's going to happen to your documentary of the tour?"

"I imagine father will have someone cut together the footage and use it to further Jack's career when the time is right. Granier, I appreciate everything you've done. Especially watching out for Jack and Bobby.

"When they let me."

"Yeah, well… we Kennedys can be stubborn."

Patricia leaned over and kissed him on the cheek. "Look at that… our first kiss. Not how I imagined it," she said.

He blushed, then something caught his eye. The

Vietnamese vendors that sold their wares around the hotel were noticeably absent. The man selling papers was also gone, and there was an absence of trishaws. Only foreigners were visible. "Patricia, do me a favor and go inside," he said.

"Why? What's wrong?" she said, looking around.

"I'm not sure. It's probably nothing. But just to be safe."

"Alright. Are you gonna be okay?"

"I know when to duck."

"Yes. Of course," she said, heading into the hotel.

Granier watched in the distance as General De Lattre's convoy turned on Rue Catinat and headed toward the hotel. "Ah, shit," said Granier.

A car pulled up in front of the hotel, and the driver, a Vietnamese man, jumped out. Granier pulled out his pistol from his pocket and pointed it at the driver. "Move that car now!" said Granier firmly.

The driver climbed back in his car and drove away. The hotel security team saw Granier pointing his pistol. They surrounded him, drawing and pointing their pistols at him. They shouted in French. Granier laid his gun on the table and raised his hands above his head. "The Vietnamese have left the area. Something is wrong. You need to move these people off the patio," said Granier to the security team.

The convoy pulled up in front of the hotel. John started to step from the backseat of the General's car when he saw Granier, standing with his hands in the air. Their eyes met. Granier shook his head slightly. John looked around as he slipped back into the car and closed the door. "General, would you mind dropping me off at the back entrance?" said John.

"Of course not," said De Lattre.

The General gave the driver orders, and the convoy turned the corner to the back of the hotel. "Is there something wrong, Congressman?" said De Lattre.

"I'm not sure," said John.

Watching the convoy disappear around the corner and with the congressman safe, Granier let out a sigh of relief and relaxed. Better safe than sorry, he thought, his hands still in the air, a security guard searching his pockets.

A car parked across the street from the hotel entrance where the General's car had been only a few moments earlier exploded, sending several pedestrians flying through the air, their bodies torn to shreds. Granier and the security guards were blown off their feet by the powerful blast. Plates and glasses from the tables flew through the air smashing against customers and the walls. The windows on the hotel facing the blast shattered. Glass shards rained down, ripping holes in the cloth overhang above the café. As patrons struggled to their feet, they were pelted and cut by flying glass.

They ran for cover inside the hotel. Blood flowed soaking into the carpet and furniture fabric. Patricia appeared in the doorway, shocked by what had happened. Granier, his face bloodied, saw her and waved her back inside, "Find Jack and Bobby. Get to your room and lock the door."

"Are you okay?" she said.

"Go, damn it!"

She obeyed and disappeared inside. A fire engine and police sirens approached from a distance. Those not killed from the explosion tended to the wounded.

In the park across the street, a second bomb inside a mailbox exploded, sending shrapnel in all directions, killing and maiming more passerby, and again knocking everyone in the surrounding area off their feet. A man flew off his motorcycle and landed in the street, where he was run over by a car careening out of control. His motorbike skidded across the pavement until it hit a curb, then flipped up into the air, and landed on a pedestrian lying on the sidewalk, a victim of the second blast. A baby carriage flew through a store window and knocked over several mannequins. The baby tumbled out of the mangled carriage, screaming but safe. The baby's Algerian nanny, missing several limbs, laid on the sidewalk outside bleeding to death.

The streets and sidewalks cleared as survivors ran for cover, leaving the wounded to fend for themselves. Nobody was willing to risk a third blast. Granier and the hotel employees helped those that they could until the emergency vehicles arrived. The carnage from the two explosions was massive – over twenty dead and hundreds wounded.

Granier and the Kennedys sat in the rooftop lounge. Granier was covered with cuts from flying glass and bruises from being thrown off his feet. The Kennedys were mostly unscathed, except for a cut on John's hand, where he pulled a glass shard from a woman's forearm. He used his tie as a restriction bandage to slow the bleeding and his shirt to wrap her wound until she could be taken to the hospital for stitches.

It was crowded. The rooftop bar felt like the only

safe place to get a drink, which everyone needed to calm their nerves. The waiters served free cocktails, nuts, and French fries. Patrons were visibly shaken, some in shock just stared, expressionless. Other relived the experience telling their stories of what had happened to them, reminding those listening of their own horror stories.

The police were interviewing everyone trying to rebuild the scene before the bombs went off, hopefully, to identify some suspects. A police sketch artist was overwhelmed. Everyone had a different version of who the bombers might be and what they looked like. Everyone seemed to feel that they were Vietnamese and not foreigners. Biases were strong and made most of the information useless. "You saved our lives," said Patricia tending to a bad cut on Granier's ear.

"I don't know. I missed it. I should have seen it earlier," he said as he drank a beer. He would not drink anything stronger while in-country.

"No, Granier. Credit where credit is due. Well done," said John.

"You all should think about going back to the states in the morning with Patricia. It's only going to get worse."

"No. That's what they want us to do. Run scared. It's not in our nature. We feel more comfortable running toward trouble."

"I can see that," Granier said, with a slight chuckle.

"It's good that Patricia is going."

"I thought I might stay. Things are getting exciting," said Patricia.

"Not this time, kiddo. Mom would kill me if I let anything happen to you. You're heading home," said John.

"What about Bobby?"

"She doesn't like him as much."

Bobby laughed, "It's true."

"But seriously, Bobby and I are headed north with De Lattre. If we're lucky, things are gonna heat up, and it's gonna get even more dangerous. Keeping an eye on Bobby is gonna be bad enough. I don't want to be looking after my baby sister as well."

"Alright. If you think it's best, Jack," said Patricia.

"I do. You've done a good job, but it's time to call it quits."

"I'm gonna miss you guys," said Patricia tearing up.

"Ditto, Kiddo," said Bobby hugging her.

"Granier, can I have a few words with you in private?" said John.

"Sure," said Granier.

Granier and John moved off to a corner where they could speak. "Before the bombs went off, Bobby was interviewing a couple of reporters in the lobby. They told him about the Liên Minh militia near the Cambodian border. They are both anti-communists and anti-colonialists. Their leader General Trinh Minh THe, was an officer in the French army when he broke off and formed his own militia."

"I've heard of him."

"I'm thinking he might be the leader we've been searching for. People believe in him. His ranks are growing."

"Well, the word is he might have been the one

behind the bombs in Saigon."

"I heard those rumors too. I still think we should make contact before we leave and see what he is about. And if he is what I hope he is, we need to find out if he'll play ball."

"We?"

"You."

"Ah."

"Bobby and I can head north with De Lattre while you head west and try to make contact with THe. We can meet up in Hanoi once you're done."

"After what just happened, I think we should stick together."

"We'll be fine. Besides, I really can't see Bobby and me heading into the jungle to find a rebel leader. That's your turf. You'll be able to move a lot faster without us."

Granier grunted. He knew John was right, but he still didn't like it. "Believe me, I wouldn't ask if it wasn't important," said John. "You've already done way more than you bargained for. I won't forget it."

"I don't care about that. I just want to make sure you guys are safe."

"We'll be alright."

"Okay. I'll give it a shot. But what makes you think this guy THe will be willing to talk with me?"

"That's a good question. I thought it might help to offer THe an incentive."

"What kind of incentive?"

"The kind everyone understands… money."

"Probably make him less likely to shoot me right off the bat."

"I'll arrange it before you leave. It's a pretty good

distance to the border. Any idea how you're gonna get there?"

"Yeah. I know a pilot just crazy enough to fly me there. If I can find him."

Granier went to the hotel's front desk and asked to have his passport removed from the hotel safe. He also asked for three sheets of wax paper and a handful of rubber bands. He sent a telegraph to Colonel Patti requesting the current location of the American pilot, James McGovern.

Returning to his room, he placed his passport in the middle of one of the sheets of wax paper and wrapped it up. He repeated the process with the other two sheets of wax paper then slipped on several rubber bands in different places around the waterproof package.

There was a knock at the door. Granier answered it. A pageboy handed him a telegraph from Patti. He tipped the pageboy, closed the door, and opened the telegram. McGovern, nicknamed McGoon, was in Hue shuttling transportation aircraft from the Philippines as part of the new aid package. Like Granier, McGoon worked for the CIA. They had met previously when McGoon flew the OSS Deer Team into northern Vietnam. He liked McGoon and trusted him... somewhat. McGoon was one of the few Americans that had flown in Vietnam and was familiar with the patterns and behavior of mountain fog, which could be deadly.

The next morning, Granier, with a parachute slung

over one shoulder, and a backpack slung over the other, took a commercial flight up to Hue.

After landing, he took a taxi to the military airfield, where he tracked down McGoon in the French officer's club, drinking a cold beer. McGoon was easy to spot. He was a mountain of a man, not your typical pilot. Granier walked up behind him. "Drink much more of that, and you'll break the barstool," said Granier.

McGoon turned, angry until he saw Granier. "Granier, what in the hell are you doing here? I thought you were stateside teaching tadpoles how to swim," said McGoon as he gave Granier a bearhug.

"They let me out every once in a while, to stretch my legs."

"Long ways to stretch your legs. Must've forgotten to stop when you hit Hawaii."

"Must've. How are you doing, McGoon?"

"Fat and sassy. You?"

"Grumpy and mean."

"Sounds about right. So, seriously, what are you doing here? I didn't think the agency was letting your type in the country."

"They're not as far as I know. I'm on special assignment. Babysitting a congressman."

"Kennedy?"

"And his brother and sister."

"I heard he was coming for a visit. They in Hue?"

"No. Just me. I came to find you."

"Really? This conversation just got a lot more interesting. Beer?"

"Always."

McGoon motioned the bartender for a round of

beers. "So, what's up?"

"I was wondering if you could break yourself away from playing delivery boy for a couple of days and drop me in a jungle out west?"

"Little recon?"

"Something like that."

"Any chance of getting shot at?"

"Me, yes. You, no."

"That's disappointing. I'm in anyway. No matter what, it's got to be more exciting than shuttling cargo planes. Boring as hell. Like watching paint dry."

Granier pulled out a map and showed McGoon where he wanted to go. "Cambodian border. It sounds like you're looking for trouble."

"It ain't trouble I'm after. Ever hear of a General THe?"

"I heard he's a crazy bastard. Going up against the French and the Viet Minh."

"Well, that's what I gotta find out... how crazy."

"You got a plane?"

"I was hoping we could borrow one of your cargo planes."

"Nah. Too big for a mission like that. We need to be sneaky. I'll find something. When do we go?"

"As soon as you're ready."

"I'll be ready as soon as I finish my beer."

With his parachute and backpack sitting beside him, Granier stood on the airfield tarmac waiting. He heard the buzz of an engine approaching and turned to see McGoon taxing over in a French Morane-Saulnier MS.505 Criquet – a single-engine reconnaissance plane. McGoon stopped and opened the passenger door. "Jump in," yelled McGoon.

"You gotta be kidding. It's smaller than a can of tuna," said Granier.

"Hey, if I can fit, you can fit. Let's go."

Granier put his parachute and backpack in the small space behind the seats and climbed into the passenger seat. "You sure this thing's safe?" said Granier.

"It's a little worse for wear, but yeah. It'll get us there and back. It was the best I could do on short notice."

As he taxied toward the runway, McGoon handed Granier the radio handset. "Say something in French but make it like the radio is cutting out."

"Why?"

"I didn't actually ask permission to borrow this plane. It's better they think we have radio trouble. That way, they won't send anyone to shoot us down."

Granier made up some radio jargon in French while McGoon made static sounds. The tower responded. They ignored it. Granier handed back the handset and said, "Will that work?"

"I don't know, but we are about to find out."

McGoon pulled onto the runway and took off without incident.

As John and Bobby boarded a C-47, De Lattre noticed the absence of Granier and Patricia. "Where are your sister and your bodyguard, Granier?"

"Patricia is on her way back to the states. She got a job offer in Hollywood and decided to cut her stay short," said John.

"How fortunate for her. And Granier?"

"He said he was going to check up on an old friend and that he would meet us in Hanoi in a couple of days."

"A friend in Saigon?"

"He didn't say. Honestly, I was a little perturbed at him for abandoning us. It turns out he was not as reliable as we thought."

"I see. Hopefully, he will turn up soon."

As the Kennedys boarded, De Lattre turned to his head of military intelligence, "Find Granier now. We cannot afford to have an American reconnaissance soldier loose in-country."

The military transport carrying De Lattre and the Kennedy's touched down on a Hanoi airfield. As the plane taxied off the runway, John looked out the window and saw a large group of soldiers standing in formation on the edge of the airfield. "I thought we were done with the inspections?" said John.

"The divisional commander insisted on making a show of it," said De Lattre.

"It's a waste of time."

"I assure you it is not. It is good for the men's morale to know that they are not in the fight alone and that America is with them."

"But that is not completely true."

"No, but they do not know that. Think of it as doing your part to fight the communists. It will only take a few minutes."

John sighed. "Alright."

The plane pulled to stop in front of the crowd, and the stairway was pushed into place. A military band struck up a tune. The door opened, and De Lattre stepped out to cheers from his men. John was next. De Lattre took his arm and raised it with his own as a sign of unity. John just smiled and played along. He realized that the general was using him for propaganda, but there was little he could do about it if he wanted De Lattre to give him access to his soldiers on the frontlines.

But on this occasion, De Lattre had another motive for having the American congressman with him – the pride of a father. After inspecting the troops, De Lattre escorted Kennedy to a regiment snapping to attention on the right side of the field. The general was handed a box holding a medal – the Croix de Guerre. The Kennedys stood back and watched as General De Lattre pinned the award on his son Lieutenant Bernard De Lattre.

Bernard had been commanding a platoon stationed at an outpost 20 miles southeast of Hanoi when it was attacked just after sundown. The platoon was outnumbered four to one by an entire company of Viet Minh. Several men in the platoon were immediately wounded, but Bernard stayed calm and ordered his men to return fire while the medic tended to the injured. The Viet Minh charged the outpost defenses several times, and each time the young commander and his men fought them back. The fighting lasted most of the night. It wasn't until early morning when French aircraft came to the rescue – bombing and strafing – that the Viet Minh finally broke off the attack and retreated into the jungle. Amazingly, he had only lost two men, while most of the others had at least one wound.

Bernard had just turned 23, and it was his second Croix de Guerre, the first having been won in World War II at the age of 15 when he helped his father escape from a Nazi prison camp.

John was impressed by the story and understood why General De Lattre would want him to meet his son. He was a remarkable young man and a true patriot that believed in what the French were doing in Indochina.

John was only 25 when he received his two medals – a Purple Heart and a Navy-Marine Corp Medal – for his command of P.T. 109 in the Pacific War. John thought about how frightened he was when his boat was hit by a torpedo and caught fire. But he didn't panic. His men needed a strong, confident leader at that moment, and that is what he gave them. Bernard had done the same. John also felt a kinship with Bernard as the son of a great man. John's father, Joseph Kennedy, was a politician and a well-known businessman. It was difficult standing out while living in such a vast shadow.

After the awards ceremony, there was a small reception with champagne where De Lattre boasted of his son's exploits and retold the story of the assault, much to his son's embarrassment. But the general didn't care. He wanted to tell the world of his son's heroism. Everyone wanted to shake Bernard's hand and make sure that the general saw them do it. John approached De Lattre and said, "It looks like your son is a chip off the old block."

"Old block?" said De Lattre, confused by the expression.

"Oh, ah... It means like father, like son. You're the same."

"Ah, yes. We are the same. I should be so lucky. I understand you earned two medals yourself," said De Lattre.

"It was involuntary. They sunk my boat," said John.

A caravan of cars and military vehicles wove its way into downtown Hanoi. The streets were lined with a mix of French and Vietnamese civilians cheering the American congressman and the French general as they slowly drove past. "This is ridiculous," whispered Bobby to John.

"The general certainly knows how to milk a situation," whispered John while waving politely out the window. "You'd think I was Jesus himself."

"I wish Patricia was here to film it. This could be good for your career."

"It's better that she's safe. One less thing to worry about."

"And what am I? Sliced cheese?"

"I didn't mean it like that."

"I know. I've gotten used to being the expendable Kennedy."

"You're not expendable, Bobby. I need you. I can't do all this alone."

"Well, I'm here, ain't I?"

"I appreciate it."

"Stop it. You'll make me shed a tear."

"No, you won't. Kennedys don't cry. Mother forbids it, remember?"

They both laughed at the thought as they waved

to the passing crowds.

It was a long, slow flight for Granier and McGoon. They had to stop at another airfield to refuel. The Criquet sputtered over the mountains at just over 100 mph. "You want me to get out and push," said Granier.

"Sure, smartass, but leave the parachute," said McGoon.

Granier studied some intelligence reports he had acquired from a French reconnaissance captain for twenty US dollars. "Their base camp should be somewhere along that ridge," he said, pointing.

"I hope we find them soon. We're running out of daylight."

McGoon paralleled the ridgeline for about twenty minutes until they saw smoke ascending from a thick canopy of trees. "That's probably them cooking their evening rice," said Granier.

McGoon got out his map and studied it. "Here," he said, pressing his finger on a spot. "I'll wait for you in that village."

"How do you know you can set it down?"

"Don't worry about me. I can land anywhere. It's all about confidence. I'll wait for forty-eight hours. After that, I'll assume you're dead. Anyone you want me to notify?"

"No. I'm good. Think this thing can make it up to eight hundred feet?"

"Sure. May take a few minutes."

"I'm in no rush."

Granier slipped on his parachute and pulled out his pistol. "Hang onto this for me, will ya?"

"You ain't taking a weapon?"

"Nope. I figure my cover will be a lot more convincing if I'm unarmed."

"That's the stupidest thing I ever heard."

"Yeah. Sounded pretty stupid in my head when I thought it up."

"Good luck. Beers on you when we get back."

"You got it."

Granier shook McGoon's hand and opened the passenger door. He slid his feet out and stood on the wing slats. He closed the door and looked down. He took note of the landmarks around the area where the cooking fires were burning. He waited until he was a couple of miles away from the camp, then jumped.

He waited until he was sure he was clear of the plane's gear to open his chute. At only eight hundred feet, there wasn't much time. The parachute billowed, then snapped open. He felt the familiar tug on his crotch and chest harness straps. He descended toward a thick jungle.

He crashed through the branches and leaves of the canopy, causing a cascade of foliage to fall to the jungle floor. He was lucky not to have landed on a strangling fig or palm tree with their tooth-like branches. His chute hung up on a large branch and brought him to an abrupt halt twenty feet above the ground. There was a loud crack. The branch broke, and he dropped to the jungle floor. He tumbled across the uneven ground and over a large root. He looked up to see the broken tree branch hurtling toward him from above. There was no time to get out of the way. He curled up in a ball and hoped for the best. It hit him on the side of his chest with a thud and knocked the wind out of him. It hurt like being slugged by a boxer, but he was pretty sure nothing was broken. He detached his parachute's harness and stood. His muscles felt sore, and his body bruised. He knew the pain would most likely subside once he started hiking. He gathered his chute more out of habit than necessity. He had no intention of carrying it through the jungle. He left it balled up by the base of a tree in between two large roots. It wasn't hidden very well, but he figured it really didn't matter. He slung his pack over his shoulders and took off in the direction of the cooking fires he had seen.

It was dark by the time Granier reached the camp, and that suited him. He removed a pair of binoculars from his backpack before hiding the backpack next to a tree and covering it with loose leaves and a fallen palm frond. He laid on his belly and crawled over a small rise above the camp. He used the binoculars to survey the camp. There was little light in the camp, making it difficult to see.

The sprawling camp was spread out beneath the canopy of trees. Machineguns in watchtowers protected the four corners of the compound. Camouflage nets covered the towers, making them invisible from the air and keeping the soldiers inside hidden. More nets covered supply crates and ammunition boxes. The structures within the compound were temporary and made of material from the surrounding jungle. The frons and foliage used to camouflage the structures were replaced weekly to keep them fresh and appear natural. There were gun pits dug into the soil and stacks of sandbags forming defensive perimeters around each of the structures. Several mortars were set up in the middle of the camp, each pointing toward the most likely direction of an attack. It was a well-made camp designed to fend off an aggressive enemy.

The soldiers moving around the camp wore camouflaged uniforms and blended well with their surroundings. Each carried his weapon wherever he went, always ready for an attack. In many respects, they seemed more disciplined than the Viet Minh rebels Grainer had lived with for several months while fighting the Japanese in World War II.

He tried to gauge the number of soldiers in the camp, but they were too spread out. The barracks were also spread out, and there was no central chow tent where the men would sit. He spotted an open-air kitchen under a large camouflage net and a supply hut. Next to the kitchen was a large chicken coup covered in palm fronds and surrounded by a wire mesh fence to keep the hundreds of chickens from wandering off into the jungle and keeping predators out. He backed away from the rise and made his way through the jungle until he was near the kitchen and supply hut.

He crawled down to the edge of the kitchen. He steered clear of the chow line where the cooks severed the men of the camp. The diet was mostly cooked rice with fish sauce, a boiled egg, and some raw vegetables. Several cooks stirred boiling pots of rice over fire pits. Granier made his way to the supply hut and slipped inside.

The supply hut was filled with bags of rice, which

Granier counted, then estimated the number of men they would feed for a week. It was a very crude way of measuring the size of the army, but it was all he had. He also counted the bottles of fish sauce and estimated the number of eggs stored in five large woven baskets. He figured it all added up to feed around one thousand soldiers.

As he slipped out of the supply hut, something caught his eye – a command tent with a map stretched over a table. It was in front of the kitchen, which meant he would have to cross an open area to get to it. It was risky, but he really wanted a look at that map. He decided to attempt to reach it. He figured the best way to cross the open area was to act like one of the soldiers. That wasn't easy since he was far taller and his shoulders much broader than most Vietnamese. Fortunately, it was dark, and it was starting to drizzle. He was also wearing a camouflaged uniform, and while it had a completely different pattern than the Vietnamese outfits, he wondered if anyone would notice. He figured if he stayed clear of any light, he'd be okay. Slouching would also help.

He waited until the command center was empty. He worked his way toward it using a stack of ammo boxes for cover. When he came to the end of the ammo boxes, he almost ran into a soldier smoking a cigarette, trying to keep out of the rain under the camouflage net. The soldier had set his conical hat down on one of the boxes. Granier reached up and grabbed the hat when the soldier was looking in the opposite direction. He slipped the hat on, stood up, and started walking toward the command center, careful not to make eye contact with anyone. It's all about confidence, he thought. One foot in front of the other. An evening stroll.

When he arrived at the command center, he slipped inside. The walls were open. Everyone could see him. He needed to be quick. He walked over to the map, folded it up, and stuffed it inside his shirt. He walked out across the compound and back into the jungle.

He worked his way back and retrieved his backpack, then hiked deeper into the jungle and away from the camp. He found a dry spot inside a burned-out tree trunk. Amazingly, the tree was still living even with the blackened scar. He used a flashlight with a red filter to study the map. It showed the placement of the army's units. The militia commanders used the same symbols as the French to identify their units, and there were no units larger than a platoon outside of the base camp. Granier thought his estimate was in the ballpark – about one thousand men give or take five hundred. He noticed that the platoons were all positioned near villages. He imagined the villagers supported the units in their area either by their own free will or by compulsion. He grabbed a big bite of beef jerky from his pocket, took a swallow of water from his canteen, and turned off his flashlight. He would grab whatever shuteye he could. Tomorrow would be a busy day.

The next morning just after sun-up, he traveled through the jungle back toward the base camp, his eyes scanning the ground and surrounding trees. He munched on more beef jerky and took another swallow of water as he walked. He didn't want to stumble across a patrol from THe's camp. Surprised by his white skin and large stature, they might assume he was French and shoot him like what happened to Colonel Dewey. What he really wanted was to find a booby-trap.

A few minutes later, he was crossing a small clearing when he came across a tripwire stretched between two trees. He followed the wire until he discovered the weapon – a grenade attached to the base of one of the trees. He carefully cut the wire with his knife. He moved to the opposite side of the tree with the end of the wire in his hand. He made sure none of his limbs were exposed from behind the tree. He gave the wire a hard yank removing the safety pin from the grenade. The lever flipped open, and the grenade immediately detonated with a loud explosion. Protected by the tree, none of the shrapnel hit him, but his ears rang a bit. He walked out into the clearing, set down his pack a few feet away, and stood with his hands in the air as if he was surrendering. He wanted no mistake about his intentions.

A few minutes passed before a Vietnamese patrol appeared through the jungle to investigate the explosion. They saw Granier standing in the clearing and aimed their rifles at him as if they were about to shoot. The unit commander shouted for his men to hold fire. Granier was searched and taken captive. One of the soldiers searched his pack and found it was filled with bundles of American dollars. They didn't know what to make of the strange green paper.

They had never seen an American dollar before. The commander figured it was some sort of currency and decided to take it with them. Granier's arms were tied at the wrists and elbows. He was led through the jungle toward the base camp. The soldiers kept their fingers on the triggers of their weapons as they walked, which made Granier more than nervous, but he figured it was not the best time to lecture them on gun safety.

Granier and his pack filled with money were brought before General THe. THe looked inside the pack and saw the money. Granier spoke to THe in French since the General understood little English. "What is your name?" said THe.

"Rene Granier."

"You are French. Give me one reason why I shouldn't have you shot?"

"I'm an American. I'm not your enemy. I came unarmed," said Granier.

"Granier is a French name."

"It is. But I am American."

"Do you have proof of this?"

"My passport. It's in my shirt pocket."

THe ordered a soldier to bring him the contents of the prisoner's pockets. The soldier removed Granier's passport along with everything else and handed it to THe. THe removed the rubber bands and wax paper from the passport and examined it. "Why are you here, American?"

"To offer you the contents in my pack with the promise of more once we have an understanding."

"An understanding? You Americans think you

can buy anything."

"We don't want to buy you. We want to help you."

"Why?"

"We believe our interests and your interests are aligned. You want independence from the French. We believe you should have it."

"And yet you give the French military aid."

"Because we have no alternative. Like you, we want to keep Indochina free from communists."

"You think me a fool. America wants to replace France, not free Vietnam."

"That's not true. America has no interest in Indochina beyond stopping the expansion of Communism."

"We do not need America's help to defeat the communists or the French."

"Maybe not yet. Your movement is still small. You can get by on raiding your enemy and taxing the villages you control. But that won't be enough if you want your army to grow to the size needed to defeat your enemies."

"You underestimate the size of our forces. We have over thirty thousand armed and ready to fight."

"No. You have one to two thousand."

"Are you calling me a liar?"

"No. You are a commander that fears the French or Viet Minh will attack your base of operations if they perceive your force is small and ill-equipped."

"Why do you think this?"

"Because last night I looked at your rice stores. You can only feed one to two thousand men. I am also sure you could quickly increase the size of your force if you were properly supplied."

"And America is offering the money required?"

"Yes, under the right terms."

"How do I know you are authorized to make such an offer?"

"You don't. That would take faith on your part."

"If we accepted your help, you would wish to control us."

"It's true. We would ask that you not attack civilians."

"And how exactly do you tell the difference between a Viet Minh and a civilian?"

"I know it's not easy. But slaughtering an entire village for the act of one man is not a good way to win the hearts of the people."

"We do not kill our own people. You confuse us with the communists."

"And the bombs in Saigon? You killed dozens of innocent people."

"You assume it was us that planted those bombs."

"Did you?"

"Even if we did, those people were French. They don't belong in our country."

"They were civilians."

"War is not fit for those that wear white gloves."

"We cannot help you if you terrorize civilians."

"If I agreed not to 'terrorize civilians' as you say, what would you give me in return?"

"America can be a powerful ally, especially when it comes to international recognition of the leader of a country's government."

"And what of Bao Dai, the French puppet?"

"The people do not trust him and will not follow

him."

"He will need to be removed."

"I don't think so. When the French leave, so will he. He has no loyalty to Vietnam. He will choose to live in France so he can chase women, play cards, and drink wine. The people of Vietnam should choose their leader, not the French, and not the Americans."

"You would want the people to elect their leaders?"

"Once the government is stabilized, yes."

"You are naïve. The people of Vietnam are uneducated peasants. Most have never seen the inside of a school or even own a book. How can you expect them to rule themselves? It is impossible."

"They have the right to choose who they follow. It is no different than your own men."

"They follow me because I bring them victory. When that stops, I am a dead man."

"The odds of winning are much better with America as your ally."

"And what of the French? Do you expect them to just up and leave?"

"No. It will take some convincing that they should grant Indochina true independence."

"They will never do it on their own. They are too proud and greedy."

"Well... that's why we need you."

"I will admit, I am intrigued by your offer."

"I thought you might be."

"I don't trust you. Trust takes time and experience."

"I feel the same."

"I will consider your offer. How can I communicate with you?"

"I will give you a code phrase and a radio channel that my people will monitor. Use the code phrase, and we will send someone to make contact again."

"You?"

"I don't know. I don't make those decisions. But no matter, someone will be sent to meet you," said Granier handing THe a paper with the radio channel number and the code phrase.

Without warning, three mortar rounds whistled into the camp and exploded, wounding two of THe's soldiers. Nearby gunfire erupted. THe barked out orders to his officers, then drew his pistol and pointed it at Granier. "You have brought the French."

"I did not. If I had, this conversation would not have been necessary."

THe cocked the hammer back as he prepared to fire and said, "You lie."

A lieutenant ran up to THe and spoke in Vietnamese. THe gave him orders. The officer ran off. THe uncocked his weapon. "You are lucky. It is the communists. You are free to go. I will send some of my men to escort you."

"No, thank you. You will need your men. I am better on my own."

Granier moved off in the opposite direction of the fighting and disappeared into the jungle.

Hiking through the jungle most of the day, Granier came out of the trees next to the village McGoon had identified. He was happy to see the aircraft sitting on top of a long dike ready for takeoff. He noticed that one of the wheel struts was wrapped with a bundle of bamboo.

As he approached the village, two villagers armed with rifles aimed at him. He stopped and raised his hands. They motioned for him to continue toward them.

Granier was escorted into the village by one of the guards. He found McGoon sitting in front of a pig roasting over a fire pit. "You made it," said McGoon. "Just in time for the luau."

"Where did you get the pig?" said Granier.

"I bought it from the village chief. It turns out he likes paper money. Who would have thunk it?"

"What happened to the plane?"

"Oh, that. I tried to land in a field. Broke a wheel strut. Village handyman fixed it."

"Is bamboo enough to hold it together?"

"He says it is, but I suppose we are about to find out. After supper, of course. I would hate to die on an empty stomach."

"So, how did you get the plane up on a dike?"

"They lifted it. It's pretty lightweight. Sit down and take a load off. They got a nice local liquor made from some kind of fermented fruit. I can't pronounce it, but I can verify its alcohol content. Pretty strong stuff."

"How much of that did you drink?"

"I don't know. One, maybe two coconuts full."

"We ain't flying tonight. Not until you sober up."

"You misjudge my ability to process liquor."

"Yeah, well... we still ain't flying."

"Suit yourself. I'm happy to stay the night. They

made me a comfy bed in one of the huts. It comes with a nice girl I like to call, "Betty."

"Does she think you're taking her back to Saigon?"

"Maybe. I can't say for sure. I think I promised to buy her a dress."

"You know the plane only holds two."

"Yeah, but she's just a little thing. Don't weigh nothing. We'll be fine."

"Well, I'm too damn tired to argue. Cut me a slice of that pig cheek, will you?" said Granier plopping down on the ground.

"No, but I will see that it is done. I gotta save my energy for Betty."

McGoon motioned to a middle-aged woman tending the fire and pig. She cut off a slice of the cheek, placed it in a banana leaf, and handed it to Granier. "Thanks," said Granier chowing down.

She smiled a toothless grin while looking him over.

An early morning fog hung over the rice paddies around the village. The mist stopped just below the dike, giving the impression of a miniature mountain ridge poking through a bank of clouds.

The plane's propeller turned slowly at first then quickly picked up speed as the engine sputtered to life. Granier sat next to McGoon. Betty, a teenage Vietnamese girl, sat in the storage area. She had never even been in a car, let alone a plane. "This is gonna be a short takeoff, so you might want to hold on to something," said McGoon.

"Will that help if we crash?" said Granier.

"Couldn't hurt."

McGoon throttled up the engine as far as he dared before releasing the brakes. The tail-dragging plane lunged forward and barreled across the top of the dike. The ground was bumpy, and the width of the dike barely fit the wheels. Just before running off the end of the dike, McGoon took off. Betty's eyes went wide. She was petrified. McGoon banked the plane hard to avoid a wall of trees and flew over the village. "Look, Betty. It's your village," said McGoon pointing and grinning.

Betty barfed.

The Criquet landed safely at Da Nang Air Base. McGoon abandoned the aircraft at the end of the runway. Granier and Betty hid in a drainage ditch and waited for McGoon as he switched off the engine. All three made their way toward the civilian terminal keeping their heads below the ditch edge.

As they entered the terminal, McGoon pointed Betty toward the restrooms so she could clean herself up and made hand motions like he was washing his face. Betty went inside.

Everything looked strange to Betty, especially the white porcelain urinals attached to the wall. She wondered what their use was. She thought they might be some kind of place to wash your hands because they had water in the basin. She was amazed at the big mirror above the sinks and her reflection. She had seen her reflection on a mirror in the village, but it was small and only had room for her face. She could see her whole body in the big mirror. Curious, she took off her clothes and stood naked, gazing. She liked her body. A man walked in and was shocked to see her. Betty grabbed her clothes, ran into one of the stalls, and slammed the door shut. She had not understood the symbol distinguishing the Men's restroom from the Women's.

As promised, Granier bought the first round of beers at a bar inside the terminal. With a cold beer in his hand, McGoon was as happy as a hog in a puddle. "Any day ya don't crash is a day to be celebrated," McGoon toasted, clanking his beer mug against Granier's.

"You have a very low bar for success," said Granier.

"Yep, but that just means I am rarely disappointed. Ya gotta keep a positive attitude."

"I suppose. Thanks for the help."

"Don't mention it. I'm always up for an adventure. So, what's next?"

"I'll be heading to Hanoi to catch up with the congressman and his brother."

"You watch yourself. Those Frenchies up north can be tricky bastards if they don't like what you're selling."

"Good to know. How about you? You heading back to Hue?"

"Not right away. I thought I'd take Betty to Saigon and show her around for a few days."

"A few days, huh. You know she's probably pretty fertile."

"I would imagine. I'll be safe. My wife probably wouldn't appreciate me bringing a mixed-breed back to the states."

"Probably not."

"Kid might be kinda cute, though."

Granier grunted and drank his beer.

John and Bobby sat in a military briefing on the disposition of the enemy and the defensive perimeter the French had created around Hanoi and Haiphong Harbor. A French colonel who spoke acceptable English pointed to a wall map. "The De Lattre line is now almost 90% complete. The line is comprised of 1200 reinforced concrete blockhouses. Each blockhouse holds a minimum of ten soldiers and is able to withstand shelling from 155mm artillery. The blockhouses are built in clusters of 3 to 6 to provide supporting fire when attacked, similar to the redoubts of a star fortress. The defenses are spread over 235 miles starting at the ocean in the north and stretching around Hanoi in a hook shape. The perimeter is set forward 22 miles from both Hanoi and Haiphong, preventing the enemy from shooting artillery over the line to strike the city or harbor. All the defensive lines are connected by roads capable of bearing 30-ton tanks. This gives us a robust interior line of communication to reinforce and resupply any of our units under attack quickly. Our airfields within the perimeter give us exceptional reconnaissance and air-to-ground assault capabilities."

"How is this any different than the Maginot Line which the Germans circumvented with their blitzkrieg?" said John.

"The Viet Minh do not have tanks," said the colonel, snidely.

"Yes, but they do have artillery and have shown

an amazing ability to move their forces great distances in a short amount of time. When they find a weak spot, they will surely exploit it."

"It's true that there are still gaps in our defensive line, and some Viet Minh units have penetrated deeper into our perimeter, but our patrols have picked up their movements. We have been able to dispatch them successfully before they caused too much damage. It is a far better strategy to let them attack us, then search for them in the mountains," said De Lattre.

"It's a defensive strategy that requires that the enemy cooperate. I've found from experience that the enemy rarely complies with our wishes," said John.

"Ho Chi Minh needs Hanoi as his base of operation if he ever hopes to mount a credible attack against our forces in central and south Indochina. Hanoi gives him control of Haiphong Harbor, and Haiphong allows the Chinese and Russians to easily supply his troops with vast quantities of weapons and food. Hanoi is the prize that we must deny him. He will bash his forces against our defenses, and we will wear him down until he has no choice but to sue for peace."

"I would like to see the De Lattre Line in action first hand."

"And you shall. Our intelligence reports indicate a large Viet Minh build-up to the southwest of Haiphong."

As the briefing adjourned and the Kennedys headed back to their hotel, De Lattre was approached by his head of intelligence, "We found Granier. He just got off a commercial flight from Da Nang," said the officer.

"What was he doing in Da Nang?" asked De Lattre.

"We don't know. But he was wearing dirty jungle fatigues and in great need of a shower."

"I'm not interested in his hygiene. I want to know where he—," said De Lattre stopping mid-sentence to think. "THe. He went to contact General THe."

"Why?"

"Why is your job. See that you do it," said De Lattre moving off, agitated.

Granier was waiting for the Kennedys in the lobby of the hotel – the Grand Hotel Métropole in the French Quarter of Hanoi. Guests glanced at his dirty fatigues as they entered and exited the hotel. A hotel security guard approached him and asked if he would feel more comfortable seated in the outdoor café. "No. I'm good here," he said in a don't-bother-me voice accompanied by a killer's glare.

He was left alone until the Kennedys finally showed up. "Granier, in case you hadn't noticed, you are badly in need of a shower," said John shaking his hand.

"I thought it was important that you hear my report as soon as possible," said Granier.

"It is. Did you make contact with General THe?"

"I did."

"Good. Take a shower and meet us in the lounge in thirty minutes."

"Did you bring my suitcase?"

"Oh, damn. Were we supposed to do that?"

"I can buy something in one of the shops."

"No. It's my fault. I'll give you a change of clothes. We're about the same size, I think. You can tell me about THe on our way to my room."

"I'd rather wait until we can speak privately."

"Of course. Shower, clothes, a stiff drink, and then your report."

Bobby retrieved their room keys from the front desk, and they headed upstairs.

Granier took a shower in his room and put on John's change of clothes. The shirts were tailor-made of silk and the pants of lightweight linen. The dress shoes look like they cost a small fortune. In truth, Granier had never looked so good. He didn't like it. His appearance drew attention. He placed his pistol in his front pocket. It bulged against the linen fabric. He didn't like that either. Fu-fu clothes, he thought. He missed his fatigues, which were already being washed in the hotel's laundry.

Granier met the Kennedys in the lounge. Kennedy had requested a booth in the corner away from the other patrons so they could talk privately. "You clean up nice, Granier," said John.

"Thanks for the loan," said Granier.

"They're not a loan. You keep them. A man should have a nice change of clothes. If we have time, I'll have you fitted for a suit. I hear the Vietnamese tailors are quite good."

"Thanks, but no. These are enough. I don't have much occasion to dress up."

298

John ordered Bloody Mary's for Bobby and him. Granier ordered a beer. "You sure you don't want something a little heavier? I bet it's been a long couple of days."

"No. Gotta keep my wits to do my job."

"Okay. But I think we are pretty safe here in the hotel."

"I know you think that."

"Very well."

John waited until the waiter was out of earshot, then asked, "So, General THe… is he the real deal?"

"Yes. And he has an army. About one thousand men."

"Well, I suppose that's a start."

"I saw them in action. They can fight. He's trained his men well, and they're brave."

"How did you see them in action?"

"His camp was attacked while I was there."

"The French?"

"No. Communists."

"Who won?"

"I didn't stick around to find out. But I'm pretty sure they survived. The camp is pretty well situated, and his men were well-armed."

"Good. How did he receive our offer?"

"I think he'll take the aid. He wants to overthrow the French."

"So, he's both anti-French and anti-communist as we hoped?"

"He is. But I can't say he's pro-democracy."

"What do you mean?"

"I mean, if wins, he'll be a dictator."

"We'll see about that."

"No. I'm sure. If he wins, he's keeping the crown."

"I see. That's not what we had in mind."

"I didn't think so."

"That's too bad. I thought we might have found our man."

"I'm not sure your man exists… not in Vietnam. A strong leader is the only way to rule this country, and no matter their original intentions, strong leaders tend to dictate when they come to power."

"And I think we haven't looked hard enough."

"Maybe your right. At least THe had enough guts to break away from the French. I'll give him that."

"So, the search for a third force continues."

CHAPTER FIFTEEN

The French had learned well from their defeat along Colonial Route 4. The defensive line of blockhouses and lookout towers had worked for a time and forced the Viet Minh to re-route their supply lines farther from Hanoi. But it didn't last. Because civilian traffic was able to use the road, the Viet Minh were able to penetrate the defensive line that protected it. The positioning and layout of the blockhouses were also wrong. While they could support one another, it was difficult to consolidate enough firepower to stop a determined enemy assault. But the biggest problem was that the fortresses along Colonial Route 4 were far from their supply depots around Hanoi, and there was only one road leading to the last fort. The one way in, one way out geography exacerbated the ever-increasing need for reinforcement and high probability of ambush on the supply and troop convoys.

From these lessons and more, the French built the

De Lattre defensive line around the highly populated Tonkin Delta. It was a defensive ring that started on the northern coast, extended along the mountains, then curved southward around Hanoi and back to the southern coast on the opposite side of Haiphong Harbor. Multiple roads were built inside the protected area to the different sections of the line, making reinforcement and resupply safe and quick. The line was protected by hundreds of 105mm, and 155mm howitzers placed several miles behind the front so they could not be easily captured by the Viet Minh if there was ever a breakthrough. Mobile Groups with armor were stationed at central points within the interior, allowing them to quickly reinforce any position under pressure from the Viet Minh or plug any breakthrough.

Almost 1200 blockhouses were constructed over 235 miles of perimeter. The lookout towers were also beefed up being built out of concrete instead of wood, making them more impervious to heavy assaults. While their walls were not as thick as the blockhouses, they could withstand most small arms fire and even a bazooka rocket. The fortifications were far from uniform. Some were simple blockhouses built along a road, while others were elevated on man-made hills and had elaborate designs, including perimeter walls with deep trenches to slow down the human wave assaults. All the blockhouse had 360-degree firing portals that allowed the soldiers inside to fire in all directions and had cleared fields of fire several hundred yards out.

The area protected by the De Lattre line was massive and required a large portion of the French army to man the blockhouses and lookout towers. This significantly limited operations outside the perimeter. The French had put themselves in a defensive posture that required the Viet Minh to attack.

But De Lattre calculated that Ho Chi Minh would attack. The prize inside the perimeter was too valuable to just pass up. Ho needed Hanoi and Haiphong Harbor for political and logistical support of his growing army. He needed the rice grown in the delta to feed his troops. And most of all, he needed to destroy the French army. The French had massed within the perimeter, and when the Viet Minh broke through, they would exact a heavy toll on the French troops, perhaps enough to force the French to surrender and leave Indochina once and for all.

Like the ringmaster of a circus, De Lattre was careful of what was shown to the Kennedys. Even as he pretended to be an open book, he wanted the message controlled whenever possible. His duties prevented him from conducting the entire tour himself, which he would have preferred. But he was needed elsewhere. The Viet Minh were massing once again. De Lattre was doing everything within his power to be ready. Once again, he hoped this would be the final battle that brought the Viet Minh to their knees as they pounded against his impregnatable line of defense.

The first few days in Hanoi went as planned by De Lattre. The Kennedys were chauffeured in an armored car to military bases, airfields, construction sites, and various locations along the defensive line. It was a rough ride that didn't help John's back. The air inside the armored car was hot and stale with the stench of exhaust fumes. There was almost no ventilation except for the gun portal where the machinegun had been removed so John and Bobby could look out and watch the countryside as they passed. It was a miserable experience, which was precisely what De Lattre wanted. The shorter the Kennedys' visit in the north, the better.

Even though their tour was uncomfortable, it was informative. John was impressed by the French buildup. Thousands of workers slaved away at the construction of blockhouses and watchtowers. Most of the line had been completed within the first year, an unfathomable accomplishment when they started.

While the defensive line did tie up a large portion of the French Army during construction, it also protected the major population center in the north. There was little doubt of the viability of De Lattre's promise never to let Hanoi or Haiphong fall into enemy hands. The French were here to stay. De Lattre's long term plan was to train Vietnamese colonial troops to eventually take the place of the French troops manning the perimeter defenses. Unfortunately, it was a slow process that De Lattre criticized. He felt that most of the Vietnamese government and military leaders were fence-sitters waiting to see the outcome of the war rather than pitching in with the French to defend their country. The French were far from winning the hearts and minds of the Vietnamese people and were forced to provide the majority of the defense of the De Lattre line themselves.

Unsurprisingly, the one group in-country that did support the French were the Catholic communities around Vietnam. Catholicism had grown to over 5% of the total population, and there was an exceptionally large contingent around Hanoi and Saigon. There was very little doubt that Christians, in general, would be treated harshly under a communist government. The Catholics had formed their own militias to protect their people and property. The militia leaders had volunteered to help fight the Viet Minh should they attack. While their troops were not as well trained as the French colonial soldiers, the militia did have high morale bolstered by their faith and proved to be staunch defenders.

While visiting a construction site of several blockhouses, John watched dozens of wheelbarrows and ox carts transporting tons of wet concrete from a line of cement mixers to the forms of the blockhouses. John asked, "Where do you get the concrete?"

"We are fortunate that Vietnam has an abundance of clay, limestone, sand, rock, and gravel. It also has the iron and coal mines that allow us to manufacture the steel required to reinforce the blockhouses," said the commander of the engineers overseeing the construction. "If we were in any other part of the world, I doubt this would be possible. It is an incredible engineering feat and will be responsible for the downfall of Ho Chi Minh."

"You seem confident that the De Lattre Line will hold back the Viet Minh."

"It will. It must."

Granier looked out at the surrounding jungle and

wondered if it would be enough. The French seemed well prepared, but he knew Giap was sly and would not attack where the French expected. He also hated the idea of taking a defensive stance rather than seeking out the enemy. Offense disrupted the enemy's plans and forced them to defend themselves. The Viet Minh could not advance while retreating. By sitting and waiting for the Viet Minh to attack, the French were playing into Giap's hands. It was Giap that controlled the location of the battle, not De Lattre. Bobby moved up next to Granier and said, "It all seems so very formidable. Do you think this will work?"

"The French love drawing lines in the sand and daring the enemy to cross them," said Granier. "But it's a lousy way to fight a war. Your enemy knows what you will do, and where."

"General De Lattre says he's training the Vietnamese colonial troops to take the place of the French, and that will allow his troops to go back on offense."

"This line is massive. It'll take years before they train enough men. I don't think the French have that long to wait. De Lattre hopes Giap will attack the defenses now and try to break through. He wants to smash them with his artillery and airpower."

"That's a good plan, isn't it?"

"I don't know. I'm not a general. But I don't think Giap is going to do anything that De Lattre expects. No matter what, it's going to be a bloody couple of days when the two sides meet this time."

"Enough to end the war?"

"Depends who wins and by how much. Never

underestimate your enemy's tolerance for pain."

As the Kennedys concluded their tour of the construction site, De Lattre's convoy appeared, speeding toward them. The group of vehicles stopped, and De Lattre jumped out. "How was your tour today?" said De Lattre.

"Interesting and impressive. Your men sure know how to pour concrete," said John.

"We have learned through experience. I am afraid I must cut the rest of your tour short."

"How's that?"

"Our intelligence reports a major Viet Minh build up nearby. It's best if we get you back to Hanoi now before the battle begins."

"Pardon me, General, but isn't that the whole point of us coming north? We want to see how your men fight."

"No. No. It is far too risky. You should go back now. If you hurry, you can make the cocktail hour at your hotel."

"I don't need a cocktail, General. I need the truth."

"You are presumptuous, Congressman. I am hiding nothing."

"Then let us see your men in action. We accept the risk, and I promise you we will stay out of the way."

Three mortar artillery rounds whistled into the construction site and exploded. The French engineers scrambled for their weapons, leaving the concrete to dry within the mixer. "It has begun already," said De Lattre.

"I'm sure you have more to worry about right now than our safety. We can take care of ourselves," said John.

"No. You will stay with me. My command center is nearby. You will see how we French fight the Viet Minh."

"Now you're talking, General," said John with a grin.

They climbed into the General's vehicles and drove off.

The command center was filled with maps, radios, phones, and staff officers rushing about. Granier, John, and Bobby stood near De Lattre and observed but were careful to stay out of the way. De Lattre seemed to be in complete control as the reports came in of the enemy's movements. He fired off questions about locations of his units, the range of his artillery, and the condition of his armor. His staff rattled back the answers. Everyone knew what information the general wanted before he wanted it. They were a well-oiled machine. Any pause was met with a sharp rebuke and threat of dismissal by the general. He was merciless and deadly serious. They feared him and admired him. His mind was quick. Life and death decisions for hundreds of men were made with little time to consider. Experience and confidence took over. He feared nothing. He knew how to fight his enemy like he had played out each scenario a dozen times in his mind before this moment.

The Kennedys and Granier could not help but be impressed. The battle was just beginning, but already the French were locking into their strategy and driving the Viet Minh back. More reports of attacks in other areas came in. It was an all-out-offensive with three Viet Minh divisions. As usual, the French were outnumbered, and the attacks were in an area where the roads were still under construction, making reinforcement difficult. Giap had chosen his ground wisely, but the French were undaunted.

After receiving his medal, Bernard was given command of an entire squadron of mechanized cavalry made up of armored cars and troop transport trucks. When he heard the first shells explode in the distance, he knew his men would be called into action. He didn't wait for the command before loading his troops and gear in their vehicles. They were told to carry extra ammunition and to expect a long night. Then, he waited by the radio. Within five minutes, the call came in from his commander, ordering him to attack.

He marked the position of the enemy forces with a grease pencil on his map and quickly laid out a route to reach them. His hundred and twenty men would be going up against an entire Viet Minh battalion attacking several blockhouses by the bridge across the Day River. He rode in the first armored car, and his men followed in trucks, jeeps, and armored cars. They had no heavy armor, such as tanks. Their advantage was speed and agility.

French aircraft flew at top speed in multiple directions. They were strafing and bombing as fast as possible, then returning to their bases to reload and

refuel. Because the airfields were close to the
battlefields, the French airpower was multiplied. One
aircraft could make three, four, even five bombing
raids in one day.

As the cavalry squadron drove along a half-built
road, Bernard looked to the horizon. The sun was
setting. The French warplanes would be forced to
return to their aircraft carriers and airfields. Bernard
spotted the enemy battalion with his binoculars.

The Viet Minh were attacking three blockhouses
and a watchtower at the mouth of a bridge stretching
across the Day River. The fortifications were
designed to protect the crossing and were on the
same side of the river as the city of Ninh Binh. Unlike
most of the blockhouses around the De Lattre line,
the field of fire was only cleared for thirty yards.
Buildings along the riverfront made good cover for
the Viet Minh. The French aircraft and the soldiers
within the blockhouses were keeping the Viet Minh
from advancing, but it was only a matter of time
before the Viet Minh consolidated enough troops to
rush the French defenses in a human wave. The
French would make the Viet Minh pay dearly, but it
was clear that they would be overwhelmed and
forced to surrender their position or die.

Time was running short. Bernard's cavalry
squadron was the only hope for the French troops in
the blockhouses. Bernard would make the most of the
air support that remained. He ordered his troops to
dismount from their trucks. The trucks and jeeps
would be easy targets for the Viet Minh and provided
no additional firepower. Only the armored cars and

foot soldiers would go into battle. As soon as they were in position, he ordered his men forward. They advanced quickly and opened fire on the flank of the enemy battalion.

The Viet Minh were now forced to fight on two fronts and were at a disadvantage.

The Viet Minh commander ordered his heavy mortars and machineguns to fire on the approaching cavalry while his infantry kept engaging with the blockhouses.

It was a murderous barrage of exploding shells and bullets zipping through the grass. Bernard's foot soldiers were forced to the ground while the armored cars laid down a volley of covering fire. Bernard could feel his assault stalling, and he wasn't having it. He jumped out of his armored car and joined his foot soldiers lying on their bellies. He moved to their head and said, "Follow me."

Crouching low, he advanced toward the enemy. His men followed. How could they not? They kept low. Some tried to crawl on their bellies, but they were too slow. They jumped to their feet and moved forward with their backs bent over like a hundred hunchbacks. The long grass was their only cover.

The armored car drove forward, firing their cannons and machineguns at the enemy machinegun and mortar positions. Many of the enemies fell silent, some dead, others playing dead, so their position was not discovered as the armored cars approached.

With the enemy fire subdued, Bernard and his troops were able to move quicker. When they were finally close enough to engage the infantry assaulting the blockhouse, Bernard yelled, "Charge."

The French cavalry ran forward and opened fire on the enemy.

With their flank unprotected and their comrades dropping like flies, the Viet Minh battalion recoiled and broke off their assault. The French kept firing, picking off as many of the enemy troops as possible until they were out of range. The firefight had been short but fierce. The French had won − the first round of many.

Bernard watched as the last of the aircraft headed to the north toward the airfields around Hanoi and east toward the Bay of Tonkin, where the aircraft carrier Arromanches was waiting to retrieve its children. "The aircraft are leaving. The Viet Minh will attack again. Have the men take up defensive positions and see that they receive a resupply of ammunition," said Bernard to a staff sergeant. "I'll be back in a few minutes. I need to coordinate with the blockhouse commander before the next assault begins."

Bernard moved off, keeping low. He was careful to warn the French troopers that he was a friend before approaching their lines around the blockhouses and watchtowers. He called out that day's password in French, and they called back with a reply.

He found the commander in the middle blockhouse and informed him of the disposition of the cavalry squadron and made sure they were clear on which radio channel they would communicate. Together, they would support each other's positions, keeping the Viet Minh at bay. Toward the end of the conversation, three enemy mortar shells whistled in and exploded around the blockhouses. "I've got to get back to my men," said Bernard.

"I think you are too late. The attack has begun," said the blockhouse commander.

"No. I can make it back. Good luck," said Bernard, leaving the blockhouse.

Bernard bent over to keep low and ran as fast as he could. Two more shells whistled in and landed near the blockhouse like before. A third exploded right in front of Bernard. He was stunned as he was blown backward and landed on his back. He sat up and noticed his uniform was smoking. He looked down to see dozens of holes where red-hot shrapnel had pierced the heavy cloth and was smothering inside his body. He was dead; he just didn't know it yet. A moment later, he slumped over in the long grass.

CHAPTER SIXTEEN

"Everyone stop!" said De Lattre in the command headquarters.

The room went deadly quiet, and nobody moved. Only the hiss and crackle of the radios could be heard. He studied the map showing the current enemy positions, his eyes darting around, absorbing the data, calculating the risks. "What the heck is he doing?" whispered Bobby.

"I don't know, but he'll have your head if you interrupt him," Granier whispered back.

De Lattre backed away from the map as if a thought had come to him and said, "It's not the bridge or even the city that Giap seeks. It's the river."

The staff exchanged confused glances. "He needs the river to bring down supplies and reinforcements from the north to his divisions in the Red River Delta. We will deny him that route. I want 9th Dinassaut to immediately blockade the Day River to the Northwest of Ninh Binh. No boat traffic allowed.

No exceptions," said De Lattre.

"Even after an inspection?"

"There will be no inspections. Nothing gets through. I want him to know that I understand what he is doing and why. Make it so."

Everyone went back to work. "What is a Dinassaut?" asked John.

"It's a French Naval Assault Division – Dinassaut for short. The French Navy uses them to control the rivers in Indochina," said Granier. "They're usually a mix of ten to twelve boats, mostly American landing craft modified with armor – used tank turrets and anti-aircraft guns. Some have 81mm mortars that can be used as riverine artillery."

"Why use landing craft instead of PT boats?"

"The landing craft has a lower draft that makes them ideal for operations in the deltas and rivers."

The 9th Dinassaut sailed up the Day River at top speed. None of the eleven boats were similar in design or modification. Each was custom built for a specific purpose. All were deadly war machines. Most had at least one cannon mounted in a turret and multiple heavy machineguns. Several had heavy mortars set up on the deck below the armored sides of the landing craft, so the mortar crews were completely protected from shore or river fire. There were also four support boats carrying supplies and ammunition. They, too, had machineguns that could safeguard their crew against river pirates and Viet Minh assaults from the shore.

When the flotilla reached its destination, the boats spread out across the river, forming the blockade.

The sampans transporting goods to market came to a stop upriver of the French flotilla, and the pilots complained by shaking their fists at the French. Instead of offering an explanation, the French commander replied by having his boat's machine-gunner fire a stream of bullets in the water in front of the lead sampan. It was a clear message. More and more sampans came to a stop until there was a log jam of boats waiting upriver. It would be a long wait.

When Giap received the news of the river blockade, he was furious. His troops were cut off from desperately needed supplies, ammunition, and reinforcements. It would be difficult and risky to continue their offensive with his supply lines cut. He knew there were a large number of reinforcements being smuggled into the area by boat. It occurred to him that they were in a perfect position for a surprise attack on the French Dinassaut. The only problem was they had no leader.

Giap rectified the situation by sending one of his best commanders, Captain Ton Hieu Phong. Phong had been with Giap during the raids on the Japanese Army during World War II and had fought in almost every major conflict in the Indochina War. He was both experienced and confident. In addition, Giap sent a weapons company to assist the reinforcements as they assaulted the blockade.

Phong and the weapons company moved on foot along the shore using reeds for cover on the southern side of the Day River. As they approached the blockade, Phong ordered his platoon commanders to take up positions among the reeds.

The mortar platoon made a small clearing within the reeds with their knives and shovels. They set up their three 81mm mortar tubes and moved as much ammunition into the clearing as possible. Each mortar could launch twenty-five shells in the first two minutes of the battle, then eight shells a minute at a sustained level.

The heavy machinegun platoon set up their three guns along the shore, pointing toward the river. The soldiers used their knives to cut down the reeds in front of the machinegun positions but were careful to leave enough to keep their firing positions hidden. Even with the removal of a large number of reeds, the machine-gunners could not see their targets. Once the battle had begun, the machinegun bullets would quickly clear away the reeds between them and their target, giving them a clear view of the battle. Ammunition cases were lined up next to the machineguns.

The two additional platoons were riflemen. They, too, set themselves up along the shore and on a narrow knoll that allowed them to form two lines, one shooting over the heads of their comrades. Each platoon also had a light machinegun that was placed on top of the knoll. Their sergeants passed out additional ammunition and readied their men for battle, pumping them up with political slogans and famous words from their leaders.

Phong always carried two sniper rifles with him in a well-worn golf bag. He would give the two rifles with plenty of ammunition to the two best shots in any unit he commanded and position them as high above the battlefield as possible to search for targets of opportunity. He had been trained to be a sniper by an American named Granier and knew what a sniper could do to destroy the enemy's morale. He believed that one well-placed bullet could change the tide of a battle, and he wanted every advantage possible when he fought.

Once the weapon company was set up, Phong put on a disguise of a rice wine vendor and walked along the shore with a big jug until he reached the log jam of sampans. He stepped onto the first, then leaped-frogged his way through the boats contacting the reinforcements as he served them rice wine. He laid out the plan of attack and told them to watch for his signal – a single flare fired above the French boats. The attack was to begin before dawn. He gave each group of reinforcements three grenades and told them to place one of their men in the sampan closest to a French boat. The grenades were to be used in the opening minute of the battle, killing as many French as possible. If the reinforcements felt they could take over a French boat, they were ordered to do so and turn the weapons aboard on the other French boats.

A single flare arced across the dark sky, illuminating the French Dinassaut. The flare was followed by three mortar shells crashing into the river around the French boats and exploding. The surprised marines were drenched with water but unhurt, for the moment. More mortar shells were launched toward the blockade. The Viet Minh machineguns on shore opened fire, driving the French to take cover as they

318

returned fire. It was difficult to see where the machineguns were located. Unlike the French, the Viet Minh were not using tracer ammunition. The French fired wildly at the shoreline.

The thick steel sides of the transport boat protected the French troops from the machinegun rounds and small arms fire. Even when a mortar shell exploded inside a vessel, the damage was minimal because the Viet Minh mortar shells were incapable of penetrating the hull and sinking the boats. Enclosed cannon turrets and vertical steel plates welded to the sides and deck helped protect the French troops from flying shrapnel as they returned fire.

Once the French were occupied by the weapon company onshore, the Viet Minh reinforcements made their move. Sampans were propelled forward up against the French boats, and grenades were tossed over the sides, exploding and killing unprotected French troops. The reinforcements climbed on to the French boats and fought the French marines hand-to-hand. The French pilots gunned their engines and rammed the sampans, sinking several, pushing others out of the way. But when one sampan would sink, another would sail up to take its place. The French boats were trapped and overwhelmed. Fires broke out on several of the French boats, and unprotected ammunition was baked-off in wild explosions. The first French boat listed then sank in the river as an armor-piercing round exploded, driving the shell through the hull. The French were greatly outnumbered, and there were no other French troops with boats nearby to help them.

The sky was beginning to lighten with predawn as reports that the Dinassaut was under attack came into the command center. De Lattre listened and asked pointed questions, mostly about the disposition of French forces nearby that might weigh into the battle. He was like a machine, unfeeling, focused solely on the task at hand. The Kennedys watched from close by as the general gave a string of orders in rapid succession with a clear, confident voice.

De Lattre's executive officer listened on a radio handset. His face turned ashen as he set the handset down and walked toward De Lattre. The general watched him approach and grew angry at what he thought was a disruption. "What is it?" said De Lattre.

The XO took a moment to compose himself, then said, "Bernard... Bernard has been killed."

De Lattre stopped, frozen at hearing the words. "My Bernard?"

"I am afraid so, General."

"How?"

"Mortar. Near Ninh Binh during the assault on a bridge. I'm so sorry, General."

The command center went dead quiet. De Lattre looked lost, distant. John walked over and said quietly, "My condolences, General. He was a son that would make any father proud."

De Lattre said nothing in response. He just stood staring at blank space. The Air Force coordination officer approached and said, "I'm sorry for your loss, General. But I need your orders for the Day River assault. What do you wish the Air Force to do?"

De Lattre thought for a moment and said, "Napalm."

"General, there are surely civilians on those boats along with the rebels."

"I understand. Now, burn them. Burn them all."

The officer was shocked by the order but decided now was not the time to argue. He saluted and went off to communicate the general's orders.

The squadron of Grumman Hellcats was already loaded with napalm canisters when the order came to the airfield. It took less than fifteen minutes to get the fighter/bombers in the air and on their way to the battlefield. It was a short trip. The airfield was close.

After taking a quick recon pass over the river, the first Hellcat made its run. It dropped its canisters on the log jam of sampans, and nothing happened. The canisters crashed into the wooden sampans without detonating, sinking several but causing no fiery explosions. The fighter pilot radioed the squadron and suggested hitting the shore first to detonate the bombs and let the momentum carry the fire over the sampans.

The next aircraft dove down over the land and sped toward the river. The pilot released his bombs just before reaching the water and pulled up. The canisters hit the shore and exploded in an orange burst of light. The momentum of the gelatinized fuel carried the flame over the flotilla of sampans. Fourteen boats were engulfed in the inferno. The crew and passengers were covered with the sticky fire. The instant pain and confusion of being blinded were overwhelming for most. Some dove into the water and drowned, unable to see out their scorched eyes. Others just fell and burned on the sampan decks. And still, others tried to use river water to put out the flames but only ended up spreading the napalm over more of their bodies.

The French troops of the Dinassaut cheered and pushed the burning sampans away with their rifle butts whenever they came near their boats.

The Viet Minh on the other sampans were wide-eyed as aircraft after aircraft swooped in and dropped their loads of napalm canisters, then returned for a second pass to strafe the survivors with their machineguns. The fire spread quickly. Within ten minutes, all of the sampans were burning.

The warplanes refocused their attack on the Viet Minh on the opposite shore. It didn't take much before the Viet Minh broke and ran for the lives. Napalm could destroy any man's bravado. The gunfire tapered off to nothing. There were no more targets. Over four hundred Viet Minh and civilians were dead and dying. Those wounded that made it to shore were taken captive. Most didn't live long, their bodies too badly burned.

As word spread, nobody even dared approach the French boats in the river. The blockade held. The supply lines to Giap's divisions were cut off.

Granier and the Kennedys had been up all night watching the battle unfold. John was looking unusually tired with dark rings under his eyes. "I think we should head back to the hotel," said Granier.

"Good idea," said Bobby.

"I feel like I should say something to the general before we go," said John.

"I know that seems like the proper thing to do, but I don't think he needs to hear from anyone right now. He needs to be alone to deal with his grief," said Granier.

"Yeah, you're probably right. I don't know how I would feel had I just lost my only son. Surely, he can't be expected to continue his command under these circumstances."

"I don't know. He's French and a general. That is something few can understand. I'll see about getting us a ride back."

Granier moved off. Bobby looked over at John and said, "Are you okay, Jack?"

"Yeah. I'm fine. Just a little tired," said John.

Bernard's cavalry company had been badly mauled after their commander was killed and were forced to retreat down the riverbank. Without the cavalry supporting their flank, the French troops in the blockhouses had been overrun. Some were able to escape the concrete death traps and jump in the water where they would swim to shore downriver. Most died inside the blockhouses fighting until they ran out of ammunition.

Bruno and his company of paratroopers were called in to retake the bridge. In addition to his troops, Bruno was given an American-made M36

Tank Destroyer and a squad of engineers. Having a tank as part of his command was new for Bruno. He was used to fighting with light weapons and moving quickly. He was annoyed at the delays required to move the tank into position. While waiting for the tank to move up, he laid in the grass on a low hillside studying the bridge and the blockhouses through his binoculars.

The Viet Minh were removing the French corpses from the overrun blockhouses. When emptied, the Viet Minh occupied the blockhouses, which allowed them to shoot in any direction through the gun ports. The Viet Minh had stormed the bridge and now controlled both sides of the river.

Bruno and his men were hidden on the north side of the river opposite the city of Ninh Binh. They did not have the advantage of using the buildings for protection as they advanced on the Viet Minh positions. Bruno's company would need to cross the bridge to get at the majority of enemy forces. That's why his commander gave him a tank when he was given the assignment. It was unlikely the tank destroyer's 90mm cannon would be able to penetrate the concrete walls of the blockhouses. Destroying the enemy troops protected by the blockhouses would need to be done up close and personal by the engineers. But the tank could provide some much-needed cover for his men advancing across the bridge.

Crossing a bridge while under fire was not easy in any situation, but it was especially dangerous with an enemy in fortified defensive positions. There was only one way across the bridge, and it eliminated any chance of surprise. It was a meat grinder. Bruno hated the idea of wasting his men's lives on a suicide mission. He would simply have to find another way, and he knew the best way to take an enemy position was to flank one of its sides. He sent his scouts upriver to find what he thought he might need – a gunboat.

The scouts returned and reported that they had found a gravel barge tied up on the riverbank. Bruno ordered one of his heavy machinegun fireteams and a British-made PIAT team to follow him upriver.

When they arrived at the barge, Bruno made a quick decision that while not ideal as a gunboat, it would have to do. The machinegun crew and the PIAT fireteam dug themselves firing positions within the gravel on the barge. Having worked on a tugboat before the war, one of the scouts volunteered to pilot the watercraft. "You are not required to destroy the blockhouses. You simply need to divert the enemy's attention while we make our assault across the bridge. We will begin when you float into position and engage the enemy," said Bruno.

As the soldiers on the barge continued to prepare for their assault, Bruno returned to his men near the bridge. Seeing him approach, his executive officer approached and said, "Bruno, we have a problem."

"Already. The battle hasn't started yet," said Bruno.

"The engineers took a look at the bridge. They say it should be able to hold a 10-ton vehicle."

"And?"

"The tank destroyer weighs 28 tons. It'll never make it across."

"Now see, that's why I don't like tanks. Slow and undependable. We should have just gone on our own."

"It can still give us fire support while we assault the bridge. It can make a hell of a lot of noise."

"I suppose that's something. With our luck, it'll shoot the bridge, and we'll all end up in the drink."

"I'll tell 'em to be careful."

"You do that."

"One more thing. We made contact with the cavalry company that assaulted the Viet Minh before they took the bridge."

"The one with the general's son?"

"Yes. They are pretty scraped up, and morale is not the greatest, but they are willing to give it another go if we want them."

"Hell, yes, we want them. Where are they?"

"They're on the opposite bank about a quarter of a mile downriver."

"Alright. Good. Have them take up positions as close to the bridge as they dare without being discovered. When they see the barge open fire, that's their signal to attack."

"Will do, Bruno."

"We're attacking on three sides. I like it."

"Too bad there's a bridge between the enemy and our men."

"Yeah, well… if it were easy, they wouldn't have called us. Get the men ready. We go in ten minutes… or thereabouts."

The XO moved off without saluting.

The barge chugged downriver toward the bridge.

The gun crews and their weapons were hidden below the piles of gravel. The scout in the pilothouse threw the engine into reverse thirty yards from the bridge stopping the ship's progress. He blew the ship's whistle to signal the gun crews to open fire. They sprung from their hiding positions and set up their weapons.

The Viet Minh onshore saw what they were doing and opened fire first, hoping to pick off the French gunners before they could fire.

The PIAT team was the first to set up and fired their first 3 lb. grenade. It arced across the sky and hit the side of a blockhouse. The damage was minimal, but it got the Viet Minh's attention. More men were brought up to fire on the barge.

Bruno signaled his mortar team to open fire. They launched three smoke shells toward the Viet Minh lines. The shells exploded on the pavement and sent clouds of smoke in all directions obscuring the sight of the Viet Minh.

The cavalry company was next. Their armored cars rolled up the street, paralleling the river, and opened fire with their cannons and machineguns.

The Viet Minh were being attacked from both flanks simultaneously. Some continued firing on the barge while others turned to face the French armored cars advancing on their position. Billows of smoke added to the confusion.

The heavy machinegun on the barge finished setting up and opened fire, racking the gun portals of the blockhouses, preventing the soldiers inside from firing.

With the Viet Minh distracted, Bruno, taking the

lead, motioned his men forward. The paratroopers advanced first, and the engineers carrying satchel charges in their hands followed. Bruno had given the tank commander instructions to hold back until the paratroopers were under fire before exposing his position.

The Viet Minh protecting the bridge on the northern side did not notice the paratroopers moving up behind them until it was too late. The paratroopers charged their defensive positions, firing their submachine guns. But it was the appearance of the tank destroyer firing its main gun that broke the Viet Minh and sent them scrambling back across the bridge. The Viet Minh feared the French armor as much as they feared their warplanes. The French paratroopers had control of one side of the bridge.

Bruno and his men continued their advance across the bridge. A Viet Minh heavy machinegun on the far side of the bridge opened fire. Bruno could see the gun barrel flashes faintly through the smoke. Two of Bruno's men were killed, ripped apart by the large caliber bullets. Bruno signaled his men to take cover. They used the bridge girders for protection. The heavy machinegun bullets made dents in the bridge's steel girders but failed to penetrate. "Tell the tank commander to take out that heavy machinegun position," said Bruno to his radioman.

The tank gunner realigned his gun's sights and fired a high-explosive round toward the flashes of light in the smoke. There was an explosion, and the machinegun fell silent.

Bruno signaled his men to continue their advance. They leap-frogged from one girder to the next, covering their advance with sprays of submachinegun fire into the smoke on the opposite side of the bridge.

The PIAT gunner on the barge launched another round toward a blockhouse. Fire along the shore erupted, and several rounds hit him. He fell dead on the gravel pile. His assistant picked up the PIAT launcher and attempted to load another round. He was hit in the head and fell dead. The heavy machinegun crew on the barge shifted their fire to the Viet Minh firing on the shore and killed several, driving them back, silencing their weapons. As soon as the threat was dealt with, they resumed fire on the blockhouse gun portals, once again pushing the Viet Minh inside away from the portals, preventing them from firing at Bruno's paratroopers as they continued to advance.

The closer Bruno's paratrooper came to the blockhouses, the more of his men were hit by enemy fire.

The tank fired on the blockhouses. As Bruno expected, the big 90mm cannon was not enough to penetrate the reinforced concrete walls, but the dust from the shells' explosions added to the confusion and blinded the Viet Minh.

One of the armored cars fired its cannon and accelerated toward the blockhouses. A Viet Minh sapper with a lunge mine bolted from a doorway and thrust the mine against the side of the armored car's turret. The explosion killed the sapper, and the crew inside the armored car showered with molten metal. The vehicle, smoke billowing out of the hole in the turret, careened wildly out of control and toppled over as one of its wheels hit the edge of the embankment. The armored vehicle rolled several times and landed in the river disappearing below the waterline.

With the tank destroyer's cannon firing over their heads, Bruno and his men reached the opposite side of the bridge. The three blockhouses were only twenty to thirty yards away, but the fire coming from the gun portals was intense. Bruno knew he needed to create an opening for the engineers. They would only have one shot at destroying the blockhouses before the Viet Minh counterattacked and drove them back. His mind raced as the engineers moved up into position to start their assault. He had to ensure they at least had a chance at success. He turned to his radioman and said, "Tell the cavalry to push as hard as they can for the next three minutes while we make our assault. Then tell the mortar team to switch back to smoke and use everything they've got."

Having seen their comrades killed by a lunge mine, the commander of the armored cars was not anxious to advance any more toward the bridge. But he knew his duty and complied with Bruno's request. He ordered his machine-gunners to spray the buildings along the street as they passed, hoping to drive any suicide sappers back behind cover before they realized what was happening. The French foot troops behind the armored cars would protect their backs as they advanced. On his signal, the entire company charged, and the armored cars roared forward, firing all their weapons, using up what remained of their ammunition.

Seeing the cavalry make its charge, Bruno pulled two smoke canisters from the belt of a nearby paratrooper. He pulled the safety pins, threw them toward the blockhouses, and charged. His men followed, firing their weapons and trying to catch up with Bruno to keep him safe. Several paratroopers and two engineers were hit and went down.

Bruno reached the first blockhouse and pressed his back against the concrete wall, trying to stay out of sight of the gun portals. One of the smoke canisters laid nearby, spewing out plumes. Bruno used his beret as a glove and picked it up. He held it up toward the gun portal obscuring the vision of those inside. An engineer crouched down beside him and prepared his satchel charge. "This is not going to be a safe spot when the charge explodes," said the engineer.

"Let's hope. Go," said Bruno.

The engineer crawled toward the doorway and pulled the handle on the wire fuse. Smoke seeped from the pack as the detonation charge started to ignite. The engineer leaned the smoking satchel against the door and made a run for it. Bruno followed him, running as fast as he could. The engineer was shot in the shoulder and spun around as he began to fall. Bruno ran straight at him, hitting the engineer in the stomach with his shoulder and lifting him. They both reached the embankment, and Bruno leaped as the satchel charge exploded with a burst of flame and a deafening roar.

The steel door on the blockhouse was ripped off its hinges and flew into the interior, smashing into a Viet Minh soldier and crushing him to death. Flames

331

from the explosion engulfed the other soldiers inside. Their uniforms and hair burning, they ran through the doorway and were machine-gunned by a nearby paratrooper.

Bruno and the engineer rolled down the embankment and into the river. Bruno pulled the wounded engineer out of the water.

Two more engineers used their satchel charges to blow up the remaining blockhouses, killing those inside. The Viet Minh commander was inside the last blockhouse when it exploded. He was killed instantly. Seeing the smoldering blockhouse where their commander was killed and seeing the French paratroopers charging through the clouds of smoke like banshees, the surviving Viet Minh soldiers broke and ran back into the city with the French paratroopers running after them to revenge their fallen comrades.

The French had stopped Giap's advance and regained control of the bridge.

Giap's divisions lost their momentum as ammunition ran low, and casualties mounted. The general could feel the morale of his men sagging. Try as he might to bolster their confidence, they had passed their point of exhaustion. Almost nine-thousand Viet Minh had been lost during the Battle of the Day River, and the casualty numbers were growing by the minute. Giap gave the order to fall back.

Giap had tried three times to break through the De Lattre line and had failed each time. For the first time, the Viet Minh general's confidence wavered. He needed time to rethink his strategy. Even Uncle

Ho began to question Giap's leadership of his army. Ho felt that Giap was impatient in his strategy to fight the French head-on, and it cost the lives of thousands of his Viet Minh.

If only Giap and Ho had known that it wasn't their legions of soldiers that had almost defeated the French general, but the loss of one man that brought him to his knees – Bernard, his only son.

CHAPTER SEVENTEEN

John, Bobby, and Granier rode in an armored car escorted by an infantry platoon riding in trucks. In the distance, the battle continued to rage. Granier could see that John was in pain. The armored car's suspension was firm, and they felt every bump in the road. John had been up for over 24 hours and had been standing for much of it. His back was a wreck. "Are you alright, Jack?" said Granier.

"I wish people would stop asking me that, especially when there is nothing that can be done," said John.

"We'll be back in Hanoi soon, and you can rest," said Bobby.

"Not soon enough," said John.

"Maybe we could stop for a few minutes and let him lie down?" said Bobby.

"That's not a good idea," said Granier. "There could be enemy units in the area. If we stop, we will become their target."

"I'm alright, Bobby. Granier's right. We should keep moving," said John.

The armored car slowed and came to a stop. "I told you I'm alright," said John angrily.

"I didn't tell them to stop," said Bobby.

"Our escort is stopping," said the driver.

There was a rap on the door. Granier opened it. A lieutenant stood outside the armored car and said, "My platoon has been ordered back to Ninh Binh. The Viet Minh are retreating, and we will give chase. You should go with us."

"No," said John. "We should continue to Hanoi… please."

Granier could see the desperation in John's eyes and said, "We'll go on to Hanoi in the armored car."

"I don't think that's wise," said the lieutenant. "Viet Minh saboteurs have slipped through our lines and are still in the area."

"We should be okay," said Granier taking another look at John's face, sweat beading on his forehead.

"Suit yourselves. Good luck," said the lieutenant, closing the door.

The troop trucks turned around and headed back the way they had come. The armored car continued its journey toward Hanoi.

Granier remounted the 7.5mm Reibel machinegun in the turret's portal, cranked the turret so the gun faced the tree line, and kept watch as the armored car continued to move through the countryside.

"Are we gonna be okay?" said Bobby, concerned.

"Yeah. I think so. I just wanna be ready in case something happens," said Granier, not taking his eyes off the tree line paralleling the road. "John, I'm going to tell the driver to go as fast as possible. It's gonna get bumpy. Are you going to be okay?"

"Yes. Do it. The faster we get there, the better."

"Alright."

Granier instructed the driver, and he increased speed. The armored car jostled its passengers from side to side. John groaned. He wanted to keep quiet, but he couldn't help himself. The pain in his back was too much.

Granier kept his eyes fixed on the horizon, scanning for threats. In the distance, he watched as tracer rounds from the jungle struck a watchtower along the road. It was almost a mile away. "Do you see it?" he said to the driver.

"Yeah. They're under attack. We should help them," said the driver.

"No. We should find an alternative route," said Granier. "Your orders are to get the congressman and his brother safely to Hanoi."

"There is no other way."

"There is always another way," said Granier picking up a map, studying it, then pointing. "How about this route?"

"It could add several hours to the journey, and there is no guarantee that it will be any safer."

"We'll take that risk."

The watchtower in the distance exploded from a bazooka strike. A ball of flame flared, leaving the top of the tower burning like a candle. "Alright," said the driver turning the vehicle around.

"We're going back?" said John.

"No. But we need to take a detour. Road's

blocked up ahead. It'll take a little longer, but it should be safer," said Granier.

"Alright. I trust you, Granier."

"Just hang on, Jack. We'll get there."

The driver turned onto an adjoining road and headed east away from Hanoi. Due to lack of maintenance, the road was much rougher than the main road, but there was no traffic to slow them down. They made good time, but John suffered from the additional potholes and ruts.

After a half-hour traveling on the new road, there were several loud thuds against the turret like someone was hitting it with a hammer. "Shit," said Granier.

"What's wrong?" said Bobby.

"We're under fire," said Granier swinging the turret toward the direction of the tree line. He fired one quick burst to let the Viet Minh know that the vehicle was not defenseless. He didn't want to waste ammunition firing blindly into the jungle. They might need it.

There were more thuds against the turret. "Should we turn around?" said the driver.

"No way to know where they'll be. Forward is just as good as back."

Granier saw a muzzle flash in the distance and fired a burst at it. He knew the odds of hitting someone were slim. "Did you get 'em?" said Bobby.

"I doubt it, but maybe it will keep their heads down for a moment or two," said Granier.

The fire from the tree line intensified. "I think you got their attention," said John, hearing more thuds against the armor.

"Apparently," said Granier firing back in short bursts. "How long before we hit some cover?"

"There's nothing out here but rice paddies," said the driver.

Mortar shells exploded around the armored car. Shrapnel pinged off the armor. "What now?" said Bobby frightened.

"Mortars. Probably in the tree line."

"They can't get us, right?"

"If they are small, then no. We're safe inside."

An explosion directly in front of the armored car caused the driver to brake and swerve. Everyone bashed against the hard metal inside the vehicle. There was a whoop-whoop noise coming from the right side of the vehicle. "We've been hit. I think they got the front tire," said the driver.

"Can you keep going?" said Granier.

"No. The tire will fold into the wheel-well, and we'll never get it out. I've got to stop."

"And do what?"

"We've got to change the tire. I've got a spare on the back."

"You're gonna try and change a tire under fire?"

"I don't see what choice we have. I can't drive with a flat tire. You'll just have to hold them back with the machinegun."

"That's a really bad idea. We don't know what we are facing."

"It'll be okay. The flat tire is on the opposite side of the tree line. The vehicle will protect me. I can change it in ten minutes, and we'll be on our way."

"How much ammunition we got?"

"Enough."

"Alright. I'll cover you," said Granier firing another burst.

"Should I go with him?" said Bobby.

"No," said Granier firmly.

"He may need help, and the faster we get out of here, the better."

"Alright but keep your head down."

Granier fired several long bursts into the tree line to subdue the enemy for a few moments.

Bobby and the driver exited the vehicle through the side door as bullets ricocheted off the armor. The driver released the spare tire from the back of the vehicle and lifted it down to the ground. Bobby wheeled it over to the flat tire as the driver retrieved the jack. But the driver never joined Bobby. Bobby went back to the rear of the vehicle to see what was holding up the driver. The driver was lying on the ground with a bullet hole in the side of his head. Bobby panicked and went back inside the vehicle and closed the door tight.

"What happened?" said Granier.

"He's dead. They got him," said Bobby, distant and detached.

"Damn it."

"I would have stayed, but I don't know how to change a tire. I'm sorry."

"It's alright. You did the right thing coming back inside."

"What are we going to do?"

"I don't know. If we stay here, we're dead."

"Wait a minute... Are you talking about abandoning the vehicle? It's safe in here."

"For the moment, yes. But they'll move in once

they realized we're disabled. That or they wait until we run low on ammunition. Either way, they'll overrun us."

"So, what? We become prisoners?"

"They're behind enemy lines. I doubt they'll take prisoners."

"But we're American. We're not the enemy."

"We're shooting back at them. That makes us the enemy."

"Granier's right. If we stay here, we'll die," said John.

"How are you gonna run, Jack?" said Bobby.

"If I can't keep up, you gotta leave me."

"That ain't gonna happen," said Granier. "Although we might have to carry you. Nobody gets left behind."

"Let's quit talking and get on with it," said John.

Granier retrieved the driver's rifle and all the ammunition he could find, plus a couple of grenades. He handed everything to Bobby. "Okay, here is what we are going to do. You are going to leave the vehicle first while I cover you with the machinegun. You're going to head out across the rice paddies to our right."

"And you're gonna follow, right?" said John.

"Once I know that you're clear."

"Don't leave us, Granier," said Bobby.

"I'll be there. Just keep going until you reach the dike on the opposite side of the paddy. You can rest and wait for me there. But if I'm not there is three minutes, you've got to keep going on your own until you find a village or farmhouse."

"No. No. We can't make it on our own," said

Bobby panicking.

"Yes, we can. We can do this, Bobby," said John. "One foot in front of the other."

"Alright, alright," said Bobby.

"Wait until I say," said Granier manning the machinegun.

Granier fired two long bursts from the machinegun and said, "Go!"

Bobby opened the door and helped John climb out. Bobby reached back inside and retrieved the rifle, ammunition, and grenades. They ran around the opposite side of the vehicle as the enemy fire intensified, whizzing over their heads and pinging off the armor. Granier kept up his steady bursts of covering fire as John and Bobby made their way across the rice paddy next to the road. Their feet sunk in the mud, making it a struggle to even walk, especially for John. When they reached the other side, they laid down on the opposite side of the dike out of breath. John took the rifle and prepared to cover Granier's retreat. "It's gonna be alright, Bobby," said John. "Just keep your head down."

"I'm not afraid to die, Jack. I'm not a coward."

"I know you're not, Brother."

"I just don't have your confidence that everything is going to be okay."

"I'll let you in on a little secret. I don't believe that everything is going to be okay. I just fake it."

"Really?"

"Kinda. Yeah."

"So, we really are going to die in this godforsaken country?"

"Nah. Everything's gonna work out just fine.

You'll see," said John with a grin.

Bobby laughed.

Granier appeared around the back of the armored car, running, carrying the vehicle's 7.5 mm Reibel machinegun slung over his shoulder and a 150-round pan magazine in his hand. He ran down the embankment into the rice paddy. The armored car exploded, sending a massive ball of fire into the air. "Did they hit it?" said Bobby.

"No. I think Granier blew it up," said John. "Bobby, find a couple of rocks the size of a softball. Granier's going to need 'em."

Bobby combed the side of the dike until he found two rocks the same size. He brought them back to John. "What are they for?" said Bobby.

"Machinegun mounts," said John taking the rocks and setting them down next to each other on the top of the dike.

Granier was out of breath when he reached Bobby and John. He saw the two rocks side by side and set the machinegun down on top of them, pointing the barrel back toward the armored car and said, "So far, so good. You two pull back two more rice paddies."

"I think we should all stick together," said John.

"Jack, if we ever find ourselves in the middle of the Pacific and you come up with a plan, I swear I will follow it to the T. But this is my world, and need you to do as I tell you. We don't have time to argue."

"Yeah. You're right. I'll shut up."

"How are you holding up?"

"I'm okay. I just need to rest a little."

"I just want to make sure they don't follow us.

Once we hit a tree line, we can rest until it gets dark."

"But you said the Viet Minh own the night," said Bobby.

"Not when I'm around," said Granier with a slight grin. "You'd better get going."

John and Bobby took off, running across the next two rice paddies. Granier chambered a round into the machinegun and waited. The sun was low on the horizon, setting in the direction they were heading. It would make it more difficult for the Viet Minh to spot them. Granier figured they had maybe forty-five minutes before it set. This would be simple if he were alone. But he wasn't. The Kennedy brothers were smart, but they didn't know the land as he knew it, and they didn't have the skills he had. If it came to a fight, he doubted John would be of much use even though he had been trained how to shoot. He was getting sicker by the hour, and that concerned Granier more than anything. A cough or sneeze could get them all killed when the Viet Minh were close. He needed to put distance between the Viet Minh and the Kennedys. He knew that if he could slow the Viet Minh down, they stood a chance.

Things were quiet for the next three minutes, and then five Viet Minh appeared on the road next to the burning armored car. Granier took aim and let loose several bursts of machinegun fire. He hit two of them, and they went down, but he wasn't sure if they were dead. He would have preferred that they were just wounded, so their comrades would be forced to tend to them. More Viet Minh appeared on the road firing their weapons in Granier's direction. He exchanged fire with them using short two-second bursts. They

343

used the opposite side of the road and the armored car for cover. With the sun at his back, he could see them clearly even at one hundred yards. But he was not good with a machinegun which pulled up and to the right when fired. He cut his bursts to less than a second, and that seemed to help a bit. It still felt like he was constantly wrestling with the weapon like it had a mind of his own. He missed his sniper rifle. The machinegun went silent, meaning the gun was empty. He swapped out the pan magazine and racked the bolt, chambering the next round. He only had one hundred and fifty bullets remaining. He would make them count. He waited.

With the machinegun silent, the Viet Minh rose and started across the rice paddy. Granier counted twelve in total. He assumed there were probably more tending to their wounded, but he didn't care about them. They were out of the hunt. He just needed to deal with the twelve in front of him. He imagined there might be a squad sent to flank his position, but he couldn't see anyone. Leadership within the Viet Minh was very uneven, and it was hard to predict what a unit would do. He would keep watching his flanks but not let the idea of someone lurking out there overwhelm his thoughts. Fight what is in front of you, he thought. He let the Viet Minh advance fifty yards, so they were in the center of the rice paddy before he opened fire again. He hit three more, and they went down. The rest of the Viet Minh returned fire as they crouched down in the green rice plants and muddy water.

It was hard to keep track of the number of rounds he had fired. He figured he had used up about half of the magazine, but he couldn't be sure. He decided to empty the magazine and abandon the machinegun. It was a heavy bastard, and he could move a lot quicker without it. Bullet hits kicked up the dirt on the backside of the dike. He realized they weren't coming from the Viet Minh in the rice paddy. He turned to his right and saw muzzle flashes from the edge of the dike. He had been flanked. Shit. You're in trouble, he thought. He swung the machinegun around and gave the flankers a couple of bursts to force them down. It worked. But the Viet Minh in the rice paddy started their advance again. He knew that the two groups would leap-frog back and forth until one of them was close enough to pick him off. He wasn't going to wait for that to happen. He lifted the machinegun and took off running along the bottom of the dike in the opposite direction of the flankers. He figured it would put distance between he and his hunters and eliminate the flanking move at the same time. The two groups of Viet Minh would become two fronts at different angles, which was far better than a front and a flank. He was also leading them away from the Kennedys. If he went down, the Viet Minh would probably assume that the others with him were in the direction he was running. His biggest concern was that John might play hero and return for him. He decided not to worry about it since there was nothing he could do about it right now. Bullet zigged past his head as he ran.

He made it to the edge, climbed up the dike, and jumped over the opposite side, releasing the machinegun, so it landed on the embankment. He crashed down in the paddy with mud up to his knees.

He tried lifting his legs. They didn't budge. He was stuck. He knew that when he pulled up his boots, they created suction that pulled them back down. He needed to break the air pocket below his boots and do it quickly. Twisting one of his boots to an angle, a bubble of air rose through the brown water. It was free. He duplicated the procedure for the other boot. It worked. He took several steps back to the embankment using the rice plants underneath his boots to keep them from sinking again. He laid down on the embankment and picked up the machinegun. It was covered in mud. He cleared as much mud and dirt away from the chamber and bolt as possible. He pulled off the magazine and scraped off the mud as best he could then put it back on the gun. With luck, he could get off a few bursts before it jammed. He crawled up the side of the embankment and set the machinegun on the dike. He rose his head and looked out.

Five Viet Minh were within twenty feet of his position. He fired a burst, killing two. The other three crouched down and returned fire. He aimed again and squeezed the trigger on the gun. Nothing happened. It was jammed. He gave the bolt a quick tug back, hoping that would be enough. It wasn't. He turned the gun on its side and looked at the open bolt. A bullet was lodged crooked inside the chamber. He pulled the bolt back and cleared the jam by pushing the cartridge into the barrel and released the bolt.

The Viet Minh were surprised by the silence and must have figured he was out of ammunition. They rose and charged his position. Granier stood and pulled the trigger as he swept the gun from side to side. It fired a long burst hitting all three of the Viet Minh in their chests. They fell into the rice paddy. The machinegun went silent again. At first, he thought it might have jammed again but then realized on closer inspection that the gun was out of ammunition. He threw the weapon into the rice paddy, where it immediately sank into the mud, and took off running, leading the Viet Minh away from the Kennedys. He made it to the opposite side of the paddy and jumped over the dike, careful not to land in the water. He took a quick moment to catch his bearings, then started a zig-zag pattern where he would run west along a rice paddy, then north, then west again, each time using the cover of the dikes to hide his position. He continued this strategy until the sun went down, then changed direction back toward where he thought the Kennedys might be by now.

It took him a half-hour to get back to where he thought the two brothers might be hiding, but he couldn't be sure. He looked around, but they were nowhere in sight. He cursed quietly as he continued his search. He found nothing. He realized the most likely scenario was that they had been taken captive or killed by the Viet Minh. He had failed to protect them.

Granier's head jerked around when he heard water splashing. It was pitch black and difficult to see. He crouched down in the rice paddy and listened as the splashes of water came closer. He could hear voices. They weren't speaking English or French. He pulled the pistol from his pants pocket and readied himself. He could see the silhouettes of several men approaching. One was holding a rifle. He leveled his pistol and took aim. He would take out as many as he could. He wouldn't go down without a fight. "Granier, is that you?" said a voice that sounded a lot like Bobby. At first, Granier didn't reply, wondering if it was some kind of trap. "It's Bobby," said Bobby as he stepped close enough for Granier to see.

Bobby was holding the rifle Granier had given him, and he was flanked by three indigenous Vietnamese with bows and arrows. "Who are they?" said Granier.

"I don't know. But I'm pretty sure they're the good guys. They helped us."

"I think they're Montagnard," said Granier studying the tribesmen. "Where's Jack?"

"He's back at the village. The chief's wife is taking care of him. He's in a bad way. Where did you go? When we heard the machinegun stop, I thought the Viet Minh might have got you."

"They almost did. I led them off in a different direction, then doubled back to find you guys."

"That's what Jack said you would do. We should probably get back to the village. We gotta get Jack to a hospital."

"Alright," said Granier, then pointed to the rifle. "Do you mind if I take that?"

"No. Of course not." Bobby handed him the rifle.

"I feel a lot better about life when I have a rifle in my hands."

"I bet you do."

They moved back across the rice paddy. The village was over a mile away along the edge of a forest. By the time they returned, John was burning up with a fever, and there was little the chief's wife could do for him except try to keep him cool with fans and wet clothes. "Has he been like this before?" said Granier.

"It happens when he gets tired. He can run a fever and feel even more fatigued than usual," said Bobby. "The real danger is infection. His immune system becomes weak when he's tired."

"What is it? Malaria?"

"That's what we tell the press."

"I'm not the press, Bobby."

"I know. And you deserve an answer. But it's not easy because of who Jack is. What I can tell you is that Jack has been sick most of his adult life. We need to get him to a good hospital."

"That's gonna be tough in Indochina."

"The French don't have hospitals?"

"They have a few, but they're usually overwhelmed and understaffed. They do the best they can."

"I don't know if that will be enough. This is pretty serious stuff he is dealing with."

"There is a pilot, I know. He could fly us out of the country if I can find him."

"He's got a plane?"

"He can borrow one. Just don't ask a lot of questions."

"Alright."

"First, we've got to get back to Hanoi."

"The village chief says there's a Catholic mission a few miles to the west. They may have a car or truck."

"Probably our best shot."

"Are we gonna take Jack with us?"

"No. I'll ask the chief for a guide. If the mission has a vehicle, I'll come back, and we can load up Jack. If not, I'll keep going until I find one. You stay here with Jack."

"What happens if the Viet Minh show up?"

"I think the Montagnard will protect you. It's part of their culture. The Viet Minh want the Montagnard as an ally against the French. I doubt they will create too much trouble. They'll probably leave you alone."

"I hope you're right."

"Maybe you should keep the rifle just in case."

"No. You should take it. I won't be much good with it, and Jack's down for the count."

"Alright. Here," said Granier, handing Bobby his pistol and the extra bullets from his pockets. "Just in case."

"Right… just in case," said Bobby, unsure.

Granier looked in on John before he left. John mumbled something in his sleep as sweat rolled down his forehead. He was delirious. "Hang in there, Jack," said Granier quietly.

"You'd better hurry, Granier. It's never been this bad," said Bobby.

"Right. I'll be back as soon as I can," said Granier leaving with his tribal guide.

John F. Kennedy woke to see a ceiling fan whirling above him. The ceiling and walls were painted a faint green. He could hear people talking in the hallway. Bobby was asleep in a chair beside him. "Bobby?"

350

said John.

Bobby woke and said, "You scared the hell out of us, Jack. How are you feeling?"

"Thirsty."

"Yeah. They've been pouring liquids into you through the IV. You were badly dehydrated," said Bobby pouring John a glass of water from a pitcher on the side table. He helped his brother lift his head and sip. "Where am I?" said John.

"You're in a military hospital in Okinawa, Japan."

"Japan?"

"Yeah. They've got good doctors here. They saved your life."

"What happened?"

"What do you remember?"

"The armored car blowing up and running through a rice paddy."

"That was five days ago. You got really sick. Granier and I took you to Hanoi and loaded you on a plane. The pilot flew us here. Your temperature rose all the way to 106 degrees. Doctors said they never saw someone survive with a fever that high. We thought your brain was going to boil, and you'd die. We even got you a priest. But you hung in there, and your temperature finally subsided."

"Where's Granier?"

"He's back in Indochina. Said his mission was done once we dropped you off here."

"Sounds like Granier."

"Yeah. If it wasn't for him, I don't think we would have made it."

"I gotta thank him," said Jack, his eyes lids growing heavy.

"Yeah. But right now, you need to sleep, Jack. We're going to fly you back to the states in a couple of days. Mom's got a private hospital all set for you in Boston. Nobody needs to know what happened."

"You did good, Bobby. You did real good."

"Thanks, Jack. I did my best."

John didn't hear his brother. He was already asleep.

EPILOGUE

November 14, 1951 - After several more weeks in a private hospital recovering from his illness, John F. Kennedy emerged to give a radio broadcast at the Mutual Broadcasting Network. It was a farsighted speech defining the need to reject third world Colonialism and embrace nationalism, which he felt was the bulwark needed to combat Communism. He talked about his journey to Indochina and other countries he had seen. It was Kennedy's first declaration of the need for a program of counterinsurgency, a doctrine that would eventually plague his presidency in Cuba and again in Indochina. In his radio address, Kennedy blasted American leaders and diplomats for conceding to the wishes of European powers as they attempted to hang on to their empires without understanding the needs and desires of the people in the countries they controlled. He criticized U.S. policy in Indochina that aligned America with France without requiring

353

the political reforms needed to win the war. He said it was a serious mistake that played into the hands of communists and would cost the free world dearly if not rectified. He talked about the need for a Third Force that was both anti-colonial and anti-communist and could satisfy the Vietnamese aspirations for freedom while frustrating the communists' strategy. Without it, Indochina was sure to fall prey to the Viet Minh. It was a speech that defined the time and declared Kennedy's desire to build a free world built on strength and understanding. He was far from being a pacifist and willing to pay the sacrifices required for freedom and democracy.

January 11, 1952 - General Jean De Lattre de Tassigny was the greatest military commander in the Indochina War. In his brief time as Commander-in-Chief of French forces, he turned the tide of the war and stopped General Giap and his Viet Minh. But after the death of his only son, Bernard De Lattre, the general was never the same. He became bitter and morose. His health failing, he was forced to give up his command and return to Paris for surgery. The cancer that had plagued him spread through his body like wildfire.

Within a year, he was on his death bed. In a conversation with his friend General Valluy, De Lattre said, "My only regret is that I never really understood Indochina." As he fell into a delusional stupor, his last words were, "Where is Bernard?"

It is hard to imagine what might have been the

outcome of the Indochina War had Bernard not fallen in battle and the general had continued his command. A hero of three wars, De Lattre, was elevated to Marshal of France posthumously in 1952 at his state funeral. He was buried beside his son and father at the cemetery des Invalides in Paris.

LETTER TO READER

Dear Reader,

I hope you enjoyed The War Before The War.

If you wish to read in chronological order, the next novel in the series is We Stand Alone. It's the fictional account of the longest battle in the Indochina War - the siege at Dien Bien Phu. It's fascinating history and the story that inspired me to write the Airmen Series. Here is the link:

https://www.amazon.com/dp/B07BWTP8RT

Below you can find a list of all my books and the correct reading order. Thank you for your consideration, and I hope to hear from you.

In gratitude,

David Lee Corley

LIST OF TITLES WITH READING ORDER

The Airmen Series
1. A War Too Far
2. The War Before The War
3. We Stand Alone
4. Café Wars
5. Sèvres Protocol
6. Operation Musketeer
7. Battle of The Casbah
8. Momentum of War
9. The Willful Slaughter of Hope
10. Kennedy's War
11. The Uncivil War
12. Cry Havoc

The Nomad Series
1. Monsoon Rising
2. Prophecies of Chaos
3. Stealing Thunder

Facebook Page:
https://www.facebook.com/historicalwarnovels

Shopify Store: https://david-lee-corley.myshopify.com/

Amazon Author's Page: https://www.amazon.com/David-Lee-Corley/e/B073S1ZMWQ

Amazon Airmen Series Page:
https://www.amazon.com/dp/B07JVRXRGG

Amazon Nomad Series Page:
https://www.amazon.com/dp/B07CKFGQ95

Author's Website: http://davidleecorley.com/

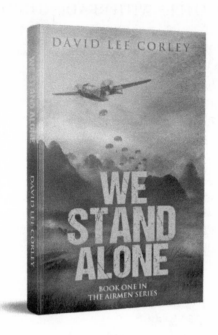

Author's Biography

Born in 1958, David grew up on a horse ranch in Northern California, breeding and training appaloosas. He has had all his toes broken at least once and survived numerous falls and kicks from ornery colts and fillies. David started writing professionally as a copywriter in his early 20's. At 32, he packed up his family and moved to Malibu, California, to live his dream of writing and directing motion pictures. He has four motion picture screenwriting credits and two directing credits. His movies have been viewed by over 50 million movie-goers worldwide and won a multitude of awards, including the Malibu, Palm Springs, and San Jose Film Festivals. In addition to his 23 screenplays, he has written ten novels. He developed his simplistic writing style after rereading his two favorite books, Ernest Hemingway's "The Old Man and The Sea" and Cormac McCarthy's "No Country For Old Men." An avid student of world culture, David lived as an ex-pat in both Thailand and Mexico. At 56, he sold all his possessions and became a nomad for four years. He circumnavigated the globe three times and visited 56 countries. Known for his detailed descriptions, his stories often include actual experiences and characters from his journeys.

CPSIA information can be obtained
at www.ICGtesting.com
Printed in the USA
BVHW031548060323
659797BV00001B/115